Nigel

~~PUFFIN BOOKS~~ PROUDLY BRINGS YOU

An autobiography about an unusual boy with a suit of armour, an unshakeable dream and a most unusual vocabulary, written by that very boy (Nigel Dorking).

PUFFIN

PUFFIN BOOKS

Published by the Penguin Group
Penguin Books Ltd, 80 Strand, London WC2R 0RL, England
Penguin Group (USA) Inc., 375 Hudson Street, New York, New York 10014, USA
Penguin Group (Canada), 90 Eglinton Avenue East, Suite 700, Toronto, Ontario, Canada M4P 2Y3
(a division of Pearson Penguin Canada Inc.)
Penguin Ireland, 25 St Stephen's Green, Dublin 2, Ireland (a division of Penguin Books Ltd)
Penguin Group (Australia), 250 Camberwell Road, Camberwell, Victoria 3124, Australia
(a division of Pearson Australia Group Pty Ltd)
Penguin Books India Pvt Ltd, 11 Community Centre, Panchsheel Park, New Delhi – 110 017, India
Penguin Group (NZ), 67 Apollo Drive, Rosedale, North Shore 0632, New Zealand
(a division of Pearson New Zealand Ltd)
Penguin Books (South Africa) (Pty) Ltd, 24 Sturdee Avenue, Rosebank,
Johannesburg 2196, South Africa

Penguin Books Ltd, Registered Offices: 80 Strand, London WC2R 0RL, England

puffinbooks.com

First published by Penguin Group (Australia),
a division of Pearson Australia Group Pty Ltd 2007
Published in Great Britain in Puffin Books 2008
1

Set in Janson Text
Made and printed in England by Clays Ltd, St Ives plc

British Library Cataloguing in Publication Data
A CIP catalogue record for this book is available from the British Library

ISBN: 978–0–141–32377–0

Nigel (the Notorious) Dorking's

Knights' Code of Chivalry for Modern Day Knights

I	Thou Shalt Crush the Monsters That Steal Our Land and Rob Our People.
II	Thou Shalt Always Extend Hospitality to All Travellers, Be They Friend or Foe.
III	Thou Shalt Never Attack an Unarmed Foe or Unhorsed Opponent.
IV	Thou Shalt Always Uphold the Honour of a Lady.
V	Thou Shalt Never Gloat, Even in Victory.
VI	Thou Shalt Always Outwit Serpents and Fight All Manner of Evil Dragons, Even Unto Death.
VII	Thou Shalt Always Practise Humility and All Other Knightly Virtues.
VIII	Thou Shalt Always Play Fair. Even to Thine Enemy, Thou Must Mercy Show.
IX	Thou Shalt Eschew Unfairness, Meanness and Deceit, and Use Strategy First, the Sword Second.
X	Thou Shalt Not Recoil from Thine Enemy.
XI	Thou Shalt Fight Injustice in All Its Forms, to Punish the Wicked, and Reward the Virtuous.
XII	Thou Shalt Always Defend the Weak and Innocent.
XIII	Thou Shalt Always Avoid Torture.
XIV	Thou Shalt Never Abandon a Friend, Ally or Noble Cause.
XV	Thou Shalt Lay Down Thy Life for the Crown, Country and All Thou Hold Dear.
XVI	Thou Shalt Never Use a Weapon on an Opponent Not Equal to the Attack.
XVII	Thou Shalt Always Strive for Excellence and to Set a Good Example to Thy Inferiors.
XVIII	Thou Shalt Always Have Faith, Even in the Face of Grave Peril.
XIX	Thou Shalt Treat Elders With the Respect They Deserve.

XX	Love and Determination and Inspiration Shall Always Prevail.
XXI	Thou Shalt Always Count Thy Blessings and Be Eternally Grateful.
XXII	Thou Shalt Exhibit Patience and Forbearance at All Times.
XXIII	Thou Shalt Always Exhibit Self-Control.
XXIV	Thou Shalt Always Persevere, Even in the Greatest Adversity.
XXV	Thou Shalt Remain Steadfast.
XXVI	Thou Shalt Never Betray a Confidence or Comrade.
XXVII	Thou Shalt Always Fight for All Damsels in Distress.
XXVIII	Thou Shalt Always Listen to Others, Even to the Dull and Ignorant, for They Too Are Important.
XXIX	Thou Shalt Always Act Honourably.
XXX	Thou Shalt Lay Down Thy Life for a True Brother.
XXXI	Thou Shalt Never Accept Defeat.
XXXII	Thou Shalt Trust in Knightly Valour, and Banish All Doubt.
XXXIII	Thou Shalt Always Accept Thy Fate with Fortitude.
XXXIV	Thou Shalt Swear Allegiance to Those Who Put Their Selves in Harm's Way to Help Others.
XXXV	Thou Shalt Fight with Knightly Valour for the Honour of Those Thou Love.
XXXVI	Thou Shalt Honour Friendship above All and Know a True Friend by His Deeds.
XXXVII	Thou Shalt Never Harbour Envy, Fear or Hatred in Thy Breast, but Instead Shalt Live a Pure and Noble Life.
XXXVIII	Thou Shalt Always Speak the Truth, No Matter How Painful.
XXXIX	Thou Shalt Never Look Down on Those Less Fortunate than Thee.
XL	Thou Shalt Always Show Forgiveness in Thy Thoughts and Deeds.
XLI	Thou Shalt Always Remain Faithful to Thy Pledged Word.

Dear Miss Murray,

I have written my hero essay for you as requested. And have written it as ~~disgust~~ discussed in class, as if it were the first chapter of a novel setting up the setting, the characters, and some jeopardy.

Though there might be a few surprises! I have taken the liberty of writing in old-fashioned language as my ~~storey~~ story is about a young knight. To be more precise, in fact, it is about a young knight called Nigel. (Aha! I hear you ~~deduse~~ deduce!) And yes, you are correct. That knight is indeed I.

I, Nigel Dorking.

So quite clearly this story I am writing is not fiction, but rather, autobiographical.

And you will probably notice I have done an unusual thing.

I have written it in the third person. In case you are unfamiliar with this, as you are only a grade six teacher and I don't think this is even taught until high school, it means I will ~~right~~ write about myself as if I were someone else. So rather than saying, *I did this noble thing, unimaginable for someone my age* (which sounds boastful) I will instead write *He did this noble thing, unimaginable for someone his age* (which does not).

After all, my ~~storey~~ story is the ~~storey~~ story of a knight, and a knight is never boastful.

Hopefully you will find this ~~littery~~ literary device as inspired as do I! For not only will it give me the ability to say nice things about myself that might otherwise sound like I was up myself, but also, it is my hope that it will help me to face unthinkable truths. For a knight is always brave, and will always face the ~~unfaeceable~~ unfaceable.

Also it will help me get a ~~bird sigh~~ bird's-eye view of my life, and hence help me to leave out bits that even though true, might not contribute to the ~~storey~~ story, bits like *and then I went to the toilet and found there was no toilet paper, and had to race out to find some, but my pants were round my ankles, so I had to hop, hoping that no one saw my ~~bear prosterior~~ bare posterior (bottom)*. For even though that did happen, it is ~~unirrelevant~~ irrelevant to my story, if you follow my drift.

So that being said, let us start this ~~storey~~ story, and let the mists of time transport us back to long ago (nine months to be precise) to the days of ~~you're~~ yore, when the world was a far safer and much happier place. When Dad still lived with Mother, Ivan, Gilgamesh and me, Nigel.

Hear ye, hear ye! Prithee listen, for, dear reader, I have a goodly ~~storey~~ story set in a time when brave, courageous, ~~valient~~ valiant and heroic knights still fought gallant battles on Saturday afternoons, and when goodly merry wives still hummed as they put their families' washed wet armour onto their clothes line to dry. There lived then a great and masterful knight, known far and wide as Len (The Lionheart) Dorking.

Abiding (living) with him in his castle on Grail Grove, just up from Ikea, were his faithful son Nigel, his faithful wife (Nigel's mother), Kelly Dorking, his son, Ivan Dorking, and his faithful goldfish, Gilgamesh Dorking.

None was happier, in this Kingdom in Camelot Heights, than this ~~close-nit~~ close-knit, happy family. And none was prouder of the deeds of this gallant and noble adventurer than Nigel.

For not only did this boy Nigel have the incredible luck of being born this noble man's son, but also the honour of being a proud spectator of his esteemed father when his medieval re-enactment group jousted with each other once a month at the old sports ground, down past the turn-off on Devil's Bend, past the old butter factory (now Crazy Clint's).

This was indeed a joy, a privilege, an honour and only two dollars per person entry.

Proudly, every first Saturday afternoon of every month, Nigel, his mother and Ivan would sit in his father's plumbing pick-up that had 'Toilets R Us' printed on the side. And together they would watch with their hearts in their mouths. (Not literally, as this is just an expression. Usually, in actual fact they had pies or donuts in their mouths from the near-buy fast-food van.) But apart from that everything was extremely authentically Middle Ages.

But I ~~tigress~~ digress, dear reader (Miss Murray, Nigel's most esteemed teacher!).

Happily, these were the golden days before the ominous (just to save you having to find a dictionary this means *portentous* – and just so you don't have to get up and find that in a dictionary, this means *menacing*) cloud had settled over their lives at Grail Grove.

Tragically, all their lives were soon to be torn asunder by the evil, father-stealing arch-manipulator, Babette.

It happened on the evening of Ivan's birthday. As Nigel lay in bed, he heard ungodly yelling from his parents' chamber. He had never heard Mother and Father yell like that before. His mother spake unrepeatable, cruel and harsh words most unwifely (words like [illegible] and [illegible] and *pig*) to his noble father.

Nigel pulled the pillow over his head to stop the terrible accusations against his ignoble father ~~impenetrating~~ penetrating his eardrums. And to further shut them out, he whispered all the rules of the Knights' Code of Chivalry, the way his father had taught him, repeatedly, again and again.

When he awoke, the next morning, to his horror, there before him, in the doorway, stood his father with his suitcase, looking stricken (his father, not the suitcase).

Like a blocked sink, Nigel's insides gurgled with tragic foreshadowing.

With a strange, ghostlike expression on his face all his father said was, 'Nigel, I have come to say goodbye.'

He then turned and left.

Nigel's tear-stained mother (just her face) (obviously) finally explained to him that Len Dorking, Nigel's father, would not be coming back. Ever.

This did not make ~~cents,~~ sense as his heroic, noble father would surely never leave him. And his father would certainly never have left his armour behind. Or his own son Nigel. Or his beloved goldfish Gilgamesh.

Len the Lionheart was noble and gallant.

What could the explanation be?

Ah, dear reader, this was a case of father abduction by enchantment. Babette, his new wife, had evilly stolen him. Like Mordrid Le Fay before her, she lured honest men into her trap and sapped their memories, so they could no longer recall their children or their wives, their birthdates or even to buy them Christmas presents.

But luckily, Nigel's father with knightly foresight had schooled his son Nigel in the ways of knights and had taught him all the rules of the Code of Chivalry. Which included loyalty, and how to fight honestly. Obviously, his father had wisely done this so his son could help out were such a tragic event as his ~~bewhichment~~ bewitchment ever to take place.

He, Nigel, would stealthily steal into her lair, and somehow lure his father back into the ~~busum~~ bosom of his family. (And of course when I say ~~busum~~ bosom I do not mean the rude version which is of course '[illegible]. Just so you know!) Then their bond would flourish . . .

This was his quest.

To save Dad, his hero.

Surely father and sonly love would conquer all ~~bewhichment~~ bewitchment? He would *make* Dad remember. Dad *would* come home to Camelot Heights.

Nothing would get in his, Nigel's, way.

Not even the deeply embarrassing personal problem he had developed the day after Dad had left. The one he could never allow his father to find out about. (One unfortunately I cannot disclose as you, ~~deer~~ dear Miss Murray, are not a doctor and have not taken the ~~hypocritical~~ Hippocratic oath.) Thisvery medical condition had tragically made it impossible for him to stay at his father's for even one night, even if he had been invited.

Even though this type of medical problem had probably also occurred in medieval times to the most gallant and noble of knights in the night-time as well (as surely it would have been hard to always get their armour off in time). Nonetheless, he did not want to tempt fate. He most definitely did not want to risk his father finding out.

Against all odds, Nigel set out on his hero's journey.

And that, dear Miss Murray, is my hero ~~storey~~ story which I commend into your hands with your lovely pearly nail polish. By the way, could you tell me which beauty parlour does them as I might give my mother a gift voucher for her birthday. Can they also help with wrinkles? And what about those funny warts you can get on the left eyelid? As these blemishes do not befit one as my mother who was so honoured to be chosen as my father's wife.

Excellent, Nigel. You've obviously gone to a lot of trouble. A-.

Plus, well thought out. But you must practise your spelling and learn to control your language.

Dear Reader and Miss Murray,

You probably found that chapter suspenseful.

I have some news.

I have decided to continue my story!

(This is due to your encouragement, Miss Murray. And thanks for the top mark in the class! You have spurred me on! Inspired me! You are my muse!)

Due to homework commitments however (well, they are pretty demanding, after all I am in grade six) I have decided to dictate my future chapters onto my digital voice-recorder, as this is far quicker than actual writing.

So I am creating an authentic medieval audio blog of my life story as a modern-day knight.

Naturally, I will continue to dictate my autobiography in the third person.

When I showed my hero's essay to Mum (my only critic besides you, Miss Murray), she also said she liked it a lot, but unlike you, suggested that writing it all in old speak was a bit 'monotonous'. I take her point that some people are a bit thick and might not comprehend my unusually large vocabulary!

But when she said she also thought I should not write it in the third person I decided it must be my mother who was a bit thick!

'It looks like you're afraid of the pronoun *I*!' she accused me.

As I said to her gently, 'I find this illogical, unintelligent, uninsightful, wrong and actually quite stupid.'

(And that's the other thing, she said it was too verbose.) (This means too many words –

unnecessary, redundant, and pointless words.)

But what would she possibly know about ~~litterature~~ literature, as she reads mainly Mills and Boon? Love books, which, in my humble opinion, if they had only one word it would be one too many.

And anyway, it is ridiculous to suggest that I might be afraid of the pronoun *I*. As knights are not known for their being afraid. Of monsters maybe, but of the word *I*? I think not. After all, it is just a letter of the alphabet. And if I were so afraid of it ~~shorely~~ surely I would use no words with this letter in them, ~~shorely~~ surely? And *au contraire* (*on the contrary* in French); I actually speak three languages including pig Latin; I think you will find many words that contain the letter *i*. Most of all, note the word *knight* for instance. Or *idiot*, as in the case of people who disagree with me. So this I firmly reject.

Yours ~~sincearely~~ sincerely, Nigel Dorking

Note, I even have the letter *i* in my name. And it features thrice in the title of my autobiography.

PS As this book will have been dictated, any errors will be the fault of the publishing company. (Obviously.)

PPS I hope you find this ~~storey~~ story insightful, illuminating, challenging and compellingly suspenseful. If you do however find any boring bits, just read them quickly. But they would also be the fault of the publishing company. They sometimes make people put in boring descriptive bits like, *the expanse of ocean lit by the golden sunlight glittered like diamonds on a bejewelled sea as the foam on the azure waves came riding in like white horses.* (Actually I might use that. But you know what I mean.)

Dear Voice Recorder, this is . . .

I, Nigel Dorking, Do Hereby Swear to Crush the Monsters That Steal Our Land and Rob Our People.

'Ahem. Ivan,' said Nigel.

Ivan's eyes flickered open.

'It is I, Nigel.'

Nigel waited for his brother to wake and for this to sink in.

'You know my conditions,' said Nigel.

Ivan drooled onto blue bear, who lay next to him.

'That you drop this ridiculous act. If you don't I cannot take you.'

'I oo,' called out Ivan.

Nigel studied his brother's face for a hint of an intelligent response.

'If you accompany me,' he encouraged his brother, 'I have decided to call us the Dauntless Duo. Due to our boundless belief in our father, our extreme courage and our extraordinary bond.'

Nigel stood very still. He did not even dare hope like he used to that his brother might weigh up his options, jump out of bed, laugh, and say, 'Okay, Nigel, you win. Come on.'

All he hoped was that Ivan showed some sign that he was slightly more intelligent than he made out.

This, however, did not happen.

Eventually he was forced to say, but did so in his most courtly manner, 'I am sorry, Ivan, but if you continue to dribble I cannot take you to Dad's. As you know, it would only remind him of why he was able to be stolen from us in the first place, and obviously that would be unintelligent, given we are trying to get him back. We need to *im*press him, not *de*press him. I hope you understand.'

Then, to soften the blow for his brother, he explained in his kindliest voice, 'It's alright, Ivan. I wouldn't let Mum come, either. She is not welcome until she becomes more ladylike, gets rid of her tattoos, tries not to use rude words, and learns to control her temper. Okay? This is so we can get Dad back. We don't want to frighten him off. Wish me godspeed.'

He withdrew graciously from his brother's bedroom. Now he would once again have to be Nigel the Notorious, the lone crusader.

Nigel tried to banish any bitterness towards his brother as he crept to the front entrance. He refused to waste even one brain cell worrying about his selfish, manipulative brother, who refused to try the tiniest bit. Not even for such an important cause as getting Dad back.

No, he would not dwell on people who didn't deserve to come. He needed to preserve all his energy for strategy and possible battle. That is, if he were going to succeed in getting Dad back by Ivan's birthday.

Nigel quietly pulled the front door at 3 Grail Grove closed behind him.

It was then, just as he stood 'twixt two worlds, when he was on the threshold of his adventure, that he saw in his own street, right outside his own home, a flash of the most brilliant red, and was startled by an almighty roar.

What could it have been? It was like a comet shooting across the skies! Except it zapped right down his street, after streaking off from a parked position directly outside his very house, and then turned right at Ikea. Nigel stared after the trail it had left, transfixed. What was it? And who was it that sat astride with such magnificence? Was it a celestial being? Or perhaps a figure from the past, a knight upon a flaming red steed?

It was the backfiring that finally made him realise it was a motorbike. The most gleaming ruby red motorbike he had ever seen. Why, however, had it been parked outside his house?

Puzzled, Nigel set off, like knights of old, towards

his immediate destination, the bus stop on Lancelot Drive, directly opposite McDonald's.

As people munched their burgers, Nigel pulled from his pocket the precious form. The one he hoped to get signed by his father that very day.

Nigel knew if Dad would just sign this, then he, Nigel, would be on the road to implementing his plan, and getting Dad back.

All he needed was to get Dad alone, away from her, Babette, so they could forge a relationship. And this form represented the first real opportunity since Dad had left ten months ago.

He re-read the form.

Dear Fathers, it went,

Please find the time to come along to the Father and Son Night on Friday 9th March at 7.30 p.m. in the school hall, prelude to Father and Son Bonding Camp on Wednesday 28th March. This camp will last just three nights and could change your son's life. Come along to the information night and find out more. We will also have a guest speaker who will talk about raising boys in our modern culture. Please sign the form below, and return with deposit for camp as directed.

He refolded it, and put it back into his pocket.

Camp could not have come at a better time. It was perfect.

For, three weeks ago precisely, Nigel's medical problem had stopped. Up until then it would have been impossible to stay at Dad's, even if he had been invited over, or to go on camp. Now, however, he was free to pursue this relationship with Dad. All he had to do was convince his father to come.

How would Dad react? He did not like surprises.

But this visit was now unavoidable. Getting this form signed was extremely urgent: Father and Son Night was this Friday and this form must be signed by Monday, the final day the school would accept them. And it was Saturday already.

Clearly there was no alternative. After all, had he not done all that was humanly possible? Had he not called Dad, repeatedly? Quite obviously Dad had been so extremely busy he was unable to return the calls. Clearly there had been plumbing emergencies galore these last ten days.

After all, Dad did live in a high-growth, high-density area. Two years ago this whole estate didn't even exist. It was just paddocks.

Ah, the chariot! Nigel spied his bus in the distance . . .

This would be his first time ever alone on the bus.

It would also be the first time ever he'd gone to Dad's.

But Nigel would not allow himself to be daunted.

He was determined to triumph. He would face the unfaceable to save his relationship with his father.

Nigel boarded his chariot, the one that would take him, unbeknownst to Mum, out of Camelot Heights, the best suburb ever, to the fortress where Dad was now held captive by Babette and her twin daughters.

This boy's perilous journey had begun!

Paradise Springs, a walled estate, was a much newer and more expensive suburb than Nigel's. But nothing could beat Camelot Heights, where both Nigel and Dad belonged.

Nigel paid his fare (naturally), and then strode proudly, head held high in a knightly way, down the aisle of the bus, on the way to his seat. He did not mind the stares of the other passengers. After all, if he, Nigel, were to see a knight in shining armour on a bus on a Saturday afternoon he too would stare.

And for once he was glad his armour was mainly plastic and silver lycra, as real armour would have clanked quite loudly.

On his way to his seat he gave an old lady who looked particularly admiring a courtly nod, and then, to a small child who was gaping and pointing, a gracious bow.

'Is he Superman with a crash helmet?' said the child very loudly.

Nigel stopped mid-bow. Ignoramus, he thought.

(Note from author, this is a term often used by intellectual people meaning 'ignorant fool'.) It was obviously a very stupid child.

He sat.

After all, how could anyone not know a virtually authentic medieval knight's suit of armour when they saw one?

Most people would be impressed. Anyone with any brains would be. And Dad most certainly would be. After all, this was why he, Nigel, had worn his armour. To impress Dad. To remind him of the old days, of their bond. Of the past. Of how things used to be, before she stole him. Babette, the family-wrecker.

As the bus jigged along Joust Avenue and turned down Gawain Parade, Nigel double-checked his Woolworths bag for his certificates. The ones that proved he was respected at school for respecting other people's property. And the tidiest boy in the playground certificate. And the proof that he had been accepted into the gifted stream in English. And most importantly his results from the WISK intelligence test proving he was in the 98th percentile, which meant he was very clever indeed.

These would most certainly impress Dad.

He imagined standing proudly outside Dad's in his armour that very afternoon, and Dad spotting him. Dad waking as if from a trance, running to throw his arms around Nigel, and promising to come home.

But with great self-discipline, Nigel told himself not to get ahead of himself. (That is something Dad had often warned Nigel about when Nigel was helping him fix toilets, and Nigel ever eager to help handed him the wrong implement too soon.)

So instead, he settled on imagining Dad signing his form. And then that wonderful moment when Dad would walk into the school hall at Father and Son Night. And then Dad on camp. Nigel and Dad on camp doing father and son things. Dad teaching the kids about swordfights and chivalry. And amazing them with his plumbing and water facts.

This would be good, as Nigel did not have many friends at school.

Actually, not any. Which was fortuitous, for as a result Nigel got to spend a lot of time in the library at lunchtime, and hence had a vast general knowledge and knew heaps more than the other kids.

Nigel stared out the bus window, imagining himself, as a result of the kids being so impressed with Dad, being voted class captain.

Suddenly he was jolted out of his reverie by the bus turning into the gates that led to the housing development where Nigel's father now lived.

He saw the great gates of the walled city with its huge mythic lions on either side, guarding the palace, and the words ‘Paradise Springs’ written over the archway that was flanked by two palm trees.

Nigel almost gasped at the enormous castle-like four-storey homes whizzing past. And as they did he couldn’t help wondering if paradise was also treeless, and lawnless, and with four-wheel drives everywhere.

Nigel pulled the cord and stood, for this was his stop.

‘Is he mental?’ he heard the foolish child whisper as he, Nigel, strode past.

Every step he took brought him closer to his father’s.

He could just see the tip of the roof of the four-storey mansion now. With every heartbeat it loomed larger. And his organs played ancient Roman twister with one another.

Any second he would actually be seeing Dad. And facing her, Babette, the viper.

I, Nigel Dorking, Do Hereby Swear as a True Knight Always to Extend Hospitality to All Travellers, Be They Friend or Foe.

From where he stood, Nigel had optimal chance of seeing into most rooms of the mansion his father now lived in with his new family.

At a glance, he could already see more ways in which his father's real family could improve to win Dad back.

This mansion was so unbelievably tidy. No rotting fences, or falling-off gates. And their white pebble courtyard was immaculate. With no weeds at all. In fact, he noticed as he scanned the garden, there were no plants at all, except one. A tall, thin cactus. He also noticed a big sign saying, *Beware of the Dog*. Probably a gigantic, vicious bloodhound-cross-wolf, for tracking Babette's enemies.

The time had come to implement his plan. Nigel knelt, and from his backpack carefully extracted his handmade weapon. This would surely get Dad's attention.

Nigel slung the modified arrows in their holder over

his left shoulder, stood to attention, held the crossbow in the correct way, loaded one arrow and stayed there, poised for action.

For he was determined not to take the easy path and ring Dad's doorbell. Not because he was afraid of the dog, but rather it was a matter of honour, for surely ringing a bell was as good as begging to be invited in. And Nigel was determined this forthcoming invitation should be Dad's idea. Only when he, Nigel, had been cordially invited into Dad's home could their relationship truly begin. And Dad would most certainly invite him in once he had spotted Nigel. After all, no knight would allow another knight to stand outside his castle without inviting them in and offering some hospitality. That would be unthinkable.

He would show Dad and his new family that he, Nigel, would never barge uninvited into his father's life (as Babette and her vile progeny had done). He would show Dad that he, Nigel, was courteous, polite, gallant, a great shot, a surprisingly good authentic medieval-weapons maker, and a wonderful inventor.

Dad, of all people, would appreciate safe medieval weaponry for modern-day usage. And Dad more than anyone would understand the genius behind such an idea. Sticking tennis balls on the pointy bit of an arrow was not just safety conscious but showed remarkable civic pride in one so young. For without the tennis balls there would be holes everywhere, in furniture, lampposts and even fences, from misfired arrows.

Nigel's plan was that he would wait until he spotted Dad, and then fire three arrows in succession past their window, just the way he had been practising at home.

This would surely get him noticed and then invited in with a most warm welcome.

His arms were aching. It was getting extremely uncomfortable holding his crossbow up. Still he had not spotted Dad.

Sweat trickled down his neck under his plastic helmet, and his visor kept falling shut, making it hard for him to breathe and see. Not to mention the fact the silver lycra knight's bodysuit Mum had made him when he was seven was giving him a most unknightly wedgie.

He hoped this would not throw his aim.

To lift his spirits he allowed himself to imagine his arrows firing, the fluorescent green tennis balls sailing past Dad's window as the brightly coloured comet tails he had made from the parachute-like material from his ex-kite unfurled. He imagined Dad being amazed as he read the messages flying past his window, for Nigel had clearly written on each of the long bits of material, in indelible black pen in very large print, *Hello Dad, 'tis I, Nigel. Look out the front.*

Then Dad would see him. And Dad would invite him in. And he and his dad would swap facts like old times.

And Dad would tell him a few interesting facts about knights, plumbing and water and then he, Nigel, would say seamlessly, *Oh, speaking of interesting facts, Dad, there is a Father and Son Night at my school next Friday*, and then he'd pull out the form and show Dad.

And then Dad would beam, and ruffle his hair, and say, *Of course*, and then sign the form.

There was movement on the second floor. Was it Dad?

Nigel squinted, tensed all his aiming muscles, and lined up his mark, ready to shoot.

False alarm, they were obviously Babette's hare-brained twin daughters he had heard about from Mum, running about in what appeared to be ridiculous pink fairy dresses or frilly ballerina gear with loads of pink tulle.

But where was Dad?

Then he spotted her, Babette, the Evil One. The father-stealing arch-manipulator with neat hair, standing with her back to him on the landing. Dustbusting.

She was tall and thin, just like the cactus out the front.

And even though she had blonde hair and was tall

with really good fashion sense, unlike Nigel's mother she undoubtedly had very stubby fingers. Mum's thumbs were her best feature.

As Nigel watched this wicked woman, he swore an oath that unto his dying breath he would fight to oust this venomous family-breaker.

He even took the liberty of sending her legs a message.

Slip. Buckle, trip backwards. Fall on your dustbuster, and let it suck your guts out.

Then he spotted Dad. Len the Lionheart had just turned and was facing Nigel.

This was it.

This was the defining moment of Nigel's life.

'Ready, aim, fire,' he said.

Nigel let his first arrow go.

But sadly it did not hit its mark, instead ending up wedged in the cactus after the tennis ball fell off. He quickly loaded another. But at the last second, just as he was taking aim, this tennis ball fell off too, and plopped at his feet. There was only one arrow left.

As he reloaded, he sent his hero a mental message.

*See me. See me now, **Dad**. Please.*

Just then, however, Babette walked into view, and abruptly closed the shutters.

A shadow fell across Nigel's heart. How dare she? he seethed.

After what seemed like a torturously long time, Nigel caught another glimpse of Dad, this time at another window.

Dad was looking out at the horizon.

Nigel steadied his hand.

'Ready, aim, fire,' he tried again, this time more successfully. He watched as the arrow issued from his crossbow in a perfect arc, only a slightly larger arc than the one he had desired.

Thwack, went the ball, with the arrow, on Dad's window. Its message had not unfurled. Nigel heard the glass shudder. He looked on with horror as he waited for it to shatter. Luckily, the window did not break, but the guard dog started hurling itself against it repeatedly, yapping, snarling and generally acting as viciously as a sausage dog possibly could.

Nigel sent the dog a big thank you. For due to this animal, his plan had worked after all. Dad looked down towards him.

Nigel dropped his crossbow and went nuts, waving his arms like a knight in the watchtower alerting his king and country that their enemy had retreated and that they were victorious. He knew Dad had seen him. Surely he had?

Though Dad did not have his glasses on, Nigel felt certain Dad must had seen him.

It was surely about to happen.

All of him grinned. Parts he didn't know could. Parts like his pancreas, his duodenum and his spleen. Every single atom in his body celebrated.

Nigel was victorious.

You are outwitted, Evil One, thought Nigel. Too late for you. Dad has seen me. Any second, he will come out and invite me in and you will be thwarted.

'Let our new relationship begin,' Nigel whispered under his breath as he waited expectantly. 'It is the dawning of a new age.'

It'd been ten minutes now. Why hadn't Dad come? Perhaps he was leaning against the banister and his knee had got caught between the bars? Or perhaps the door handle had come off on the other side of the door and he was locked in that room? Or what if Babette had him in a headlock and wasn't letting him come to the front door? What if Babette was so desperate that Dad not bond with Nigel that she had bonked him on the head and was dragging him into a cupboard?

Nigel decided he would have to go in after him. Like a real knight. Even though he had been against the idea of ringing the bell, circumstances had changed. Now, he would have to go and press that buzzer and speak into that intercom.

He strode forward, ready to do anything in his power to help Dad.

Remember who you are, he told himself. You are Nigel the Notorious, dubbed so by Len the Lionheart.

But Nigel was startled by the sound of a four-wheel-drive engine.

Like a huge rock being moved from a cave, Dad's automatic garage door whirred up, his spiked gates opened, and out of the cave, like a roaring dragon, backed a four-wheel drive, directly towards him. Really fast. With her, Babette, at the wheel, Dad in the passenger seat, looking the other way, and the girls in the back seat looking totally foolish in their pink satin and tulle.

Did he have enough time to leap out of the way? Had she seen him? If he leapt and she corrected, would she hit him? Or was she aiming for him?

The beast was roaring towards him, its back wheels spinning.

Nigel scrambled out of the tree, dazed and rubbing his grazed elbows and regretting that he had jumped out of the way.

If Babette had hit Nigel, Dad might have visited him in hospital, and best of all, Babette would have been all over the news for being an evil four-wheel-drive owner who backs over children and might possibly have been jailed.

Brushing himself down, Nigel saw the four-wheel drive, like his hopes of getting Dad to Father and Son Night, disappearing into the distance.

Except for the *No Junk Mail* sign, Dad's metal letter-box, with the slit, was quite like Dad's helmet. Dad was certainly not a junk male. He was a very fine one.

Nigel pulled out his form, grabbed a pen from his bag and wrote a note on the back of the envelope.

Dear Dad, please fill this in, it is extremely important. I will be back to pick it up before school on Monday morning. Then he signed it *Nigel*. And then (*Dorking*) in brackets in case his father knew a few Nigels. And then just to be sure in more brackets he wrote (*your son*) just in case.

(A note from author. You can never be too sure with knights as they have so much on their mind with all the virtues, and their full-time nobleness. It is a well-known fact that knights of yore often forgot their children's names. And birthdays. And even Christmas.)

Back in Camelot Heights everything suddenly looked small, and a bit dilapidated.

Nigel got off the bus. Carefully, he looked both ways, then crossed the street, only just avoiding a red motorbike that appeared from nowhere out of Merlin Crescent, and then sped past.

Nigel glared after it. Surely such vehicles should have louder motors to alert unsuspecting pedestrians!

Could that have been one of the Evil One's spies? wondered Nigel. It was most odd to have been nearly run over twice within forty-seven minutes.

Though, he decided, pulling the earphones from his ears as a safety precaution, to prevent any future possible disasters on the road, he would not listen to his iPod while crossing roads in future.

Once he'd arrived safely at the kerb, Nigel turned towards home. At least things couldn't get worse, he thought.

Which is when things got worse.

Out from the tall trees a football came bouncing. And the heads of Bruno, Reece and Hope appeared on the horizon, like axed-off heads in medieval times that had been stuck on pikes as a warning to other possible evildoers, and then hung high over a city. But these were red, puffing alive heads, with necks, now torsos, now legs, coming towards Nigel.

He was about to make a quick detour when he decided that, being knightly, he should always give people the benefit of the doubt. True, they were school bullies, but this might be a good opportunity to impress them. And who knew, perhaps once they had seen him in his armour they might treat him with more respect in future, and stop groaning whenever he answered questions in class or when he was the last person left in sport and they had to choose him for their team.

Armed with these hopes, Nigel faced the blackguards.

'Good afternoon,' he nodded politely, keeping his voice even so as not to betray any fear.

He was glad that at the last second he had decided not to add *squires and damsel*, as on close inspection they looked about as civilised as crocodiles in a moat before breakfast.

Nigel waited while they sauntered up with their backwards caps and the sunscreen on their noses and their sneers.

He did not run away, as a knight would not ever do that.

A quest is not a quest without possible danger, without possible monsters, and possible grave peril.

And Nigel happened to have all three right in front of him.

I, Nigel Dorking, Do Hereby Swear Never to Attack an Unarmed Foe or Unhorsed Opponent.

'Well, look who,' scoffed Bruno. 'It's a real knight in armour. Be scared. Be very very scared.'

'I'm quaking in me boots,' laughed Reece, badly acting a terrified cringing peasant before his master. 'Don't 'urt me, Sir Nigel.'

'A knight never attacks an unarmed foe,' Nigel explained. 'And actually, I am not an actual knight in armour, in fact. It is *virtual* amour. And in case you do not understand the meaning of the word *virtual*, it means *almost real*. In actual fact,' he continued, 'in case you didn't know, actual knights do not exist any more.'

'Oh really,' said Hope with mock shock. 'Duh! Idiot!'

'This is just for medieval re-enactment,' said Nigel, ignoring her, 'which, like football, is a sport I, Nigel, and my father, Len the Lionheart, play on Saturdays. Though my father has real amour.'

'Why don't you play a normal sport like a normal kid, you freak?' said Hope.

'Medieval re-enactment is a far superior sport,' retorted Nigel as he glared with contempt at the offending football, which Bruno was attempting to spin on his finger. 'Kicking a ball around a field so you can get it between two posts seems to me to be a particularly pointless and loser pastime. But staging historically correct battles that are completely authentic is most definitely not.'

Nigel suspected from their exaggerated sneers that they were trying to mask a newfound admiration.

'And not only do we have real swordfights,' he added (he hoped not too boastfully), 'but we also get Fanta at half-time.'

'So does your dad wear a dress too?' jeered Bruno, quite obviously from extreme jealousy and ignorance.

'Ah no,' Nigel corrected him, 'neither of us wear dresses. This is a medieval squire's tunic. And for your information, even though my sword is plastic, it is an authentic imitation, whereas my chain-mail top however is actually completely authentically authentic. You may touch it if you like. It is, in fact, extremely expensive. My father got it for me from the Tower of London actually, where, in case you don't know, many famous people were imprisoned, and also beheaded, including Sir Thomas More, Anne Boleyn, and Catherine Howard, Guy Fawkes, and Sir Walter Raleigh.'

'Shut up, loser,' said Bruno, in obvious awe of Nigel's superior knowledge.

'Though of course going to jail these days, people do not get beheaded,' Nigel added very quickly. 'Unless of course it is for quite a serious crime.'

Bruno was looking at him strangely.

Probably though, one would be prone to looking at people strangely if one's father were in jail for burglary. Which is quite a serious crime . . .

Bruno pushed Nigel hard and he fell.

Nigel stood up.

And then Reece pushed him. Then Hope. From one to the other. And Nigel could do nothing, as they were unarmed, and a true knight never attacks an unarmed foe.

But while they were shoving him, Nigel made a mental note. In future, he would avoid mentioning serious crime and jail in front of Bruno, and he would definitely not go out in public in his knight's armour again. Not unless it was a matter of life and death, which obviously today was, or unless of course he was going to medieval re-enactment with his father.

'You big girl,' Bruno was yelling.

'There is nothing wrong with being a girl,' said Nigel (using a soothing sort of voice, the sort one might use to a tantrumming toddler, or an escaped lunatic). 'I just do not happen to be one.'

'Are so. And so's your dad,' Reece added.

'Yeah! He's a freak who dresses up on weekends,' yelled Bruno. 'Like Dorko.'

This was an unprovoked attack.

Still he would try to remain in control.

'Yeah, you're both spazzos like your brother.'

'Yeah, they're a family of vegetables,' laughed Bruno.

Now, Nigel's whole body was shot with fury.

Suddenly he could not be reasoned with. Even if they were extremely jealous, no one attacked his brother and got away with it.

'Take that back,' he demanded, his hand gripping his sword hard, his jaw set. 'You pathetic scurvy brains. Perhaps if you ate some vegetables you wouldn't be so deficient and you would know the difference between a vegetable and someone who just happens to have cerebral palsy with intellectual disability, which is far less disabling than being narrow-minded idiots.'

Nigel's foes roared with laughter.

Doubtless this was to mask their extreme fear because they had just realised how deadly serious Nigel actually was.

'Ooh, watch out, the brave sir knight is going to get us with his plastic sword.' Bruno grabbed Nigel's arm and started twisting it behind his back as Reece got ready to boot him.

There was a deafening screech, like the Grand Prix at take-off. And suddenly right beside them, up to the kerb, swerved a gleaming, glistening brilliant red motorbike, the same one that had earlier appeared in front of Nigel's house, its engine roaring.

'Oy! Leave him alone,' thundered a deep voice from under the helmet.

The bike revved menacingly a few times as Nigel's brave assailants ran. (Note from author. That was sarcasm as they were not really brave. Sarcasm is a form of wit.)

'Excuse me,' said Nigel. 'I must formally thank you. But who are you?'

But the mystery bike-rider said nothing, and instead sped off.

Who could it possibly be? Who was this faceless, helmeted protector? Why had they saved him? Was it really the same bike as earlier? Could it be that this inscrutable being was a knight after all? A modern-day knight on a ruby red charger? A protector he, Nigel, could conjure into the modern day?

Nigel dashed to the walk-in cupboard to change. And to be alone.

'Nige! How does shepherd's pie for dinner sound?'

Even though heavy-hearted, Nigel congratulated himself on having made it home before Mum noticed he had disappeared. This he had deduced from her casual question about dinner – a most appetising-sounding culinary delight.

'Most excellent, Mum,' he called.

He was peeling off his knight's gear when the sun came out, and from the high window opposite in the hallway a shaft of golden light slanted in, directly hitting Dad's armour. Nigel gasped involuntarily.

Dad's shield, breastplate and helmet all lit up, gleaming and glinting golden in the slant of the late afternoon sun. Was this a sign, meant to remind Nigel of Dad's courage, his bravery, and his nobility?

Nigel reached out to touch Dad's helmet, and the visor, which had been open, clanged shut. As if the head were nodding *yes*.

'Helmet o' Len the Lionheart,' Nigel whispered. 'What am I missing? How could a brave man ignore his own son?'

Nigel waited.

'Or could the visor shutting mean Dad didn't see me?'

He then decided to rephrase his question.

'If I am right, and Dad did see me, are you saying *yes* to Babette being a witch who has entrapped my father with dark magic? If so, please keep glowing.'

The answer was undeniable. Dad's armour kept glowing like Uluru at sunset, for 3 minutes and 27 seconds.

Now Nigel's heart hardly dared beat.

This confirmed his gravest fears.

His battle to save Dad was a true quest against evil. Against the dark side.

The armour finally dimmed.

Nigel stood there, overawed by the incredible mystical moment he had just experienced, and by the revelation that had just occurred, that he was absolutely right in his assessment of the situation and that he, Nigel, had been specially chosen to undertake the quest of safely returning his father to his family.

'Lemon meringue pie for dessert,' called Mum.

Nigel ran to his bedroom. He was too awestruck to be hungry.

For it had just occurred to him that he, Nigel, might have magical powers. Momentarily anything seemed possible in this twilight world.

And even though he was an intelligent and logical boy he was not without a small hope.

'Let there be a bolt of light,' he said as he smote the air with his raised arm. But nothing happened. Instead, however, he was filled with a surge of joy, even though he had just discovered that he was indeed a Muggle. The truth of what had happened earlier outside Dad's had just struck him afresh.

Dad had ignored Nigel for noble reasons! Not because he was afraid, which of course Nigel could now see was a ridiculous idea! Dad must have known that Babette had dark powers, and he had been trying to save Nigel from her.

This gave Nigel hope.

The ability to fight on.

And restored his faith in Dad.

He raced over to his computer and Googled *counteracting spells*. Then *jinxes*, then *hexes*.

'Nige, love,' called Mum all too soon. 'Dinny din dins! It's ready!'

'Mmm, especially delicious tonight,' said Nigel at dinner. 'I think the lumps in the potato add texture.'

'Thanks, love,' smiled Mum.

Then, just to ruin the moment with his usual horrible timing, Gordon walked in.

'Hello, all. Sorry I'm a wee bit late,' he called.

A wee bit thick, more like it, thought Nigel.

Nigel glared at the intruder. The one who was about to sit in Nigel's father's chair at Nigel's father's dinner table with Nigel's father's wife and sons.

Was it possible for a human being to be thicker than Gordon's pathetic and incomprehensible Scottish accent?

Had he, Nigel, not had a very clear and stern word with Gordon just under three weeks ago about the fact that they, Nigel and his brother Ivan, did not want

Gordon, the interloper, in their lives?

Some people do not know when they are not wanted, thought Nigel.

'Say hello, Nigel,' said Mum.

Nigel said it very quietly.

'So Gordon can hear,' insisted Mum.

Mum gave Nigel a glacial glare.

Enough to chill his heart.

'Hello, Gordon,' said Nigel eventually but most reluctantly. 'From what cave did you emerge?'

'Nigel!' interrupted Mum.

Gordon calmed her with a comforting hand on her shoulder.

Nigel saw Mum shoot him a grateful smile.

Nigel's heart felt even blacker. He knew exactly what Gordon was up to. This was all for show just so Mum would see what a nice guy he was.

Gordon then winked and smiled at Nigel.

Nigel shuddered, and did not smile back.

They ate in silence, until Gordon got up to clear the dishes.

'Nige, I've been thinking,' said Mum quietly, 'if Dad can't come on this Father and Son thing perhaps –'

Nigel did not let her finish. 'No way,' he said, possibly too loudly. And then more quietly to himself, 'hell would freeze over before I would allow that knuckle-dragging moron to come to Father and Son Camp.'

I, Nigel Dorking, Do Hereby Swear Always to Uphold the Honour of a Lady.

Nigel had to prove to Mum that they did not need Gordon. That is why he had been up since dawn, digging the compost and fixing the side gate himself. It would certainly bang no more in the wind, now he had taken it off completely. And Dad would appreciate this when he moved back in. Nigel had also replanted the cactus from out the back, right into the middle of their front lawn, just where Dad obviously liked them.

Coming inside from the bright sunlight outside often made it quite difficult to see. It was as if the whole kitchen were underexposed. Everything seemed terribly dark, except for the hot spots the sun had burnt into his retina.

As Nigel walked into the kitchen, the scene in front of him took the words *Good morning* right out of his larynx.

There, he thought, is Mum at the breakfast table, in her dressing-gown. (Not unusual.) And there, sitting nearby in his booster chair, is Ivan (also not unusual).

But there, with his back to Nigel, near the stove, is Dad, wearing his dressing-gown. Now, this is very unusual.

Nigel's visit had worked!

Dad was back!

Nigel's heart did the dance of joy. It was definitely Dad, standing there in his blue velour dressing-gown. It had remained in Dad's wardrobe since Dad had left. And now Dad was in it.

Slowly Dad turned to face Nigel.

Then, just as the sunspots in Nigel's eyes dimmed and allowed his eyes to feast on his beloved father's features, Nigel saw red.

Red hair. And a red beard. And freckly white skin on his arms, and he realised it was not Dad at all, but Gordon wearing his father's dressing-gown.

'Nigel, me lad,' beamed Gordon, acting pleased to see him.

How dare he? What an affront! Masquerading like this. The usurper. What could his explanation possibly be?

'What are you doing still here?' demanded Nigel sternly. 'And why are you in my father's dressing-gown?'

'Don't be rude – Gordon is our guest. And, love, it's just an old dressing-gown,' Mum said in an oily, treacherous voice, 'so I thought it was better than having him in the nuddy . . .'

Nigel was in deep shock. That his own mother

should prove to be so duplicitous was one thing, but that she should go for this oaf, this Orc, whose knuckles almost touched the ground, this ginger-haired, bearded interloper, was an abomination.

He had quite clearly stayed the night.

Gordon winked at Nigel.

'It's not what you think, wee laddie,' said Gordon.

Wrong, thought Nigel. It is exactly what I think.

Nigel shuddered.

Gordon would never suck Nigel in. Or Nigel's brother, once he, Nigel, had explained to him, Ivan, what Gordon was doing! Gordon would never take their mother from them. Over Nigel's dead body.

No way was this stupid, stinking Orc from right out of Tolkien's Middle-earth going to slide any further into their lives, Nigel decided as he, Nigel, slid into Dad's chair at the head of the table.

Then he heard that noise. The one Ivan always made when he was having a fit.

Nigel raced over to help Ivan avoid crashing into things and doing himself damage. This was Nigel's job. Not some interloper's! But Gordon in his desperate and pathetic attempt to suck up had got there first.

'You'll be alright, poor little man,' said Gordon.

'He is alright,' said Nigel. For it was now clear that this was a false alarm and that Gordon was milking it for all he could.

Nigel was the one having a fit now. And he was only just managing to keep it inside him.

'If you want to take him to see the neurologist,' sucked up Gordon to Mum, 'I will get some time off work and drive you to the city. How do you feel about that, young Ivan?'

They all spoke to Ivan as if he understood. Which of course Mum claimed he could not. But in reality Nigel was not so sure that Ivan was quite as backward as he made out.

Not that he'd ever say it to Mum again, about Ivan putting it on a bit. Not after the last time.

'Why on earth would he do that, Nigel?' Mum had turned on him. Ivan was clearly her favourite. 'What would he get out of choosing to live like this?'

All your attention for one, he would have said, but he'd seen tears in Mum's eyes. So Nigel had shrugged and decided to say nothing. For Mum had never responded well to gentle suggestions that Ivan was a manipulative brother with rat cunning who just wanted all her attention and that that was why Dad had left.

'You're an intelligent boy, Nigel,' she had yelled. 'Why would you say such a stupid thing?'

Nigel tried to ignore the small hairs prickling all over his back and arms at the memory, and wiped away the annoying beads of moisture that had sprung unbidden to his eyes.

He watched as Ivan played his favourite game of tossing his spoon onto the floor. Mum wearily bent down to pick it up.

Ivan tossed it off again.

Obviously, thought Nigel, as he watched his easily manipulated mother replace it back on Ivan's tray, she cannot understand my position, as she has never been desperate to have a functioning brother. Or a father who lived with his real family.

Nigel glared at his brother.

Even if Ivan wasn't putting anything on, Dad leaving was still his fault. Until Ivan came along, life was perfect.

Ivan pushed his plate of porridge, and it landed on Mum's head.

Nigel sighed at the pathetic sight of his mother with porridge dribbling down her face.

'Ivan?' cried Mum.

'Boo,' said Ivan with a crooked smile as his mum's head appeared above the tray with an upside-down plate on it.

Mum didn't laugh. Nor did Nigel. But Gordon did.

Nigel was incensed. How dare that walking abomination try to usurp Nigel's father and Nigel himself, and then laugh in the face of Nigel's disabled brother and unfortunate mother! What an outrage!

The Code of Chivalry Rule Number I says *Thou*

Shalt Crush the Monsters that Steal Our Land and Rob Our People. That also surely included stealing mothers by sucking up to their disabled sons.

That afternoon Nigel spotted Gordon outside, tinkering with Mum's car.

Nigel took that opportunity and wheeled his brother into the TV room, and put on Ivan's favourite DVD, the test pattern. Nigel then sat lovingly, but with great authority, next to his brother and explained their dire situation.

'Gordon is trying to worm his way into our mother's affections again. You must not respond to him. Okay? Can you give me a clue, just the smallest one, that you understand?'

'Oo,' said Ivan.

'Boo, Ivan,' sighed Nigel.

Nigel stared into Ivan's grey eyes. Were those hundreds of hours he had spent teaching him the alphabet and counting totally wasted? What about all those nature documentaries he had forced Ivan to watch? And all the facts Nigel had read to him from the *Encyclopedia Britannica*?

He gazed intently into his brother's roving eyes, scanning and plumbing their depths. Even stem cells wouldn't help if Ivan didn't try intellectually.

If only he, Nigel, could just get a hint that Ivan was

faking it the tiniest bit. He just needed something to work with.

'Mum says you are as helpless as a newborn baby. But I do not think so. You are eight years old. Soon to be nine, Ivan. But I have noted the way you always laugh when you throw things on the floor and when Mum picks them up. Newborn babies do not have senses of humour. And remember when you were four? Remember you were able to walk for a while? True, only a few wobbly steps, and with help, but still you did do it. A couple of times. And a new baby most definitely can not walk. Do you understand me? Why did you stop?'

Ivan gazed out the window at the tree as the wind rustled through the leaves, and the branches made a creaking sound as they pushed against the house.

Nigel felt hopeless. Like he was drowning.

Deep down he feared his mother was right about Ivan.

All his fury at his brother dissipated in a wave of helplessness, and hopelessness.

'I don't hate you, Ivan,' he whispered. 'Not all the time. It's just sometimes . . .'

Just then the Orc walked in all covered in grease and winked at Ivan.

Nigel was shocked. It almost looked like Ivan had smiled back.

Perhaps Ivan's mouth had just twitched involuntarily, Nigel decided. Otherwise it would be an outrageous act of betrayal.

Or perhaps it was wind.

Nigel threw Ivan a *You are under suspicion* look.

'How goes it, Nige?' called out Gordon.

Nigel ignored him.

Nigel hated the way Gordon called him that, *Nige*. He had no right to.

As every honourable person knows, you must earn the right to call someone a nickname. You can't just take a short cut by sleeping with their mother. That's outright cheating! And in actual fact more likely to require you to call them a much longer name, for instance Master Nigel Constantine Dorking Esquire.

'Laddie, just so you know,' said the Orc, 'I stayed on the couch here last night. Okay?'

The Orc pointed to the couch in front of the telly.

'Your mum was exhausted, and I thought I'd give her a wee break from gettin' up to his highness in the night, that's all.'

Even though he felt relieved, Nigel gave Gordon no indication of this. After all, getting up to Ivan in the night was surely just part of this cunning knuckle-dragger's plan to impress Mum.

'And, Nigel,' Gordon continued, 'I shouldna borrowed your dad's dressing-gown. Can ya forgive me?'

From the glare Nigel gave him it was clear that *No* was Nigel's answer.

Nigel scowled and looked darkly at the interloper. Just then Ivan cried out.

'Ahhgeeoo!'

'Och, wee Ivan,' said Gordon. 'Come on, laddie, I reckon you need a wee walk.'

'Don't you mean "a wee wheel",' said Nigel, 'as in case you haven't noticed, he cannot walk.'

Ivan gurgled.

Nigel glared at Ivan.

'Would you like to come, Nigel?'

'I most certainly would not.'

Chapter V

I, Nigel Dorking, Do Hereby Swear Never to Gloat, Even in Victory.

'Die, Sporkular, thou fiend,' cried the valiant knight.

Nigel the Notorious stood victorious, one foot on the partially slain beast who lay almost lifeless on the ground at his feet, his sword raised high for his final blow.

However, as fate had decreed, just as he was about to claim victory and avenge evil by thrusting his sword into the lower intestines of the drooling monstrosity, in walked his mother with a heap of green enviro shopping bags.

'Nigel!' she cried, dropping them on the bench.

(Note from author. Even in ancient times, whenever it was the least convenient, mothers would walk in.)

Nigel Dorking replaced his sword into its plastic scabbard. He dearly wished his mother had not just witnessed that scene as she was likely to misunderstand Nigel's noble intentions.

Ivan had begun wheezing.

'I'll get the Ventolin,' called Nigel responsibly as he

dashed to the medicine cabinet.

Nigel gave his brother the Ventolin. He struggled to get Ivan off the floor and into his wheelchair.

'Oh, Nige! He's getting too big for you, love,' Mum called, racing over to help.

'Mum, don't,' Nigel warned her. 'Your back, remember? And I can do this.'

With manly strength, he lifted Ivan up off the linoleum and into his wheelchair and Ivan gave a particularly goofy grin. Dribble ran down his left cheek.

Despite himself, Nigel found his mouth smiled back. Sometimes he found it was really hard not to give in and love Ivan just the way he was. And Nigel wanted to. Quite a lot, actually. But that would mean defeat, Nigel reminded himself sternly.

He would not go soft on Ivan, particularly in front of Mum. He, Nigel, needed to set a good example.

After all, had the Principal at last year's information night not said, 'If you have high expectations, your children might just fulfil them?'

Nigel's smile quickly faded. And so did that warm squishy feeling he'd had inside.

For Ivan's sake. And for Mum and Dad's – Nigel knew he must not give in to mushy feelings.

It was a lot easier when he reminded himself that it was exactly when Ivan had been born that the fights between Mum and Dad had started and that from there everything had gone downhill. Ivan was clearly the reason Babette had been able to capture Dad so easily.

Nigel felt his heart harden.

Later, Mum came in and sat on Nigel's bed and leant over to give him a kiss.

He sensed she wanted to talk about *him*, Gordon. And he, Nigel, did not want this.

'We won't play Sporkular again,' Nigel promised unbidden. 'It is not a game I even enjoy. It was for Ivan.'

'Nige, love,' laughed Mum, 'I don't mind if you play Sporkular. It's just better if Ivan isn't the one, 'cause of his asthma, who has to lie on the floor. Wouldn't it be better if you played the role of Sporkular the Evil?'

That really stung Nigel.

Obviously he never intended to play this game again, given it was so childish. He had only done it for Ivan.

But it was the principle.

'Mum, Ivan is Sporkular,' he tried to explain. But she didn't seem to understand.

Was this evidence that brain cells started to die off at an alarming rate once people hit forty?

How could Nigel convey to her that Ivan was better qualified? That Sporkular had to be evil, and terrible to behold – a six-headed dragon monster that pretended to be helpless, and that when kind knights happened upon him he would try to suffocate them with his terrible drool? And that the kind knight was forced to save the world and kill him?

Mum would only get angry and stick up for Ivan.

'If I played Sporkular,' Nigel said carefully, deliberately choosing small words with few syllables, 'that would mean Ivan would have to be the knight.'

Nigel hoped this would be self-explanatory, and would settle things. But quite clearly it did not.

'And what's wrong with that, love?' asked Mum.

This shocked Nigel.

Until this moment he had never realised quite how limited intellectually his mother actually was, and where Ivan might have got his condition from.

Wasn't it perfectly obvious? Ivan couldn't possibly be the knight. He couldn't even hold a sword properly. He'd probably suck it.

'Mum, he doesn't even have a suit of armour,' explained Nigel patiently.

'You could lend him yours,' suggested Mum.

'Mum,' said Nigel, taking a different approach, 'it's just that lying down is one of Ivan's skills. And I am better at standing up. And knights always stand up to beat evil monsters.'

'Couldn't he be a knight in a wheelchair?' suggested Mum.

Nigel was appalled. No wonder there were no noble female knights if she were typical of her gender.

'Mum, that is a most unsensible suggestion,' he reprimanded her. 'If you look through the legends of the great knights there is not one single knight in a wheelchair. And what's more, given we are not going to play it any more it is non-relevant.'

'Okay, Nige,' Mum smiled. She then leant over and kissed him on the forehead. 'Nighty night, knight.'

And then, once she reached the door she turned and whispered, 'By the way, love, give Gordon a go. It'll do you good to have a male role model around.'

'I already have a male role model,' said Nigel, turning away from his treacherous, weak-minded mother.

Mum sighed.

'I know, love, it's just Gordon's got more time on his hands. He's around more. And he relates to people rather than water flowcharts and plungers.'

'He is not my father,' insisted Nigel emphatically. 'And he's a moron.'

'Nigel!' reprimanded Mum. And then she continued in a much nicer voice, 'Did you know that Gordon is actually descended from ancestors that were real knights?'

'There were some knights,' frowned Nigel, 'who pillaged, and were pitiless, brutal, and very cruel.'

Mum sighed.

'They even have a coat of arms if you are interested.'

'I am not,' said Nigel.

I, Nigel Dorking, Do Hereby Swear Always to Outwit Serpents and Fight All Manner of Evil Dragons, Even Unto Death.

'Leavin' early, laddie?' called Gordon this morning (Monday), as Nigel passed the kitchen. Milk from his mushed Weetabix dribbled into his red beard. Nigel shuddered.

'If you can wait a wee minute I'll give you a lift.'

'I would rather walk,' said Nigel, who then added quietly so Gordon couldn't hear, *'through hell.'*

Nigel stood outside Dad's. He took a deep breath, summoning the courage to ring Dad's bell. Then he thought of Gordon, sitting in Dad's chair.

This was urgent.

His finger pressed the intercom buzzer by the gate, and the gate creaked open as if by magic. Nigel walked through, towards the front door.

The front door opened. And there in the doorway stood the ice queen, Babette, only her head visible as she peered suspiciously at Nigel and restrained the vicious sausage dog by its collar.

'Remember me? I'm Nigel.'

'Oh, hello, Nigel. I don't believe we've met.'

'Not formally, no,' said Nigel, who wanted to add, *and I believe your name is Cruella*. But he fought this desire.

'And what is his name?' said Nigel, pointing to the snarling beast.

'Her,' corrected Babette. 'She is a bitch.'

Nigel just stopped himself saying, *No, that is you.*

'Lotsa is her name. So what do you want, Nigel?'

He did not say, *For you to spontaneously combust and for your gizzards to be fed to wild animals.* As he would never inflict such poison on innocent creatures.

'Is my father here?' he said instead, as haughtily as he could.

'Your father isn't here. He had an emergency.'

'Oh, did he leave a signed form behind for me to pick up?'

'No.'

Nigel had not expected this. Outright lies. Or sabotage. Had she hidden the form from Dad? Would she stoop so low? But then he remembered her attempt on his life on Saturday and realised she would stop at nothing.

'But I most definitely left a form for him on Saturday with a note,' he said sternly, not budging.

'Look, Nigel, we're very busy so . . .'

'Well, actually it is quite important,' insisted Nigel, taking a step forward and not allowing her to close the door, 'so if I could come in and have a look on his desk?'

'Well, no. This is not a good time.' Her mouth smiled but her eyes did not. 'I've got the girls in the car, ready for school.'

'When is a good time?' he demanded. 'Tomorrow?'

'No,' she said, 'he will be starting very early and working extremely late tomorrow.'

Then, pushing him out, she closed the door in his face.

Nigel stumbled backwards, and had it not been for some unusually nimble footwork, he would have fallen over.

'You foul witch,' he muttered, momentarily succumbing to unknightly language, 'you are dead meat. If indeed it be flesh you are made of. But I actually suspect it is more likely that you come from the eggs maggots lay, you ghoulish, writhing, foul green evil stench. And unto that you shall return.'

Nigel's schoolbag was heavy on his back.

He had promised Miss Murray he would have his signed form in today.

And he particularly wasn't looking forward to school.

'Hey, there's the knight in a shining girl's dress,' yelled a familiar voice from behind him as Nigel approached the school.

Nigel put his head down and walked more quickly.

How could he defend himself?

Then he remembered. The brain was one weapon you were allowed to bring to school. And Nigel, being in the 98th percentile on the WISK test for kids his age, had an extremely potent weapon at his disposal.

'Okay now, hands up those who have their forms ready for Father and Son Night and Father and Son Bonding Camp.'

Nigel tried just with the power of his mind to make his own molecules smaller, hoping as a result that he might shrink into his chair and that consequently no one might notice he was the only boy in class who did not have his hand up.

'Haven't you got a dad?' asked Jeremy Fry who sat next to him. Jeremy, the new kid, the most annoying kid in the world. Why had he even come to this school? Why couldn't his mother have stayed living in the outback?

'Of course I have a father,' Nigel retorted in a whisper. 'It is virtually impossible for a living organism not to have a father unless of course you are a microbe.'

'I know that,' whispered Jeremy stupidly. 'I meant –'

'Hey, Dorko,' sneered Bruno. 'Isn't your dad coming?'

Nigel glared at Jeremy. This was his fault.

'Is there a reason why you don't have your hand up, Nigel Dorking?' asked Miss Murray as she approached.

'Ah well, of course my father is coming,' said Nigel. 'It is just he doesn't want to promise until he is absolutely sure he can, as he is a modern-day knight and they never go back on their word.'

'And seeing my father has such an important job,' he continued, 'it is very difficult for him to get time off. I imagine it is similar for the Prime Minister or the Governor-General or some other such indignatories.'

The whole class groaned in what Nigel knew to be outright envy.

'You are so up yourself, Dorko,' sneered Bruno.

Knowing this attack was prompted by extreme jealousy helped Nigel to ignore it.

'Excuse me!' said Miss Murray, trying to regain control of the class.

'Well,' Nigel went on, gallantly helping Miss Murray by speaking in a much lower tone, 'if I am "up myself", that is probably because I am in the ninety-eighth percentile of intelligence for kids of my age on the WISK test, if you must know.'

'Bragger,' said Hope Henshaw.

'Oh,' piped up Jeremy Fry, 'I am in the ninety-ninth percentile!'

Jeremy looked thrilled.

You are the most annoying living creature on this planet or any other, including blowflies, gnats, and leeches, thought Nigel as he battled an almighty urge to put both hands around Jeremy's scrawny neck and to squeeze tight.

'Oooh! Nigel's got competition!' teased Stella. 'Jeremy Fry is smarter than Nigel Dorking. Ooh! Gunna cry are you, Nigel?'

Nigel could cheerfully have banged both their heads together and put Jeremy and Stella out of all of their misery. But sadly there were rules against that sort of thing.

'It was just a test,' scowled Nigel. 'And actually I wasn't particularly well on that day.'

Kids were now hooting with laughter. At what, Nigel could not tell. But as the saying goes, empty vessels make the most sound. (Meaning, idiots are noisy.)

Miss Murray rapped the wooden metre ruler on her desk to regain control.

Thwack!

This was all Jeremy Fry's fault for drawing attention to Nigel not having his hand up.

'You big girl,' whispered Bruno.

'Hey yeah,' called out Hope. 'How come girls don't

get a father and daughter camp?'

'Duh!' called out Kyla. 'It's harder for boys because they're like totally immature wimpo losers who become like totally maladjusted and start beating up old ladies and spearing kittens and stuff if they don't get special time with their daddies.'

An antagonistic roar went up in the class from the boys. Hope sat there looking very satisfied, her hand in the air making a big L sign, for losers.

'Enough!' roared Miss Murray, glaring at them all. 'Hope, hand down.'

'You're just jealous, Hope,' whispered Bruno.

Miss Murray turned her quelling laser-beam eyes on Bruno and then the others in the class. Finally her gaze came to rest on Nigel and her beautiful eyes softened.

'Right, Nigel,' she said, 'if your family are having problems paying for Father and Son Bonding Camp, see me at recess. Now, everyone, not a single word!'

'Ah, just one word if I may,' Nigel said politely. 'There are most definitely no financial difficulties at all, in fact, on the contrary, it's quite the opposite, we are actually quite rich, actually. For your information, we have three toilets.'

'Who doesn't?' scowled Hope.

'What did I say?' said Miss Murray.

'Well, people with two or one toilet obviously,' said Nigel scathingly.

'Enough!' roared Miss Murray, her eyes flashing. 'No more baiting Nigel. And next person who speaks will cause the whole class to stay in at lunchtime!'

'But let me just say –' blurted Nigel.

'Right,' said Miss Murray, whizzing round and facing him. 'I am sorry, Nigel, but the whole class will now have to stay in at lunchtime because of you.'

The whole class groaned.

Suddenly Nigel felt he knew how the people on the *Titanic* must have felt when they realised their ship was sinking. Except they weren't being jabbed in the back by a lead pencil at the same time.

'I'll get you for this, Dorking,' threatened Bruno, withdrawing his lead pencil. 'We were gunna practise for the inter-school footy match on Saturday at lunchtime. If our school loses you are dead meat.'

Even Jeremy scowled at him. Jeremy, the most unpopular boy in the school!

'Alright!' called Miss Murray. 'In an orderly fashion head to your lockers please and grab your sports uniform as PE is next. And today, I believe, is football.'

Nigel had dearly hoped it would be table tennis.

'No groans, Nigel!' she chastised him, but with a smile that only Nigel could detect, one that said, *Ah, the extremely intellectual students always despise sport.*

I, Nigel Dorking, Do Hereby Swear Always to Practise Humility and All Other Knightly Virtues.

Nigel spied Jeremy Fry trailing behind the A-team players.

'Shouldn't Jeremy Fry be with us, the B-team?' suggested Nigel extremely helpfully.

'No, Jeremy has been chosen for the A-team,' said the coach.

'Favouritism,' complained a voice near Nigel, but quietly so Coach couldn't hear.

This was extremely galling. It was an outrage.

Jeremy was a flea. A squib. A total wimp.

It was also an insult. An affront. Nigel himself had not been picked for one A-team, ever. Not even for the egg-and-spoon race. And he had been at this school his whole life.

'Listen B-team,' said Coach, 'one of you will be chosen as a reserve for the footy match on Saturday, so show me what you're made of. Run to the far tree. Ready, set, go!'

It must have been a mixture of sunstroke, and a

small desire to make the coach realise he had been a total idiot choosing someone as inferior as Jeremy for A-team. For in the heat of the moment, he, Nigel, totally forgot that he did not want to play football of a Saturday afternoon. Or any afternoon. Ever. And unfortunately ran his fastest. (Which is actually surprisingly fast.)

And even though he remembered just in time and slowed down before the peppercorn tree for Alyssa to overtake him, it didn't help at all. For Coach then did a most spiteful thing.

'Alyssa and Nigel,' he said, 'you are my reserves.'

'Unfair!' puffed Nigel who clutched his side due to a stitch. 'You said you only wanted one.'

But as everyone knows, sports teachers are unusually unintelligent with short memories because all their blood rushes to their legs for running and their arms for catching, leaving none for their brain for thinking.

'No I didn't,' Coach either lied or forgot.

So, now he, Nigel, would have to attend the football match on Saturday.

What an imposition! And a waste of his extremely precious time.

And it was all Jeremy's fault.

Though the two kids he had beaten on B-team did look at him with newfound respect, particularly Emily, who was very inferior at running possibly partly due to her prosthetic leg.

Finally, the lunch bell went. Miss Murray came to speak with Coach, and all the kids were rounded up and told they had fifteen minutes before coming in for the detention, so they must eat their lunch quickly.

Nigel tried to ignore their accusing looks. Instead, he went to the library.

'I cannot find *One Thousand and One Medieval Facts*,' he complained to the librarian.

'Someone else must have it out,' she said.

Nigel sat in detention, making a medieval invitation for Dad for the Knight of Knights, the trivia night being held at the school for the end of term. He was certain Dad would come to this. And they'd win.

Finally the end-of-school bell went.

It was amazing how fast Nigel managed to get home at knights' pace – twenty paces running and twenty paces walking for when there was no available horse. He did not actually want to run due to not wanting another stitch. Or blister. After all, it was a long way, almost two whole kilometres.

Perhaps Dad had got the form and had sent it to him, he hoped, his heart beating fast as he walked into his driveway. Perhaps Babette hadn't intercepted it after all.

In that case, he could race it back to school this afternoon as technically it was still a school-day until four o'clock.

But Nigel was sorely disappointed.

He raced knights' pace back to the school.

'Could I please have two forms for Father and Son Night and the Camp?' he asked at the school office.

Mrs Pile looked at him suspiciously. Though, Nigel reasoned, women in the school office always did that. Probably because they are bitter about being women in the school office. Anyone would probably give people suspicious looks under those circumstances. Even civilised, helpful people.

He knocked on the staffroom door.

'Miss Murray,' he entreated, 'Dad would most definitely like to come on camp. It's just that his form has been held up probably by the inefficiency of Australia Post. I promise I'll get it to you tomorrow. Is that alright?'

'Alright, Nigel,' Miss Murray said.

To thank her, Nigel remembered what he had in his pocket. He quickly whipped out one of the business cards he had designed for his dad and printed out on his computer at home.

It read,

Plumbing or toilet installation needs?

Call Day and Knight Plumber and Son

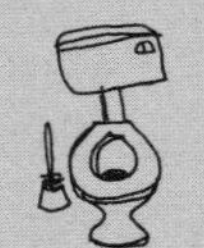

(Formerly of Toilets R Us fame)

042108095

Prompt, Professional, Chivalrous

'Oh,' said Miss Murray, trying to hide her obvious admiration.

'Just in case,' smiled Nigel as he inclined his head ever so slightly with just a hint of a courtly manner as he backed away. He needed no thanks. Just the possibility of being part of a plumbing team (the business-card designer) that saved a possible future damsel in distress was enough reward.

Then, to his astonishment, out of the staffroom walked Jeremy Fry with *1001 Medieval Facts* tucked under his arm.

'Oh,' said Nigel, affronted. 'I believe the staffroom is for teachers only. And also, I would suggest that the book you are carrying on medieval facts is actually due back in the library.' He took off, the precious forms flapping in his hand as he ran.

'I would like to send this by registered mail,' explained Nigel to the man in the post office a few minutes later.

'So does that mean it will have to be given directly to the person I am sending it to and that they will have to sign for it?'

'Yes,' said the man.

'Good,' returned Nigel.

And just in case she, the Evil One, intercepted it with her magic, and managed to undermine the whole of Australia Post, he would deliver the second personally to Dad, on Wednesday after school, seeing Dad was so busy on Tuesday. She, the Evil One, would not outwit him!

After dinner, Nigel sat at his desk in his bedroom making ticks and crosses next to the list of items he would need for camp. He was disturbed by an unfamiliar night noise that caused him to race to his bedroom window, and peek through his curtain.

It was that red bike. And it took off with an almighty roar, like a perpetrator from a crime scene, when Nigel opened the curtain. Obviously he, Nigel, had been spotted when that chink of light from his bedroom window had shone through and given him away.

Nigel stared into the darkness, still dazzled by the after-image of the flash of the bike. He stood wondering who it could be. Until at least nine o'clock.

Was this her doing?

I, Nigel Dorking, Do Hereby Swear Always to Play Fair. Even to Mine Enemy, I Will Mercy Show.

The next morning, before school, after Nigel had got ready in his uniform, he noted Gordon's van was once again parked outside their home.

He had obviously arrived after nine o'clock the night before or Nigel would have seen him while he was looking out for the mystery rider. Late to be arriving at anyone's home!

This was getting way too serious. Gordon never used to stay the night. Obviously things between Mum and Gordon were out of control. Intervention was clearly now needed.

But to make a pre-emptive strike, Nigel needed more information about Gordon.

He had a plan emerging. But first he would check the couch in the living room.

Gordon had even gone to the trouble of leaving a slept-in-looking sleeping bag and pillow there, just to trick Nigel. Clever, but not clever enough.

Gordon had Mum's car bonnet open, his head stuck inside, as he tinkered with things. Nigel walked over to him, and stood near by. It even crossed his mind that were he to let the bonnet down the Orc problem would be gone.

But Nigel reminded himself of the Knights' Code of Chivalry Rule VIII, *Thou Shalt Always Play Fair. Even to Thine Enemy, Thou Must Mercy Show.*

What was that stench? Nigel was overcome with the fumes. He remembered how in Tolkien's Middle-earth the Orcs stank. Then he recalled the strange deodorant he'd spied in the bathroom earlier, bright orange with the words *exotic garden freshness* written on it.

He can try to impress Mum by camouflaging himself and trying to smell like an exotic garden, thought Nigel, but he won't fool me.

'Good morning, wee laddie,' said the Orc.

'I am not wee,' said Nigel. 'For your information, I come up to my mother's bosoms.'

Gordon chuckled his disgusting chuckle. 'Care for a Lolly Gobble Bliss Bomb?'

Nigel stared with distaste at the bag of sweets he was being offered.

'No, thank you. I do not happen to want to keep dentists in business.'

The Orc chuckled again.

Nigel shuddered. Imbeciles often chuckle a lot, he decided.

He couldn't stand anything about this man, his big, red, bristling beard, his stupid, ignorant laugh.

'It's only fair to warn you,' said Nigel, 'that Mum and Dad are getting back together very soon. In fact, it is imminent.'

'Oh. Is that so?' Gordon said.

'Yes, it is,' said Nigel.

'Well, there you have it!' Gordon said.

This was a fairly stupid thing to say under the circumstances as it meant absolutely nothing.

'And oh,' said Nigel as casually as he could, pretending to study his nails, 'I thought you should know my mother does have some pretty bad habits.'

Gordon looked surprised.

'Really? Is that so?' he asked.

'Well, yes,' said Nigel. 'Not only can't she cook, but she doesn't even care that she can't. And she burns things you didn't think were possible. Like water. And you should see her drawers. She's got underpants in her sock drawer and jumpers in her bra drawer.'

To Nigel, this was a travesty, but Gordon didn't look as shocked as he should have.

'Oh well. To each his own,' he said, and began whistling.

So Nigel pulled out his big gun.

'And sometimes she waters the vegetables without any clothes on.'

Gordon threw his head back and laughed. Uproariously.

He must have seen her, thought Nigel, outraged. It was most unkind to laugh that hard, and for that long!

Don't worry, thought Nigel, I will get you.

Then Nigel seamlessly brought up the topic of front door keys. And the ridiculous places some people left theirs.

Then, having all the information he needed, he walked back inside, hoping he had not done his mother a disservice. But if he had it was for a noble purpose.

For this emerging Gordon situation was now extremely urgent.

'Your camp form, Nigel,' Miss Murray prompted him in class. And Nigel felt his cheeks betray him.

'Unfortunately, Dad probably can't get it here until tomorrow,' he explained, 'due to his heavy workload, due to his extreme popularity, and importance. But he is trying very hard.'

Miss Murray sighed.

'Len Dorking? Isn't he that dunny-can guy?' hissed Bruno. 'People must be crapping heaps at the moment.'

'Yeah, big giant poos,' joined in Reece.

'Right,' said Miss Murray, whizzing around to face them. 'Meet me at one o'clock, here. To pick up papers at lunchtime. Only speak when asked.'

The class was now quiet.

Unnaturally quiet.

Nigel could not resist. His father's honour and reputation were now at stake. And a strange out-of-control feeling was taking over.

'If I could just say,' Nigel interjected politely, putting up his hand, 'that in actual point of fact, my father used to run Toilets R Us, which, if you must know, for your information, did not stock dunnies as you call them but rather the very top range of porcelain water-saving toilets, in a range of colours and sizes with the half- and full-flush options.'

'Nigel!' warned Miss Murray.

Nigel had still fully intended to further explain about his heroic father. But Miss Murray's face would have made the Viking ships turn back, head home and forget all about invading Britain.

The words caught in his throat.

Her arms were crossed, and her normally melting Mars Bar eyes had hardened like they'd been in the freezer for a month.

'Do you want to keep the class in again?' she asked.

The whole class seemed to be staring at him.

'No,' whispered Nigel as he wondered whether in

future he might try to find maidens in distress who were less scary. And more distressed.

For their last class they had library. Nigel was scanning the shelves for *1001 Medieval Facts* when Jeremy tapped him on the shoulder, causing him to cry out in great startlement.

'Do not do that,' chastised Nigel. 'Never ever creep up on someone else, unless they are an adversary.'

Nigel did not like Jeremy one bit. He regarded him coolly. Especially as he was now doing star jumps in the library.

'Well, what do you want?' said Nigel. 'And I think star jumps are uninappropriate for the library.'

'Quiet ones are,' insisted Jeremy.

Nigel did not like being contradicted, particularly by an annoying idiot. And Jeremy was the most annoying of the lot. Ever since Jeremy had started at the school that year he had put Nigel out of a job. Nigel was certain he himself had made a much better library monitor. And a better whiteboard monitor.

Though, in Jeremy's favour, he had replaced Nigel as most unpopular boy in the school.

'Well,' said Nigel curtly. 'I haven't got all day.'

Jeremy cleared his throat as he looked down at his feet. And for the first time stood still. Not even any buttock or jaw crunches.

'Well, it's just that we are supposed to settle before Father and Son Night who we are sharing tents with on the Father and Son Bonding Camp. And I was wondering if you and your father would like to share a tent with me and my father?'

Nigel stared back, appalled.

'Not to put too thinner point on it, no,' he said quite firmly, 'and I would have thought that being library monitor, you should know there is no talking in the library.'

'I think you meant "fine a point",' said Jeremy.

'No,' said Nigel. 'I meant "thinner".'

'Shh,' glared Miss Rubens directly at Nigel.

Nigel stood there stunned. Not only was it the first time the librarian had ever had to tell him to be quiet, but it was all Jeremy's fault.

'Would you care to come and practise football with me at my dad's?' suggested Jeremy.

'No, I would not care to,' said Nigel.

Chapter IX

I, Nigel Dorking, Do Hereby Swear to Eschew Unfairness, Meanness and Deceit, and Pledge to Use Strategy First, the Sword Second.

Nigel knew exactly where the Orc lived. This was the right street. Guinevere Street. Gordon's street.

It was 4 p.m., exactly the perfect time to do a background check on him. For Gordon would be out driving all the handicapped kids home in the special bus. Though not for long.

Technically, Nigel had to admit, this was a break-in, but Nigel knew his purpose was noble, and that he was in fact bringing justice to the wicked.

It's true he was nervous. But when he remembered he was doing this for Dad, so Mum would be available for him when Nigel had split Dad up from Babette, he felt full of new resolve. For then he could resume a real relationship with Dad.

As a result of an earlier inquisition, and his incredible deductive powers, Nigel knew exactly where Gordon kept his spare key.

Nigel had prompted the Orc, that very morning,

'Some people leave spare keys in the stupidest of places, like under a pot at their back door.'

And the brain-cell challenged Orc had laughed and actually said, 'Hey! That's exactly where I leave mine!'

As Nigel stole down the side path, towards Gordon's back door, he had the odd sensation of being followed.

If Jeremy has followed me, he thought, fury overtaking him, I will use him for archery target practice, without the tennis balls.

He found the key. Exactly where Gordon had said.

Nigel wasn't certain what to expect from the headquarters of an Orc-like person. Probably cave-like, he thought, with straw for sleeping on, and an open area for a fire, probably with bones strewn everywhere from his horrible human feasts.

But on entering, he didn't find any human remains, or any foul stench, but something much worse: it was the messiest house he had ever been in.

Nigel set about searching. He had to do this. He needed solid evidence. Of what, he wasn't quite sure.

In the living room he was greeted with something most surprising. Possibly very incriminating evidence. All in bits, strewn over the floor were about three wheelchairs, various implements and pumps, and a welder. Why would anyone have such things on their floor if they were not involved in some wheelchair-stealing racket? This was an outrage.

This shocked Nigel. Of course Gordon was in the perfect position. He was the one who helped the disabled in and out of his bus.

Mum would not want to marry a wheelchair criminal. They were the lowest of the low. Despicable.

Nigel spotted more evidence – a framed picture.

It was just what he was after. Gordon with another woman, who was clearly not Nigel's mother.

Then, from behind him, Nigel heard footsteps.

Coming from the laundry.

He made a quick dive behind the couch, and was planning on grabbing a fire poker, when someone grabbed him.

'Hey,' yelled an angry-faced youth with dreadlocks and a biker jacket. 'What are you doing here?'

Nigel's legs went to porridge and his heart felt like it might detonate.

'Who are you?' he managed, though not as authoritatively as he had hoped, as it came out as more of a squeak.

'Ray,' said the man with a wild look in his eye. 'Gordon's son.'

Nigel was stunned but remained in masterful control of the situation.

'I'm Nigel,' he said.

'You are too,' said the startled intruder, who now looked vaguely familiar. 'You're the kid who belongs to Kelly, the old man's new squeeze.'

After translating what this intruder had said into English, Nigel still did not know what he meant.

'Kelly is my mother,' said Nigel to this man who looked about eighteen, and was pretty scruffy. 'I am Nigel. Nigel Dorking.'

Nigel held out his hand.

Ray shook Nigel's proffered hand, his face breaking into a smile. 'You're the very dude I've come to town to see.'

'Me?' said Nigel.

'Yeah,' Ray said, plonking himself down on the couch. 'And the old man. But I hadn't planned on today.'

Ray patted the space on the couch next to him. 'Relax, Max,' he said.

'Ah, Nigel,' Nigel corrected him.

Ray grinned as Nigel sat beside him.

It was weird. Even though Ray looked very untidy, which in Nigel's book was a crime, and even though he had a poor grasp of the English language (also a crime), Nigel still found he quite liked him. In fact, he realised he was feeling very sorry for him, particularly having a father like Gordon. So instead of being judgmental, Nigel was trying to be understanding and friendly.

'Sorry for freakin' you out before, man,' said Ray, scratching his head. 'It's just . . . your mum is the first girlfriend the old man has had since . . .' his voice trailed off.

Nigel didn't like to interrupt. In case this person was nuts. So far he seemed unpredictable. And right now he seemed far away.

'Since me mum died,' he said finally, looking directly at Nigel with forget-me-not blue eyes. 'And I just can't handle it. I'm so jealous, man.'

Nigel was stunned. 'Of what?' he ventured. 'Mum?'

Ray sat there, nodding as he thought.

'No, man. You.'

Now Nigel was staggered.

'Me?'

Ray sighed. And then scratched his head again and said with an apologetic look, 'It's just I can't handle the idea of me old man havin' another son. A replacement one.'

'But I'm not his son,' said Nigel emphatically. 'And I never will be.'

'Thanks, man,' said Ray, holding up his hand, his palm facing out.

Nigel was stunned. He realised Ray wanted to high five him.

Nigel put up his palm, and they hit hands.

It felt good. Nigel's hand buzzed. He had never been high fived before.

Ray now sighed deeply and then laughed. 'What a dope I am, hey? I'd been imaginin' you as some real perfect kid and you and Dad gettin' on so great. And truth is, you're not. You're just a normal kid.'

'Not exactly,' said Nigel.

'You're cool,' Ray continued.

Nigel decided it was best to keep his mouth shut and not wreck this image. It was nice, someone thinking he was cool. Ray was obviously quite smart despite his grammar. And perceptive.

'Truth is, man,' Ray said after a while, 'I've been plannin' on confrontin' you. And the old man. All week. I just haven't had the guts.'

Nigel was astonished. Ray looked like he would always have the guts.

'Yeah,' said Ray sheepishly. 'I've been ridin' past your joint every day since I've been back.'

'How did you know my address?' asked Nigel after decoding what *joint* meant.

Ray dug his hand deep into his pocket and pulled out letters. A bundle of them.

'All from Dad,' he said forlornly. 'Raves about you, bro.'

This stunned Nigel into silence. Nigel had rarely

been struck dumb in his life, but the knowledge that Gordon had written glowing letters about him to Ray momentarily took away his ability to speak. This was perplexing. But it certainly felt good to have someone calling him *bro*.

Nigel even wondered if there were some way he could keep Ray in his life but still get rid of Gordon.

'Every day I've been waitin'. Waitin' out there on my bike. For hours sometimes, just tryin' to find the courage. But ah, I just can't find it in me. Was gunna blast him.'

'Did you say *on your bike*?' asked Nigel.

'Yeah,' said Ray distractedly.

'Motorbike?'

'Yeah.'

'A red motorbike?'

'Yeah,' said Ray, obviously still mentally confronting his Dad.

'It was you!' said Nigel. 'You scared my assailants off.'

Ray shrugged. 'Hey, man, I wanted to give you a bad time, but when I saw you stridin' along in your armour like that, that's when I thought, wow.'

Nigel felt proud.

'Most kids your age wouldn't have the guts. I like that.' Ray had a faraway wistful look. 'I knew a kid like that once,' he continued. 'Though he didn't use such big words.'

'Do you still see that kid?' asked Nigel.

'No,' said Ray sadly.

Nigel would like to have known more, but Ray changed the topic abruptly.

'Anyway,' said Ray, 'that's how come I was waitin' outside here. Saw some figure disappearin' round the side just before. Sorry to freak you out, man. But I thought you were, you know, a burgular.'

Normally, Nigel would have corrected anyone who said 'burgular', but he didn't.

It's true, thought Nigel, he does look a lot like Gordon. Though Nigel tried not to hold that against him.

'So you think Mum and Gordon are pretty serious?' whispered Nigel after a while.

'Yep,' said Ray, looking forlornly in the direction of the photograph. That's when Nigel realised the photo was of Ray's mum. 'From these letters.'

They both sat there in silence together. For ages.

'It'd be kinda nice to have you as a little bro I reckon. Now I've met you.'

'I know all the rules for the Knights' Code of Chivalry,' offered Nigel.

'Wow,' said Ray, obviously impressed. 'But I'm not ready for this, man. No disrespect to you or your mum. I'm sure she's great.'

'I'm not ready for this either,' agreed Nigel.

'Any ideas?'

'Nope,' said Nigel, adopting Ray's lingo. 'But in case I do have any, where are you staying?'

'In Dad's shed as of last night,' said Ray. 'Been sleepin' in the park till then. Hey, here's my mobile number. Just in case.'

Ray scribbled it on a piece of paper. Nigel folded it neatly and put it in his school bag.

'Cool,' said Ray after a while.

Nigel nodded, 'Cool.'

They sat there for a long while, the both of them, nodding like a pair of nodding dogs and rapping.

'Wanna lift home?' asked Ray eventually.

Nigel had never been on the back of a motorbike before. It was incredibly exhilarating. Probably like being a pillion passenger on a steed, he thought. As everyone knows, knights often had to go pillion in medieval times, as there were often not enough horses to go around.

'I'll just drop you here,' Ray called into the wind when Nigel pointed to his driveway.

Nigel leapt off the bike and handed Ray his helmet.

Ray strapped it to his bike, grinned at Nigel, and then said, 'Hey, bro, don't tell the old man you saw me. Don't know if I'm ready to face him yet, cool?'

'Cool.'

Nigel raced inside.

No one had ever called him *bro* before. And he would never tell Ray's dad. Ever. A knight would never betray a comrade.

Chapter X

I, Nigel Dorking, Do Hereby Swear I Shall Not Recoil from Mine Enemy.

Nigel stood in the bathroom with Ivan. Ivan, who had just finished on the toilet chair and seemed to be holding out his arms.

'Or Oor,' he called, which sounded remarkably like Ivan was trying to say *Gordon* but without the consonants.

Nigel turned, and sure enough, standing there in the doorway, was Gordon.

Surely not? Ivan had only ever bothered with names of family members. Not blow-ins like Gordon.

How dare Ivan! What a traitor! It was quite clear that Ivan was asking Gordon to wipe his bottom.

No one in the history of the family had ever had the honour of wiping Ivan's bottom, except Nigel or Mum. Not ever! Not even Dad.

At that precise moment, Nigel knew that if his brother had any intelligence that he was most definitely on the enemy's side. This was a declaration of war if Ivan had even a modicum of a functioning brain.

It was a treacherous deed.

What a weasel. What a worm. What a lowly and despicable act.

Nigel glared at Ivan and narrowed his eyes to let Ivan know that he was onto him. It was a look that said *If you are capable of understanding me, understand this: I will unmask you, see if I don't. As of this moment, you are an ex-brother. I hereby dub thee 'Ivan the Terrible'.*

And Ivan the Terrible just stared back at Nigel the Notorious with eyes crossed and drool on his chin.

At dinnertime, he could tell Mum was trying to look cheerful as she laid out the silver cutlery they hardly ever used.

Then the Orc put the tacos on the table and sat down.

It was when Mum lit the candles that Nigel knew something was most definitely wrong. Mum only ever lit the candles on *very* special occasions.

They sat.

'Well, loves,' said Mum, too brightly, 'Gordon and I have an announcement to make.'

Mum looked at Gordon and squeezed his hand.

'May I be excused?' Nigel said.

Nigel got up from the table, just as Mum said, 'No, you may not. Sit, Nigel. This is important . . .'

This sounded ominous.

'. . . Gordon and I are planning on getting married.'

Nigel waited a beat, and then repeated his question.

'Now may I be excused?'

'No, Nigel,' said Mum. Not so brightly. 'Aren't you going to say anything?'

'No,' said Nigel firmly.

He was getting that out-of-control feeling.

But he could put things right. All he had to do was break them up, break Dad and Babette up, make Mum see how wonderful Dad was, make Dad see how less chaotic Mum was than she used to be, kill Babette, put her twins in an orphanage, and find a good owner for their dog. Oh, and cure Ivan.

And it shouldn't be that hard breaking up Mum and Gordon. Especially when Mum found out what a terrible father Gordon was.

'I'm telling you this, Nige,' said Mum, 'just so you know that I am taking this relationship with Gordon seriously. And that he takes you boys seriously. He's not going to leave us.'

'That is a shame,' said Nigel.

'You don't have to push him away,' continued Mum, ignoring Nigel's interjection.

Though she did gaze at him in a most particularly penetrating way. But Nigel said nothing. He stared straight ahead at his meal, ignoring all Mum's chastising looks and Gordon's lame attempts to get a smile out of him.

Those faces were not funny, they were unfortunate and stupid and he hoped the wind changed.

Dinner was eaten in silence.

Throw a fit, Ivan, Nigel sent his brother a mental telepathy message. *Redeem yourself. Let them know how you feel.*

But Ivan didn't.

'I think it's stupid, this whole pathetic wedding,' finally screamed Nigel at his mother. And as he turned to run, he dragged the tablecloth from under their dishes.

Crash.

'Nigel!' shouted Mum.

Then he ran to his room, yelling behind him, 'And if you leave us, Mum, I will never speak to you again. Ever.'

He remembered from the night Dad left how shock feels. Everything feels woolly and goes in slow motion.

His chest felt so tight he could almost not breathe and this time he did not have his chain-mail top on.

'Nige,' Mum whispered, as she popped her head into his bedroom. 'I will never leave you. Not ever, okay?

But that doesn't excuse you behaving like a maniac.'

Nigel said nothing.

'Apologise,' said Mum. 'So I can hear it.'

'I'm sorry,' said Nigel. 'Now please go.'

After Nigel had graciously deigned to clean up the mess in the dining room, he went back to his bedroom. Mum followed him in.

'Go away,' strongly suggested Nigel.

'Lovikins,' said Mum. 'Gordon would just join us, that's all. It's not going to happen soon. I wanted to give you some time to get used to the idea. And, love, he won't try to replace Dad, but he can perhaps do some things that Dad can't.'

'Like what?' challenged Nigel.

'Like be here,' said Mum. 'I just want you not to be shocked when you see Gordon around a little more often than he used to be. For you to understand that we are serious, so that if he stayed the night, that you wouldn't be upset if . . . .'

'If what?' asked Nigel.

'Lovely, you'll get used to it,' said Mum. 'You might even learn to like him in time.'

'Never,' returned Nigel through clenched teeth.

He so desperately wanted to yell after her, *Mum, Gordon rejected his own son. So don't go thinking he's a great father figure for me and Ivan.* But of course due to the Knights' Code and his allegiance to Ray, he could not divulge this evidence about his enemy the Orc's character.

Mum sighed as she padded down the hallway.

Where are you, Dad? Nigel sent him a mental telepathy message, his face in his pillow.

The only person who really understood was Gilgamesh. Nigel put one arm out and curved it around Gilgamesh's bowl, which sat on his bedside table. It felt cool, but he knew Gilgamesh's heart was warm.

Nigel left for school early. For two reasons. To avoid Mum and to find Ray and warn him. But Ray wasn't there, so Nigel had to leave a note.

Ray, it said, *Meet me after school. Three thirty-five at the Jousting Place park. Urgent.*

Nigel shoved it under the shed door at Gordon's after receiving no answer to his knock.

He could barely concentrate on school. He didn't even care when Miss Murray inquired about his form.

All he could think was *Mum is getting married. I have to stop this. This means Dad will never come back.*

Nigel ran knights' pace all the way.

There, across the park, was Ray. The red glinted in

the afternoon sun. And that was just his hair as he sat astride his magnificent, gleaming red beast.

He had come.

'Hey, bro,' Ray grinned.

Nigel couldn't help notice that when Ray smiled his whole face shone.

'Hey,' called Nigel, running over. 'Sorry about this.'

'It's cool.'

'It's just, I've got some not such great news.'

'I've seen a happier expression on a hangman,' smiled Ray. Then his expression changed. 'Is the old man okay?'

'Yes,' Nigel hastened to allay his concerns. 'But last night they announced their engagement.'

Ray just sat there looking like he'd been socked in the guts.

'Crap,' he said after a while.

'My sentiments exactly,' said Nigel. 'I mean, yeah.'

Ray looked away, and seemed to be in his own private world.

'I yelled at them,' offered Nigel. 'But it didn't make any difference.'

'No bull, I can't handle this,' sighed Ray after a while.

'Me neither,' admitted Nigel.

Ray had a strange look on his face. And didn't seem very talkative.

Nigel waited.

'Sorry, dude. I'm a gutless wonder.' Momentarily, Ray looked crestfallen. 'Wish I was more like you. I should confront Dad now. It's getting urgent, eh?'

'You're not a gutless wonder,' corrected Nigel. 'It is a well-known historical fact that when a brave knight was waiting to ambush someone, the waiting was often the scariest bit. For instance, I have to go to my dad's right now on a certain task. And I feel quite unwell. And I will be very glad when it is over.'

'I just can't seem to make myself.'

'There is always an opposite side,' said Nigel. 'For it is also a well-known fact that a smart knight is always tactical and will always bide his time and choose the right moment. I suspect that is what you are doing.'

'Thanks, man,' sighed Ray.

'Well I'd better get going.'

'Cool,' said Ray. 'Wanna lift?'

'Thank you, but there are some things that need to be done alone.' He decided not to say the bit about Dad probably not liking the idea of Nigel arriving on the back of a bike.

Ray nodded. 'Thanks for the pep talk, man.'

With much trepidation, Nigel caught the bus to Dad's.

I, Nigel Dorking, Do Hereby Swear to Fight Injustice in All Its Forms, to Punish the Wicked, and Reward the Virtuous.

The front gate opened, and Nigel for the third time in five days walked towards Dad's front door.

Nigel stopped himself from running when he saw it was actually Dad at the door. He needed to act calm. Confident. Like the sort of kid whose dad always comes to school functions.

'Hi, Dad,' said Nigel, his voice disobeying him and going high like it sometimes did when he was really excited.

'Oh hello, Nigel,' said Dad in the monotone Nigel loved so much. Dad's voice thrilled him. It was like the default automatic voice on the phone recorder before you record your own message. Nigel looked forward to his own voice becoming like that one day.

Nigel noted Dad looked a bit like Gilgamesh did when you tapped on his bowl. Kind of stunned.

'I've just dropped by because I wasn't sure if you received the form I put in the letterbox for you the other day,' explained Nigel.

Dad looked puzzled.

'Form?'

Aha, deduced Nigel. She did hide it from him.

'Oh well,' said Nigel, as breezily as he knew how. 'Things do go astray. So here's another form for Father and Son Night and Father and Son Bonding Camp.'

'Oh,' said Dad.

'What about the one I sent by registered post? Did you receive that?'

'No,' said Dad.

Nigel heard the guilty clip clop of someone running in high shoes on polished wood.

Babette appeared, carrying a washing basket full of clothes, as if she were a mild-mannered suburban mum, and not a fiend of mammoth proportions. She skidded to a halt at about the same time her henchdog did.

'What's this?' she said suspiciously, all wild eyed.

'Yap yap,' went the slavering, salivating sausage dog as it launched itself at Nigel and started to tug with its teeth at his trouser leg.

'Ah, perhaps call the dog off,' suggested Dad mildly.

This was Nigel's chance to dob the Evil One in.

'Babette has probably explained that I came over on Monday morning to pick up the form as it was due in then,' Nigel said conversationally.

'Well, no,' said Dad, looking mildly surprised.

‘I haven’t had a chance,’ Babette said defensively, her eyes flashing. And then she glanced at the form. ‘You can’t go, Len. Sadly you are busy then.’

Dad looked most uncomfortable. Babette flashed a smile at Nigel as if to say, *I win. And I always will.*

‘It’s actually really important, Dad,’ said Nigel, swallowing hard.

Daggers were coming out of Babette’s eyes and heading straight for Nigel’s heart.

Both Babette and Nigel knew that Dad was far too noble to disagree with anyone, and was consequently a person who did not welcome conflict in his life.

‘Well, er,’ said Dad. He looked nervously at Babette. ‘Perhaps we can think about it.’

‘No,’ she said. ‘You can’t. That is when the girls have their concert. And you are fully booked workwise.’

Nigel hated putting Dad in this position. He looked so miserable. It is so hard, thought Nigel, when you are noble and you want to please everyone.

‘Look ah,’ said Dad, glancing at his watch. ‘It is quite late, Nigel. And I think you might have missed the last bus home. I’ll give you a lift.’

Nigel’s heart danced. This was Dad’s way of saying we’ll discuss it in the car. Away from her. Yes!

‘No you won’t, Len Dorking,’ said Babette icily. ‘We have a dinner engagement.’

‘Oh,’ said Dad, torn.

Nigel couldn't bear it – Dad looking so miserable.

'It's alright,' said Nigel. 'I'm sure I'll get the bus, Dad. Don't worry. But can you just think about it? Call me tomorrow? I'll come and pick up the form.'

Nigel heard the door slam shut and Babette's high-pitched voice yapping at Dad.

Nigel knew he had missed the bus. It would be a long walk. But he had done a noble thing.

Slowly he inched towards the bus stop, his legs feeling like lead. He knew that near the bus stop there was a phone booth. A sanctuary.

He crouched there for some time, thinking he would have to ring Mum. She'd probably have called the police by now she'd be so worried.

Finally he was ready to dial.

Nigel sighed, and then he remembered something. He searched his bag and found Ray's mobile number.

He put the emergency coins in and dialled.

Nigel rode pillion on the way home, his arms around Ray's middle.

He had no idea he had just been quite so upset. To have blubbed to Ray like that was possibly extremely embarrassing. And to have said that stuff about Dad being a coward. If only he could retract it.

As Nigel got off the bike and handed Ray his spare

helmet, he said, 'Even very logical people like famous scientists can get emotional sometimes.'

Nigel noticed as Ray strapped the spare helmet to his bike that he looked wistfully towards the special bus parked in Nigel's driveway.

'It's cool, bro,' said Ray.

'Um, that stuff about Dad. I didn't mean it.'

Ray's motor was suddenly revving. Loudly. Ray's face looked stern as he put his helmet back on.

'Catchya later,' called Ray behind him. 'Remember, it's our job to be optimistic, man.' Then his bike sped off at what seemed to Nigel a frightening speed.

On the way inside, Nigel worried that he had put Ray off, that his tear ducts misbehaving like that had made Ray think he was useless. That he might not see Ray again.

Oh well, he told himself, I do not care. That is his problem.

But deep inside he didn't believe that. Nigel wanted Ray to like him. Ray was the only good thing about Gordon. And he needed his brother-in-arms.

That was what he was thinking when he arrived home.

'Is that you, wee Nigel?' called out Gordon. 'Your mum has gone across the road to meet the neighbours. She asked me to tell ya.'

Relief. Mum wouldn't be furious, as she didn't know he was late and Gordon was so useless he didn't even realise.

Nigel stared at the retreating figure of Gordon.

'Nigel, lad,' said Gordon, turning around. 'I know you wouldn't want it, but if and only if your dad can't come, I'd find a way to come on camp.'

'You are correct,' said Nigel. 'I would not want it.'

Nigel saw Gordon do that thing he could do with his eyes. He made them look all moist like he was a tender, loving fatherly man when in fact he was quite the opposite.

Quite obviously he was very skilled at hoodwinking people, for most people would have put a foot wrong by now. But not Gordon.

Mum popped her head into Nigel's room.

'Nige,' she said, looking puzzled. 'Dad just called. Did you go and visit your father after school?'

'Yes, in fact, I did,' said Nigel, gazing directly at her.

'Nigel!' said Mum. Then she ranted for five minutes about her always needing to know where he was.

Nigel waited patiently for his hysterical, irrational mother to calm down.

'And so, getting back to the subject at hand, what exactly did Dad have to say?' he finally asked.

'Well, he's coming to Father and Son Night. And to Father and Son Bonding Camp. He says he'll get the form to the school office tomorrow. There's a turn-up for the books.'

Yes! Every part of Nigel wanted to yell and jump up and punch the sky. Dad had chosen him over the spawn of the Evil One. He had won. This was an incredible victory.

But he remembered he must not allow Mum to see him happy. She must be made to suffer. That was his only weapon. Surely if she thought she was making her children miserable she wouldn't get married?

And maybe now he had another weapon up his sleeve. Perhaps when he found out more from Ray about Gordon he would have enough evidence to turn Mum right off him. Because quite obviously he was a very bad father to Ray.

'But, Nige,' said Mum, popping her head back in. 'How did Dad know about me getting married? Did you tell him?'

'No,' said Nigel. 'I most certainly did not.'

'Odd,' said Mum. 'We haven't told anybody. How very very strange.'

'Did Dad ask you not to get married?' asked Nigel.

'No,' said Mum. 'He said, "Congratulations."'

Typical, thought Nigel, stunned at Dad's selflessess.

Nigel could feel his lip start to tremble, he was so overcome with the nobility of his father.

At school, Miss Murray said in front of the whole class, 'Oh, Nigel, I got your form. A courier dropped it off. I am so glad you and your father are coming to Father and Son Night, and Camp.'

'Who are you going to share with?' nagged Jeremy.

'Shhh!' said Nigel.

When Nigel got home late after the dreaded and infuriating football practice, Mum gave him a letter addressed to him in a very unfamiliar handwriting.

'*Hey, dude,*' it said, '*gone away for a couple of days to think. Enjoy Father and Son Night, love, Ray.*'

Nigel was transfixed. He couldn't take his eyes off it. The word *love*. Even though he knew people wrote that in letters sometimes. Still he could have written *yours sincerely*, or *cheers* or *from Ray*. But he chose to write *love*.

'Who's it from?' asked Mum.

'Oh, no one you'd know,' said Nigel.

I, Nigel Dorking, Do Hereby Swear Always to Defend the Weak and Innocent.

Nigel stood parting his hair in his bedroom mirror. 'Tonight is the night I see my dad,' said Nigel to Gilgamesh.

He was a little tired, as he had learnt interesting facts to impress his father with until late the night before.

He glanced down at Gilgamesh in his bowl next to him on the bedside table, and smiled fondly. Gilgamesh, who used to belong to Dad. Nigel was glad he had inherited him. It was like owning a little bit of Dad still.

'Tonight,' confided Nigel, 'is actually the most important night of my life so far.'

Nigel thought he heard a motor revving, and raced to his window, hoping to see Ray. But it was just odd Mr Bolger across the road whipper-snipping his hedge into the shape of a hedge.

In a blinding flash, Nigel realised how it had transpired that Dad was coming tonight. Ray. Of course. Ray must have gone over there! And that is how Dad knew that Mum was getting married.

Nigel wished he had time to ring Ray and thank him for his knightly deed, but Mum had just called out.

'Come on, Nige, I'd better drop you off at the school now, love. Father and Son Night starts in half an hour. Can you get Ivan into the car?'

Ivan? thought Nigel, stricken. This he had somehow not considered.

Dad should not be reminded of Ivan. Not yet. This could ruin everything!

It's hard enough for *me* to impress Dad, worried Nigel as he raced to get ready. The last thing he needs right now is to be reminded about Ivan. Dad seeing Ivan must wait until one day in the future when Nigel had spent more time with Dad. When they had a really strong bond.

No, Dad must definitely not see Ivan tonight. Nor should any of the kids at school for that matter.

'Mum, does he have to come?' Nigel called out. Where was Gordon when you needed him? 'It's just that it is a very bright day outside still, and you know Ivan has fits in the car when it's too bright.'

'Nige, I reckon we can risk it. Ivan'd love a trip out. Come on, let's go. You'll be late otherwise.'

Nigel did not want to remind the kids at school about Ivan. Or Dad of course.

So he grabbed the tea towels.

Nigel raced out to his mother's old blue car.

This was an extra precaution, even though Mum had tinted windows.

On the side his brother would sit, the passenger-side, he wound down the window a little. He then rigged the two tea towel ends so they were like curtains over the glass, and quickly wound up the window, catching the ends in its bite. This way, no one could see in (particularly Dad) and also Ivan would be shielded from the direct sunlight.

Nigel only just managed to get his brother into the booster seat in the back of Mum's car. Ivan could be quite a dead weight. And he could be quite distracting when there was a difficult task, like trying to sit him upright in his seat. Particularly the way he kept grinning and coughing all the time.

He carefully strapped his brother in and wedged the large pieces of foam into place next to Ivan's head, between his torso and the plastic seat, and firmly either side of his neck and head. He then fixed the padded tray in front of his brother.

Satisfied that his brother was safely in, Nigel sat next to Ivan. This was always his spot. Partly to help entertain Ivan and also partly so his mother could keep her mind on the traffic in case of a fit.

Nigel stared darkly at his brother.

'Even if it isn't an act at all,' he whispered, 'you have still made my life hell.'

Kids always stared at him once they knew Ivan was his brother.

He shuddered. It was despicable. He was so careful never to go shopping with Mum these days just in case. Never to go anywhere with Ivan. And it wasn't just the kids, it was the parents and teachers.

It was the way they pitied him and his family, and silently congratulated themselves on being the sort of people not to have a brother like that, which really got to him.

Pitied him for having a brother in a wheelchair.

A brother with weird spastic hand movements and a jerking head.

A brother with the IQ of a young baby.

A brother who had taken up all Nigel's mother's time since the moment he had been born.

A brother who always had fits in public.

A brother who always made weird noises and screamed for no reason whatsoever.

A brother whose eyes rolled around in his head like balls on a billiard table.

A brother who was eight years old but couldn't even crawl around on the floor like a baby.

This is why Nigel had to hide Ivan.

'And,' whispered Nigel to Ivan a little more tenderly, 'even if you are totally for real, I still have to hide you because it is part of the Knights' Code. For I have sworn always to defend the weak and innocent. And I do not want kids calling you names.'

Ivan did not respond.

Nigel put the sunglasses on his brother.

'Why the sunglasses, Nige?' Mum asked when she got into the car.

Nigel did not want to admit to her that it was to stop anyone, including Dad, recognising Ivan. Mum would go berserk about such a thing.

'Oh, to cut down on the light,' explained Nigel breezily. 'That is also why I have put those tea towels in the window.'

But Ivan threw the glasses off.

Mum started the car.

I, Nigel Dorking, Do Hereby Swear Always to Avoid Torture.

They'd arrived twenty minutes early and Nigel leapt out of the car.

Luckily Mum couldn't wait out the front to make sure Dad arrived, because Ivan was fitting again. But she'd given Nigel her mobile phone in case Dad didn't show.

'Mum, he will come,' Nigel had said sternly. 'A true knight does not go back on his word.'

'Yes, love,' Mum had said, not looking entirely convinced, and then she'd called out, 'I'll pick you up. Just in case.'

'No, Mum,' Nigel had insisted as she chugged off. 'Trust me. Dad will come.'

Nigel could see a few dads and sons trickling into the hall, but most were gathered down by the sports field.

Of course, remembered Nigel as he peered at the smattering of people on the field. The big football match is tomorrow. They must be having a quick practice.

The ball was high in the sky. Nigel walked closer, and

saw it heading towards Jeremy Fry. But Jeremy seemed to be making no attempt whatsoever to mark it. Was this an unusual strategy? The ball landed directly behind him. On closer inspection, Nigel saw that Jeremy had no strategy at all, and that he was in fact facing the wrong way completely. He had not even seen the ball.

The coach was flinging his arms in the air in exasperation and the team and their dads were all shaking their heads in disbelief and groaning in despair.

Nigel waited outside the school hall for Dad while all the other boys in the school now streamed in with their fathers.

'Hey,' called out Bruno as he pointed to Nigel, 'on the way here, I saw his mental brother peeing into a bottle, and Dorko was holding it!'

Nigel hoped one of the nearby dads might intervene, but they were too engrossed in their own conversations.

'What, holding his thing?' asked Reece disgusted.

'Er, sick,' called out Bruce. 'You are right off, Dorking.'

'Actually,' said Nigel, 'my brother wears a nappy, so that is in fact a provable lie. But did you know when pigs urinate they do a whole six litres?'

Nigel had hoped that a fascinating fact might distract them.

'A nappy, ha ha!' cried Bruno.

It appeared that imbeciles did not know a possible fascinating fact when they heard one, as they did not have an available brain cell to perceive it with.

From their scowls, Nigel decided it was best to make himself scarce. He sped off and hid behind a particularly short but usefully porky father. Then he took the opportunity to look inside.

It was a sea of backwards caps, grinning faces, and leaflets being made into moronic paper planes nose-diving everywhere. And sadly, that was just the dads' behaviour.

The modern world, thought Nigel disapprovingly. What's it coming to? People don't even have enough intelligence to wear their caps the right way around.

A paper plane hit him in the head.

People wouldn't have done this is the Middle Ages, thought Nigel indignantly. And not just because they hadn't invented aircraft yet, either. They'd have had better things to do. Like not die of the plague.

Nigel looked around for Dad. It was twenty-five minutes to eight. The talk was supposed to have started five minutes ago. The dads had all moved in. It was only a few undesirables who were coming back outside, for the express purpose it seemed to Nigel of baiting him.

The last few people trickled into the hall.

Nigel tried to convey with his casual stance, to anyone who might have been watching, that his father, a highly respected plumber, would be here very soon, probably within the next 27 to 28 seconds.

'Come in, it's started!' called one of the dads to all stragglers.

Nigel walked into his school hall without his father.

Reluctantly, but showing respect, like knights of yore, he switched off his mother's mobile phone.

Until this very moment he hadn't been aware how cavernous the hall was. He felt as if it could swallow him up.

At assembly, Nigel had often walked towards the stage to collect his certificates, but this time the walk felt torturously slow.

As he walked, Nigel couldn't help noting that the dads in the hall looked pretty proud, and their sons sitting next to them looked pretty smug too.

But, Nigel thought to himself, I bet they don't know that the German for *Father* is *Vater*. And that in Latin it's *Pater*. And in pig Latin it's *Atherfay*. This gave him the confidence he needed to face them all. Feeling a bit superior often did this.

Finally Nigel had made it. He sat in the spare seat he had spied up near the far-right side entrance, just near the stage.

'Hey, everyone,' sneered Bruno. 'Guess whose dad's got something better on tonight, like other people's sewerage to clean up!'

Nigel felt ill.

The guest speaker droned on about fathers and sons who do bonding things together, like going to father and son nights and camps.

And then he congratulated everyone there for taking the trouble to make the time to come.

'After all,' he said, 'that's what love is all about. Making the time for your loved ones by doing things like coming to a father and son information night.'

This speaker was unlikeable and his credentials seemed quite spurious.

Quite clearly the man was very foolish. It was as plain to Nigel as the wart on the speaker's upper lip that people loved each other long before father and son nights had ever been invented. What about fathers who were in hospital in traction? What about fathers who were delivering aid to the starving people in Sudan? And what about extremely busy plumbers?

But still Nigel felt like a shining beacon in that darkened hall. Exhibit A, a boy whose father had not come.

Now Nigel couldn't concentrate on a single word the speaker was saying.

He'd just had an idea.

Perhaps he *could* get Dad here after all. He remembered blue bear.

Of course!

It made him feel a bit uncomfortable recalling it. How he had appropriated (or some might say stolen) blue bear from Ivan, strategically dropped it into their toilet, and then flushed the toilet so blue bear would get stuck, so a plumber (e.g. Dad) would have to be called.

For that one afternoon, five months ago, Nigel had managed to get the pleasure of Dad's company, even though Dad had his arm and head down a toilet bowl for most of the visit.

His plan started emerging.

If it worked it would be a masterstroke!

After all, if Dad saved the sports field, realised Nigel, the very field where tomorrow's interschool football match was to take place, he'd be a hero. With the boys and their dads. And the school.

It was a win–win–win situation.

I, Nigel Dorking, Do Hereby Swear Never to Abandon a Friend, Ally or Noble Cause.

As if he were merely an innocent person in need of a pee heading towards the toilets, Nigel managed to slip out the assembly hall side door, close to the stage.

He stole a look both ways and then raced over to Reece's dad's pick-up, and from the back borrowed the most likely looking weapon, a mallet.

In the shadows, he made his way over to the school field. The very same field that could not be used tomorrow if it were flooded. The same field, if everything went according to plan, that Dad would be saving in approximately fifteen minutes precisely.

His hands above his head, Nigel stood wielding the heavy mallet in his hands ready to summon all his strength and aim. His arms trembled. He was poised to do the worst thing he had ever done. But, he told himself, a knight could not abandon a noble cause. And saving his father's reputation and letting them all see Dad's hero status was definitely that.

He would not have been doing this unless he'd been absolutely desperate.

He hated water wasters. More than anything. But this was for a particularly good cause. Almost noble.

Nigel thwacked the mallet down with all his might upon the fire hydrant.

Jackpot. Kaput. Crunch. Clang.

Whoosh!

Water hurtled out of the hydrant. Floods of it. Spurting with a gigantic force. Everywhere. Right out, halfway across the pitch.

Nigel was momentarily stunned. He was ready to run when, 'Hey,' cried an indignant voice.

Nigel froze.

In the dusk he could only dimly make out a small figure. Running backwards around the field.

Surely not? Jeremy Fry? What was he doing out there? Surely not running around the track at this hour? What was his problem?

Nigel ran, dropping into the bushes the unwieldy mallet he had fully intended to return to its rightful owner.

Jeremy Fry, he thought darkly as he fled, wrecks everything.

Nigel found himself in the boys' toilets. This was one thing he had not counted on, a witness.

He pulled out Mum's mobile phone.

He dialled his father's special work number, which was only for work calls. This was a plumbing emergency.

Ring Ring.

Ring Ring.

'Please, Dad, answer!' whispered Nigel.

Dad had to get there immediately in order to save the sports field. It would be no good if other people saw and reported it to other plumbers. Then there would be a flood of plumbers.

Ring.

'Hello, Len Dorking.'

Nigel swallowed.

'Dad.' His voice did not sound as composed and in control as he would have liked. 'It's Nigel. This is an emergency. I am at the school and there is a fire hydrant broken. It's flooding the sports field.'

Then Nigel sat perched on the edge of a toilet with its lid down, in a cubicle. He waited.

'Hey,' he heard a man's voice yell on cue. 'There's a burst main near the field.'

Nigel raced out. He could see Dad's emergency flashing lights arriving.

Yes! Dad was on his way. Dad had come to save the day. In his silver charger. Well, his white charger to be precise.

I, Nigel Dorking, Do Hereby Swear to Lay Down My Life for the Crown, Country and All I Hold Dear.

Joy.

Nigel saw Dad open the driver's door of his white van that now had sprayed on its side *Ablutions Solutions* instead of the far more true and honorable name, *Toilets R Us*.

Ablutions Solutions was doubtlessly a stupid, sucky-type name trendy Babette had come up with.

Now Dad was racing over in measured strides to attend to the emergency.

Dad's orange lights flashed, creating a dramatic strobing effect. Lit, dark, lit, dark.

Nigel craned his neck and caught a glimpse of his father bent over, working quietly.

His heart pinged like a wine goblet being lightly tapped by a human finger. And a surge of love overwhelmed him, swamping his entire body. This was Len the Lionheart, the father Nigel knew. Nigel wanted to race over and throw his arms around him. But he knew not to. That was not his father's style.

Word had got around. Everyone from the hall had gathered there. The jetting waters were quite a sight.

No one spoke while Dad worked. It was as if doing so might break the spell.

Nigel stood watching Dad plumb, and waited for his father to see him. This would be a glorious moment indeed, their reunion.

But he must wait. Right now Dad was frowning, and concentrating.

It reminded Nigel of the olden days.

He hardly dared breathe. It'd been months since he'd seen his father actually plumb.

In this blinking night light it was easy to imagine Dad standing there in his armour. Dad saving everyone. Dad, Nigel's hero.

'That was lucky,' said Reece's dad, finally breaking into applause. 'Heck!'

'Yeah, footy match might have been called off otherwise,' agreed Mr Rollo.

Dad had stemmed the flow. He was finished. He was extremely quick. And professional. Everyone was clapping now.

Dad nodded modestly.

Meanwhile the coach called out, 'Three cheers.'

'Hip hip, hooray. Hip hip, hooray. Hip hip, hooray!' they chorused.

Nigel could tell from the admiring looks of the crowd that his plan was working. Dad was a hero.

Nigel was now dredging up the courage to say hello.

But he didn't.

Dad was peering into the bushes. Nigel saw him lean over, study something, and then pick it up.

The mallet.

Dad came back to the fire hydrant looking very stern. He cleared his throat.

'In my capacity as plumber,' he said, 'I am informing you that whoever did this, it was a criminal act. And a criminal waste of water.'

He held up the mallet.

'I have found the weapon with which this barbaric and illegal act was performed, and I will be counselling this school to prosecute and will hand this matter over to the police, who will check this alleged weapon for fingerprints. If the culprit wishes to own up now they might get a more lenient sentence.'

Deathly silence.

Nigel was glad it had got dark. He suspected he had gone a ghostly white.

'Has anyone got anything to say?' prompted Dad.

That's when Nigel spotted Jeremy in the crowd. Jeremy, who was totally sodden.

Every molecule in him felt like it was going to spontaneously combust.

Was it all over with Dad? Was Jeremy going to blab?

Time seemed to stand still as he waited to hear his voice ring out in the crowd, and ruin any possibility of a relationship with Dad for all time.

Unless, of course, he could convince Dad that Jeremy was delusional? That he saw things that weren't there? Things like whole human beings holding mallets?

Jeremy put his hand up.

Any moment now Dad would ask him what he had to say.

I will never forgive you, thought Nigel. Ever. Unto my dying day.

It was then Nigel noted that both Jeremy's hands were up, now down, now up again. He was doing his star jumps.

He, Nigel, who had always thought star jumps foolish and a waste of time, was delighted to see this. The ground once again became solid under his feet.

Jeremy made no sound.

For the first time ever, under the mask of darkness, Nigel smiled at Jeremy Fry. Not a smile of liking exactly, but rather sheer relief.

Nigel saw Dad in his van, starting his engine.

In all the commotion Nigel hadn't managed to talk to Dad yet.

Dad was taking off.

Dad had said nothing, nothing at all. Not even hello.

In fact, he'd acted as if he hadn't seen Nigel at all. Not even a blip on his father's radar. As if Nigel had been invisible. A nobody.

Had Dad guessed about the mallet?

He couldn't have, reasoned Nigel. Surely Dad would never suspect Nigel of doing such a deplorable, despicable and apparently unknightly thing?

Not wanting Bruno to see him, Nigel Dorking, do an unknightly thing, like blub, or twig that he, Nigel, had been left there without a lift, Nigel walked quickly away, with his head down.

What would he do? How could he get home? Why had Dad left without speaking to him?

Perhaps terrorists had done something terrible to the town's water supply? Blasted a hole in the dam? So the city folk would die of thirst?

'Why did you do that?' interrupted Jeremy, who was suddenly standing directly in front of Nigel, looking stunned. 'You could have wrecked absolutely everything.'

'Yes, but I didn't, did I?' said Nigel. 'And as luck would have it my father saved the day.'

'Luck? Or did you call him on your mobile phone whilst sitting on the toilet in a cubicle in the boys' lavatory?' asked Jeremy.

'I do not know what you are suggesting,' said Nigel, feeling as affronted as he sounded. 'And I do not like being spied upon!'

Nigel decided to slip away via a back route. A route that most people did not drive. He'd walk. After all, it wasn't far.

He did not want to risk being seen by other boys or their dads. The one thing he did not want was other kids' dads feeling sorry for him. He imagined Bruno or Reece's dads driving past and insisting they must stop and give poor Nigel Dorking a lift. Nigel, whose dad hadn't given him a lift home. And Nigel wouldn't be able to say a thing.

What could he say? For security reasons, national emergencies could not be spoken about. There could be no leaks. That's how Dad would run his ship. Everything would be watertight. Otherwise, people would panic and the results could be disastrous.

Unless of course, it was her. This insight struck Nigel with almost as much force as the water gushing from the hydrant. A hex could make you do anything.

And Dad had left in a zombie-like fashion!

Nigel slunk off to cut across the pitch. That is when he heard it. That horn honking.

Shh, Nigel wanted to yell. The last thing he wanted was to be noticed. Which was why what happened next was most unwelcome.

'Wee Nigel,' called a loud Scottish voice. About as subtle as bagpipes before 6 a.m. on a Sunday, thought Nigel scowling.

The special bus was there waiting for him.

'Hop in, wee laddie,' cried Gordon. 'Your mum's asked me to get you. She tried to call yer but your mobile wasna switched on.'

Nigel glared up at the intruder, appalled, his insides sinking.

'Sorry about the bus, but your mum's car isn't working. She had a spot of engine trouble after dropping you off.'

Nigel realised why Gordon had been tinkering with Mum's car so much. Why had he not realised this? Gordon wanted Mum's car to break down so Mum would have to rely on him!

Nigel felt shocked by this terrible revelation.

Gordon had just done a U-turn in the special bus and pulled up right outside the hall, where the crowds were now headed.

'Ha! Spazzo,' Bruno called out as Nigel reluctantly alighted the bus.

'Hey, retard. Did your dad leave without you?'

And then Bruno started making the sound of a siren. And the kids near Bruno started laughing and pointing.

'Actually,' said Nigel as haughtily as he could as he

stood on the top step, 'for your information, special buses don't have sirens. That is a common misconception. And also for your information I am not retarded as I happen to have an IQ of one hundred and thirty-one on the WISK test which means I am in the ninety-eighth percentile. Which I suspect is a lot higher than you. So if I am retarded what does that make you? And my father is at least saving our planet, which is more than I can say for your real father, Bruno.'

Nigel noted that the kids had all stopped laughing. Everyone had gone horribly quiet.

'I'll get you for that, Dorko,' cried Bruno.

Nigel wished he hadn't said that.

Something told him school was going to be even less pleasant than usual on Monday morning.

Particularly if a certain football team didn't win tomorrow afternoon.

I, Nigel Dorking, Do Hereby Swear Never to Use a Weapon on an Opponent Not Equal to the Attack.

Nigel did not feel at all chatty on the way home. That is why he didn't respond to Gordon's questions. That, and the fact that over the roar of the engine it was difficult to understand Gordon's stupid Scottish accent.

Particularly as Nigel had chosen to sit down the very back of the bus.

Nigel needed to think. What would he say to Mum? How could he stop her blowing her stack when she heard about Dad not turning up and then ringing him up and accusing him of being all sorts of terrible things she would most certainly accuse him of?

He considered telling her about the enchantment but decided on balance she would not understand.

No, he had to somehow stop Mum ringing Dad. It was an extremely unfair match because Mum was much better at arguing. Commoner folk often are.

And given a real knight could never stand by and watch someone use a weapon on someone else who was not equal to the attack, he, Nigel, could not stand by and let this happen.

Any second now, Mum would be asking him questions. And that would land Dad in big trouble.

Unless Nigel were to dash in first, before Gordon, and pretend to have arrived separately, as if Dad had driven Nigel home. As if Dad had come along to Father and Son Night after all. And as if Gordon had arrived afterwards, separately.

Though of course he wouldn't actually say Dad had attended, as obviously that would be a lie. But he could technically say he had seen Dad, as after all that was true.

And even though it would be slightly misleading it would be for a noble cause.

'I'll just take a wee look at your mum's car, laddie,' called Gordon as he grabbed a torch from the back of his van.

Yes! thought Nigel, feeling enormously relieved that he would get to see Mum on his own without Gordon there to correct his version of events.

Though he could not resist letting Gordon know that he, Nigel, was on to him.

'Yes,' said Nigel. 'Though after all the car-fixing you have done for Mum lately, I would suggest in future getting someone who knows what they are doing.'

Nigel felt Gordon stare after him as he dashed inside.

He found Mum and Ivan at the kitchen table, the fluorescent light flickering on and off.

Mum was looking crumpled, like she was in need of a good iron. And next to her, slumped in his toilet chair, was Ivan, with his forehead resting on the tray in front of him. Ivan had pumpkin in his hair. Pumpkin was also splattered across the wall.

'Hi, Mum,' said Nigel as casually as he could. 'Hi, Ivan.'

Ivan jerked his head to the side. Nigel noted that his brother looked particularly pale. Ivan, who never saw the sun because he couldn't stand the sunlight, was paler than the hospital sheets he had last been in after contracting pneumonia.

'Shocker of a night,' said Mum, attempting to smile. But Nigel could tell she was being brave. Her normally sparkling blue eyes looked as faded as the kitchen curtains.

'Poor old Ivan. Got to get his chest seen to. And he's had three fits,' Mum explained. 'I'll have to get you to your neurologist fast, and the paediatrician. Won't I, Ivan? Something's got to be done, Mister Rattly Chest.'

Mum was onto her third glass of beer. Nigel knew, because she'd gone through one and a quarter bottles.

It made sense to Nigel that she had drunk three glasses, given the three fits. But he couldn't help thinking that Miss Murray would never drink even one bottle.

Ivan's grey eyes jerkily followed Nigel around the kitchen as Nigel made himself a milkshake.

'But spill, love, how did your night turn out?' asked Mum.

Nigel's stomach lurched.

'Oh, it was very informative,' he said, trying to steer a path between keeping the peace and the truth. 'It was great to see Dad, too.'

Nigel had his fingers crossed behind his back as he smiled at his mother to show how great it had been.

'Oh,' said Mum, sounding and looking puzzled. 'But Dad left a message while I was dropping you off saying he couldn't make it tonight due to some emergency. Which is why I sent bugalugs down to get you.'

'Oh . . . yes,' said Nigel.

Mum stared at him uncomprehendingly with her tired white face.

'He didn't make it to the actual Father and Son,' Nigel amended his story. 'There was a water emergency at the school. The fire hydrant. And he came and fixed it.'

Mum looked even more puzzled. Her worried brow furrowed further. 'So why didn't he give you a lift home, love?'

'Oh,' said Nigel as breezily as he could. 'Gordon was there, so he didn't need to. And anyway doubtlessly Dad had another water emergency on.'

Nigel saw his mother's eyes flashing again.

'He was there and he didn't give you a lift?'

'Mum,' said Nigel. 'Calm down.'

'Nigel, tell me honestly. I need to know this. Did Gordon arrive before or after Dad left?'

'Mum! That is unirrelevant!' he tried to calm her down. 'And you know you make emotional decisions when you get like this.'

'Nigel, there is nothing wrong with emotion,' seethed his mother. 'Honestly, your father could do with some. Just the tiniest bit. What on earth could he be thinking?'

'Well, probably about drains, and S-bends and washers and toilet augers and things like that,' Nigel defended his father.

'Exactly,' cried Mum frustrated. 'He's got a one-track mind. If just for once he could think about someone else. He is astounding. One measly lift home. What is wrong with him? Sometimes I think I could murderate your father.'

Nigel couldn't help himself.

'Actually, there is no such word as *murderate*.'

That's when she snapped and stormed over to the phone and started dialling.

'No!' yelled Nigel, 'Stop it!'

But Mum was not to be stopped.

It was because of the yelling that Nigel now lay in his bed with a pillow over his head.

He'd have done anything to have spared Dad this agony. And now he'd have so much repair work.

Why did she blame Dad for everything? Couldn't Mum see it was Babette's fault? And Ivan's?

Tonight she was really letting fly.

The last time he had heard Mum yell at this volume was that night. The terrible night after which Dad left.

It all came flooding back to Nigel.

How the skies had also opened up that night, and the winds had howled along with him.

He couldn't help remembering how he'd waited most of the next morning for Dad to come home. How Dad never did.

One day, Nigel determined, after Dad had been elected Father of the Year (Nigel had nominated him ages ago), and when Mum finally saw what Dad was really like, what a hero he was, surely Mum would have to admit she was wrong and beg him to come back?

That's if Dad would have her. And of course if Nigel could get rid of Babette. And naturally only if Ivan had been cured. And if Mum had improved her personality, and gone to anger management workshops.

I, Nigel Dorking, Do Hereby Swear Always to Strive for Excellence and to Set a Good Example to My Inferiors.

Nigel heard a gentle knock at his bedroom door.

'Nige, love?'

He quickly turned his pillow, just in case. There is nothing like a sodden pillowcase to make mothers jump to conclusions. If challenged, he would point out what a strong swimmer Gilgamesh was and how he could make quite a splash. Even onto pillows.

Mum turned the light on, and came and sat on his bed. Nigel lay with his back to her.

'Sorry about that, love, I really am. Your father reckons . . . well, he was being Dad. You know what he's like. His people skills leave a lot to be desired.'

Nigel refused to nod. As far as he was concerned, Dad's people skills were perfect. And he, Nigel, would never speak to his mother again.

'And he reckons the reason he didn't give you a lift was because after leaving a message here to say he couldn't make it, he'd assumed I'd be picking you up. And he said to apologise to you that he didn't say hello.

He thought you had already gone.'

'See!' Nigel attacked his mother with great vehemence, forgetting momentarily about never speaking to her again. 'You shouldn't jump to conclusions about Dad.'

Though he didn't feel too angry with Mum any more because he was so pleased that Dad hadn't really ignored him.

How could he even have thought such a thing?

A few small bits of moisture of joy threatened to spring from his tear ducts at the mere thought of Dad's exoneration.

'Nige, he doesn't have a great history where we're concerned, does he?' sighed Mum. 'But to make up for not seeing you tonight, I have strongly suggested to Dad, and he has agreed, after a bit of intimidation, to invite you to stay for three days at his place from next Sunday.'

'Really?' asked Nigel, trying to keep his voice steady and unsurprised. Then suspiciously, 'Instead of camp?'

'As well as,' beamed Mum.

Nigel was lost for words. (A most unusual state for him!)

This was brilliant.

'It's a done deal. Which is great for me because I need to take Ivan to the city to see his specialist. And

I reckon while you're on camp, I might even take the opportunity and go into respite care myself just to take a rest. I know I've been a bit on edge recently.'

Nigel was stunned. Delighted. Overjoyed.

He allowed his mother to kiss him on his forehead. Instead of not speaking forever he would withhold hugs for three days. She must be taught a lesson. And he could tell she was itching to hug him.

'I need to sleep now,' he said, dismissing her. Well, he did not ever want to encourage her saying negative things about Dad.

And then he had the craziest thought. Ray didn't have anything to do with this outcome, did he? Had Ray paid Dad another visit?

And as he lay there he found himself fantasising that Ray, not Ivan, was his real brother.

Nigel guiltily crept into Ivan's room. 'Ivan, it's me, Nigel,' he whispered in the dark. 'Ivan. Next Sunday I am going to Dad's. You could come too if only . . .'

Then Nigel had an idea. A brilliant idea. Why had he never thought of this before?

Excited, only the way you can get at midnight when all ideas seem good, he crept out, stole Mum's laptop from the living room and took it in to his brother. Nigel opened the computer and switched it on.

'This is really important,' he explained.

Ivan blinked in the light.

'You may be aware that I have not been happy with you lately. However, you could redeem yourself by concentrating really hard, okay, and by letting me know if you really are intelligent. I realise of course you have never had access to a proper computer, only your communication aid, which is quite primitive compared to a computer. This as letters, rather than pictures. But there is a guy like you who can't control his movements. Stephen Hawking. He communicates through a computer. It's okay. Don't worry. People still have to do stuff for him, but he is really smart. He's a famous scientist. So will you give it a go . . . ?'

Nigel opened a file in which his brother could type. Then he placed it carefully, directly in front of his brother on the bed.

'This could be your lifeline,' explained Nigel. 'I want you to use it right now. Okay?'

Nigel wondered if all those hours he'd spent with his brother over the years (when he was desperate for a brother he could play with) trying to teach him the Dewey system at the municipal library, and the alphabet, might now prove to have been beneficial. If so, he would open a school one day for the so-called profoundly retarded and prove they were smarter than most people thought.

Ivan seemed to be gazing at the computer.

Nigel wondered if Ivan might be shy so he closed his eyes, to coax him to try, and listened intently instead.

All he could hear was the erratic beat of his own heart and the thudding of his temples.

Nigel knew this could be a very telling moment. Possibly a life-changing moment. And even though Nigel was desperate that his brother show intelligence, there was a small part of him that was hoping he didn't show too much. No more than, say, he himself had. But then there was another voice that told him there was little chance of that.

Nigel heard the clatter of the keys. His stomach leapt. He couldn't help peeking. He was a little disappointed to see his brother's elbow on the keyboard. But, he told himself, people have their own methods of working and this might be his. After all, there are people who do paintings with their toes.

And even though he was desperate to read the screen, he decided he'd give his brother more time.

Nigel's imagination started to race. What if he looked and his brother had written 'Federation was in the year 1901,' or 'The American War of Independence was in 1776'? Or even better, 'Nigel, I love you.'

Nigel felt tears well up in his eyes at the mere possibility. Then he imagined all the great things he and his brother could do together. And how delighted their father would be. Nigel felt certain Dad'd invite Ivan over once he knew he was smart. That's if Nigel could also cure Ivan's weird spastic movements. And his bedwetting.

Nigel summoned all his courage, unscrunched his eyes and moved around behind his brother to see what he had written.

The decisive moment had arrived. He held his breath. He read:

'dBthvmieneom/loMMD/.XMXMVK..X'

'You're not trying, Ivan,' he cried, frustrated.

But then, for a moment, for one wild second, he wondered if 'dBthvmieneom/loMMD/.XMXMVK..X' might be code for something. Something like, *I do not want Mum to marry the Orc. Please tell her.*

Then Nigel heard footsteps. It was only when he saw Ivan's door opening and Mum's face there that Nigel hurtled back to earth with a thud.

The light in the bathroom opposite was switched on, bathing Ivan's room in borrowed light.

Why had he thought this might be a good idea? Had he temporarily lost his brain? Why did ideas that seemed so great in the dark seem somehow pathetic and ridiculous by the light of a fluorescent bulb?

The light flickered, off, on, off, on.

'Turn it off, Mum,' instructed Nigel, forever Ivan's defender. 'It might trigger a fit.'

'Nigel! What on earth are you doing?'

'Nige,' Mum said, once Nigel was back in bed, 'I won't go on about it. But I want this to be the last time. Accept Ivan the way he is, love. It's not fair on him. You're a smart boy. What can't you understand?'

Nigel said nothing.

'Wait a sec,' Mum called to Nigel as she raced off to attend to Ivan. She clearly had not finished with Nigel yet.

Nigel had managed to calm down. He heard Mum padding back down the hallway towards his room.

'Nige, love, there's something else.'

Nigel remained perfectly still. His stomach turned. There was something ominous in her tone.

'Don't be offended by me asking this . . .'

He already felt offended before he even knew what it was. For surely someone would not say that unless they intended to offend you?

'You had nothing to do with that fire hydrant, did you, pet?'

'No,' he managed, feeling quite outraged.

'Alright, Nige,' she said. 'I wondered, that's all. Because of the blue bear episode . . . it's just, if you did this, it is pretty serious.'

'I need to sleep,' said Nigel.

How dare she suspect him! That showed how much faith she had in him! His own mother! Who was supposed to love him.

If Ivan were normal she would never suspect *him* of such a thing.

Eventually when Nigel calmed down about the outrageous accusation, he was almost astonished when he had to face the fact that actually he had performed the terrible deed of which he was accused.

It seems, he thought, feeling deeply sad for the whole human race, that human beings become quite indignant and deny an accusation far more vehemently if in fact they are guilty.

But why had Mum suspected? Would Dad suspect? Would he, Nigel, end up in jail? How serious was it?

He lay there anxiously, unable to sleep.

It should have been the happiest night of Nigel's life so far, given Dad had invited him over, and was coming on camp. If only he hadn't just been caught testing Ivan and if only he hadn't just lied to his mother. And if only he hadn't committed a criminal offence against his father. And his country. With a mallet.

Chapter XVIII

I, Nigel Dorking, Do Hereby Swear Always to Have Faith, Even in the Face of Grave Peril.

The water. It was spurting out with such a rush. Such power.

Water everywhere.

Mayhem.

Nigel was startled awake. It had been such a powerful dream. In fact, he could still feel a deluge.

Then he lurched into full consciousness.

'No,' he whispered.

It couldn't be. Surely? He'd been dry at night for a whole three weeks and three days now.

Very slowly he put his hand out to feel the state of the sheets and his worst fears came true. The sheets were sodden. Again.

Nigel's insides avalanched.

The water. It wasn't from the fire hydrant at all.

His eyelids flicked open. A giddying nausea overwhelmed him.

Nigel lay there, dread fermenting in the pit of his stomach.

What would this mean for all his plans with Dad?

Nigel threw back his bedcovers.

That's when he looked down towards his groin, and caught sight of the culprit.

Its pink helmet head was poking through the slit in the damp crotch of his navy-blue pyjama bottoms.

Now I can't go to Dad's! How could you have let this thing happen? Nigel wanted to demand of his penis. *You ignoramus nitwit twit life-wrecking dickwit who would score zero or even negatively on the WISK intelligence test! Don't you get it? Because of you, I can't go to Dad's. Which means I can't form a relationship with him, which means I can't win him back. You are ruining everything.*

But he didn't.

He used to yell at his penis when he was younger, but not now. Obviously he was far too mature.

Instead, he would ignore his urge to grab it with both hands and strangle it, hard.

Nigel got his sheets from the washing machine, hoping they would be dry by the time Mum woke up, which he hoped would not be any moment soon. And tiptoeing, he headed out towards the clothes line.

It was torturous watching his only real chance of staying with his father evaporate like urine on a sheet in the early morning sun. His big opportunity. His dream.

After all, Dad had never asked him to stay before. But he could not risk going. Dad would think he was like Ivan. And that would never do.

It's all Mum's fault, thought Nigel bitterly as he remembered how often she blubbed in movies, even the *Rugrats* movie. Mum comes from a very leaky family. But why did I have to inherit my penis from my mother's side of the family? Why couldn't I have been more like Dad around the penis?

And right then, even though he was incredibly proud of his father, Nigel couldn't help wishing his father was a parking inspector, or an accountant, or even the person whose job it was to make sure there were never enough sultanas in Sultana Bran. Anything but a plumber who had dedicated his life to getting rid of things that leaked.

Nigel sighed deeply.

Where can I stay, he worried, instead of Dad's?

As he pegged the last peg to the bottom sheet, the sheet blew up against him. The cool wetness of it felt good. Enlivening.

There was one small chance – that he might find a cure for wetting. And then he could still stay at Dad's! Perhaps the recurrence of this problem was just a one-off? Or maybe he could stay at Ray's. That's if Ray hadn't gone off Nigel.

'Oh, Mum,' called Nigel after lunch. 'I have to go down to the football match as unfortunately I am one of the reserve players.'

'Nige,' cried Mum, sounding delighted.

'This is against my will, and I would like to formally register a protest and say I will never do this again.'

Nigel hoped he had made himself clear.

On arriving at the field, Nigel immediately spotted Jeremy. Jeremy, who seemed to have forgotten there was a game going on and was instead kickboxing invisible foes like a ninja.

Nigel also noticed the other reserve player was not there.

Luckily everyone else had turned up.

The oval ball came towards Jeremy, the crowd yelled, and Hope careered into him as she tried to catch it instead. Jeremy fell over, and the ball hit him in the chest as he protected his head.

'You loser, Jeremy Fry,' screamed his team-mates.

How humiliating, thought Nigel. Particularly for Jeremy's father. Nigel scanned the crowd, wondering which poor sod it was. No wonder he had left Jeremy and Jeremy's mum. Poor man, thought Nigel, who couldn't help imagining the look of horror on Jeremy's dad's face when he'd heard Jeremy had moved with his mum from the outback to town to be closer to him.

At half-time Jeremy limped off in total disgrace.

It even occurred to Nigel that he might give Jeremy a sympathetic smile from the sidelines, one that said, *I am glad it is you and not me*. But on second thoughts, he decided he would rather not be seen smiling at Jeremy. Today of all days.

'Where is she?' Nigel heard Coach yelling. 'Where's our replacement?'

But she was nowhere to be found.

Nigel felt a heavy hand on his shoulder.

'Nigel,' he heard Coach's voice. 'Looks like it's you, mate. Quick smart. You'll have to play this half.'

Nigel stood paralysed. The ball had just bounced towards him. He stared at it. Uncertain what to do.

For there behind the goalposts with his torch, studying the ground beside the fire hydrant, was Dad.

'Go for it!' the crowd yelled.

Nigel managed to mobilise his legs.

Suddenly he had the ball, and was running with it. Was Dad looking at him? Kids were jumping up and down, some yelling his name. He could hear Coach hollering.

'Kick it, Nigel, kick it!'

All he could think was, I, Nigel Dorking, have got the ball! See me, Dad. See me!

Any second, Nigel noted in his peripheral vision,

he was about to be tackled by a St James brute. They obviously got junk food for lunch at their school. He was enormous. Nigel just managed to dodge him.

Dad was still there. Nigel saw a flash, and for one second thought Dad was taking a photo of him, but then it registered what Dad was doing. Taking photos of the crime scene from the night before. Probably doing a forensic investigation!

That is when everything became a terrible jumble.

Nigel couldn't make out what his team-mates were calling. It was all garble.

Nigel booted the ball anyway.

It was a mighty kick.

Without even having had time to line up the ball, Nigel watched it head directly mid-centre of the goalposts.

And as if in slow motion, like a replay on the telly, right in front of Nigel's unbelieving and incredulous eyes, he saw it sail right through. The perfect goal!

Kids were screaming as car horns tooted and parents cheered. Jumped up and down and hugged each other.

Nigel glanced towards his father. Had he noted Nigel's exhilarating moment of glory?

But it was then that Nigel became aware that none of the kids from his school were smiling at him, only the kids from the other school.

It was just as the thunderous faces of Bruno and Reece came into view that reality dawned.

He had kicked the ball through the wrong posts, for the wrong team.

Dad was disappearing into his car just as Nigel wished he, Nigel, could disappear for ever.

Had Dad seen his moment of mortification? Would it be in his photo? Proof of what a pathetic son he was, immortalised? Had he shamed his father for ever?

That the other team should have won by one point, thought Nigel miserably as he trudged alone off the field, was possibly just unfortunate. But for Dad to turn up just as Nigel was kicking the ball was surely more than plain old bad luck. And that Nigel should even be playing in the first place? What were the odds of that? Of the coach not being able to find Alyssa? And of Jeremy hurting himself? And then of Nigel kicking the ball through the wrong goalposts, just as Dad took the photo?

No, this was far more than bad luck.

'That was a good kick,' said Jeremy, cheerily coming over, trying to be friendly. Jeremy, who, Nigel noticed, was not limping.

'I thought you were injured,' said Nigel, affronted.

And Jeremy most definitely blushed, and then started to limp again. But on the wrong foot.

'Jeremy,' called Mr Fry. 'Come on.'

'You were faking,' Nigel accused him. He was stunned.

Jeremy shrugged and then limped shamefacedly away.

'Coming, Dad,' called Jeremy, heading towards Coach's car.

That's when Nigel realised. Coach was Jeremy's dad.

Now it started to make sense. Of course, Mr Fry, Jeremy Fry. He had never connected the two. Now he understood the whispers of favouritism when Jeremy had made A-team.

What an outrage.

So once again, Nigel's humiliation was actually all Jeremy's fault. How typical and how pathetic, all because he didn't want Coach to see him playing like a loser.

That night as he lay in bed, Nigel was assaulted repeatedly by images of Dad possibly seeing his 'goal'. Of Dad deciding Nigel couldn't be his real son.

Nigel decided that he could bear it no longer. Everything felt stacked against him. And then he remembered Ray's words.

It's our job to be optimistic, man.

Yes. He would not allow these negative thoughts in. Instead, like Ray, he would think positively.

Dad would not have seen Nigel. He was concentrating on the crime scene.

After a while, Nigel started to feel convinced this was the case.

He then decided to also employ a positive-thinking regime with his penis and his bladder.

I wonder, Nigel thought as he lay in bed.

He'd heard of people coming up with brilliant ideas while they slept, so he asked his brain to work hard that night. An invention is all I need, he decided. One that helps people with medical conditions like mine.

For under no circumstances can I allow a father like Len the Lionheart to realise he has a boy who not only ruins football matches, but also wets his bed. Furthermore, would such a boy not be the obvious water-wasting mains-smashing culprit?

But that night Nigel had the dream where you dream you're on the toilet.

Please, not that stupid pathetic dream again, he thought on waking.

Nigel couldn't believe his bad luck, until the truth dawned.

Of course, he realised in a blinding flash. Doubtlessly, Babette has heard that Dad is inviting me over to their place so she has doubled her dark magic.

And suddenly he knew in his guts his theory must be true. For then it clicked. The day after Dad'd left, his medical problem had started.

And she would know that no father wants a

child who does something as humiliating as wet the bed. Particularly if that father has a new wife and family. Particularly if that father is a plumber who has dedicated his life to stopping things leaking.

So to have this happen again now, just when he had been invited to stay, was too much of a coincidence.

There were no depths to which she would not sink.

Obviously, thought Nigel, using positive thinking, she is afraid that the Father and Sonly bond will overcome all. Even her black magic. Which is why she has had to double it. Because she could not risk me coming. Because she knows I will succeed in stealing Dad back. So this gives me confidence.

I will find a way, Len.

Chapter XIX

I, Nigel Dorking, Do Hereby Swear to Treat Elders with the Respect They Deserve.

Sadly Nigel's brain did not work hard enough. And doubly sadly, what Nigel had predicted might happen on Monday at school, did.

There was a certain pleasure in being correct, but a certain displeasure in the way the day was unfolding.

'Reckon your spazzo brother would play footy better than you!' stirred Bruno.

'Well, that is ridiculous as he can't stand up,' said Nigel.

'Yeah but he wouldn't be able to kick a goal for the other team either!'

Miss Murray, who was halfway around the class collecting the hero stories from classmates who were very slow writers, turned and faced the class.

'Stop that immediately!'

Nigel did not like Miss Murray thinking he was being victimised.

'Miss Murray loves Nigel,' taunted Hope in a whisper.

'Hope! Out!' demanded Miss Murray.

While Miss Murray was outside the classroom telling off Hope, Bruno shoved Nigel up against the side wall.

'Loser. We won't win this season now. And it's all your fault.'

'Well, football is a very ludicrous game,' said Nigel. 'And as I have said before I cannot see the point in it. My stance is philosophical –'

He would have gone on but Bruno was now choking him.

'And don't you ever talk about my dad,' Bruno whispered. 'Got it?'

It was now quite hard to talk properly as Nigel was being strangled around the Adam's apple. 'Perhaps you should not talk about mine either then,' he managed to say. 'Or about my brother.'

'Oy,' yelled Mr Bower, the Principal, who had just popped his angry head in through the door. 'My office, at recess.'

Miss Murray kindly stuck up for Nigel to the Principal, explaining that he was not usually a troublemaker. That it was in fact Bruno who had caused the situation.

'If I had my way,' Nigel helpfully suggested to the Principal once Bruno had been sent away, 'I would bring back the stocks like in the Middle Ages. I am certain if criminals like Bruno had their heads and hands locked into the stocks and were stuck in the middle of the playground where kids could throw rotten fruit and other bits of their lunch at them, and where birds could poo on them to their hearts' content, that might cause a marked improvement in their behaviour. Or perhaps even public floggings?'

'Sadly, Nigel, the stocks and public floggings are illegal,' said Mr Bower.

'And they call it progress,' responded Nigel equally sadly.

Nigel and Mr Bower shared a moment.

'And I am also aware,' Nigel continued in an advisory capacity, 'that if you get Bruno and his lot into too much trouble, they will only attack me more so I would suggest the best strategy might be –'

'Nigel, allow me to be the principal,' suggested Mr Bower. 'Now, where was I?'

'Ah, not allowing me to suggest a strategy,' prompted Nigel helpfully.

Mr Bower chose his words carefully. He looked over the rim of his glasses. 'Nigel, bullying is never excusable, or acceptable. Now, I will discuss a few strategies with your teacher for the classroom. But do you think there could be any behaviours you might be displaying that could possibly be magnifying your situation?'

'Ah no,' said Nigel. 'Most definitely not. Only displaying intelligence, and that can be like a red rag to a bully, particularly if that bully does not understand big words like *extracurricular* or *antidisestablishmentarianism*, which in case you don't know the meaning means –'

'We know what it means, Nigel,' said Miss Murray.

But Nigel had spotted the adults exchanging a mutually admiring look about their very excellent student.

After Miss Murray left to get back to the class, Nigel retired from the Principal's office, because it seemed like the right thing to do. And also because Mr Bower had told him to get out.

Nigel successfully eluded Bruno and his gang for the rest of the day.

It was the last hour of school, and his favourite subject, creative writing.

Nigel looked back down at his work after what he felt certain was a fond and encouraging look from Miss Murray.

That is when Bruno started.

'Dunny-can dad and wee-wee spazzo brother!'

What happened next astonished the class, but astounded Nigel even more. He had no intention of doing it. Normally he was a very rational, non-violent person.

Afterwards he felt he'd been over taken by an insane swirling fury, one that when it had finally lifted left him, Nigel Dorking, sprawled across Bruno with his hands around Bruno's neck, and with Miss Murray trying to pull him off.

After being marched to the Principal's office again, twice in one day, Nigel awaited the verdict.

'Nigel was provoked,' Miss Murray explained on his behalf before once again dashing back to her unruly class.

'Yes,' explained Nigel, 'like Zidane at the World Cup, I believe.'

The Principal sighed and sent Nigel off to make an appointment to see Mrs Bent, the school psychologist, on the double.

Chapter XX

I, Nigel Dorking, Do Hereby Swear that Love and Determination and Inspiration Shall Always Prevail.

Nigel dreamt of many things that night. But mostly of Camelot. Of a terrible mist descending. Of having to save King Arthur, who Nigel knew in his heart was Dad. He dreamed of Guinevere, who looked strangely like Mum, and Lancelot, who strangely had red hair and a Scottish accent.

And Guinevere had fallen in love with this Orcish Lancelot. Poor Dad.

Nigel knew he would have to battle Lancelot unto death. His father's honour was at stake.

With much trepidation, and heavy of heart, he went down to the lake, and there where the townsfolk had gathered Nigel saw the sword Excalibur, wedged into the rock.

It was beautiful to behold. Glinting silver in the morning sun.

Others tried to pull the sword from the rock, but were not successful.

Then it was Nigel's turn.

With a thudding heart, Nigel gently pulled the handle of the magical sword, and to his amazement, and that of the crowd, the sword slid easily from the rock. The crowd cried out in awe for not only had the magical sword been unsuccessfully pulled by grown men far stronger than him, and even by the odd tractor, just then the mystical Lady of the Lake had appeared.

None had seen such a beautiful apparition before.

A strange hush descended. Then the wondrous lady spoke unto him.

'Nigel Dorking,' she said, the lake around her glistening like jewels.

In her presence, Nigel's heart felt like a rose petal in the breeze, gently, gently falling.

'Wakey-wakey, chookums,' called Mum.

Nigel surfaced into wakefulness.

Only to find the Lady was his mother and the Lake was his bed. And to remember that his mother was ruining all his plans by getting married. And that the day he had to go to Dad's was fast looming. And he had no cure for his bedwetting. Or Ivan.

Tuesday, Wednesday and Thursday, Nigel felt unwell and stayed at home. Mum kept trying to bring up topics he did not want to discuss. He refused to respond. She was only trying to help, but as any knight in armour would know, a mother trying to discuss delicate matters like water-main smashing is just not on.

By Friday, 16 March (only twelve days before camp), he was back at school, and wishing desperately that he was not.

For he had just been dragooned permanently now onto the football team.

'Nigel,' Mr Fry said, 'Jeremy is right, that was a good kick on Saturday. You have the makings of a good player if you could just work out whose goalposts are whose.'

Even though the kids laughed, and even though he was against football in every possible way including philosophically, Nigel felt pleased. Though this would interfere with his plans. For he needed every spare second before going to Dad's on Sunday to either find a cure or a place to stay.

No way would he risk wetting at Dad's.

Thankfully the match on Saturday did not go too horribly awry. Nigel congratulated himself, for he had managed not to touch the ball once, which meant he had done nothing drastically wrong. True, he had collided with Jeremy. Or Jeremy had collided with him. But everyone on the field had done that. Some, multiple times. Poor Jeremy. It was very pathetic watching him trying so desperately hard to impress his father. Though Nigel did not feel sorry for him for long, not after he marked a ball that was clearly Nigel's. He was like one of those sticky flies in summertime, always landing in the wrong spot at the wrong time. In fact, for Jeremy Fry there was no right spot, or right time.

'Mine!' yelled Jeremy.

No, thought Nigel, actually it is mine. That is when they collided.

And Nigel took no responsibility for the fact that Jeremy's tooth had gone into his own lip.

After changing, Nigel stood at the water fountain, drenched.

'Ha ha,' laughed Bruno.

Nigel ignored him.

For he had just made a discovery.

Of course! This must be how the world's most brilliant minds make their best discoveries. Through applying their extraordinary logic to the very ordinary things in life. For Newton an apple, for Archimedes a bath, and for Nigel, a water fountain.

Nigel had tried to have a drink from the fountain which had squirted him in the face, and all over his clothes. On close inspection he found that a small piece of gravel had been deliberately wedged in the hole where the water comes out, diverting water.

Nigel knew it was deliberate by the giggling going on behind him. But taking Miss Murray's advice, he did not dignify it with a response.

This is my great chance, he realised, of saving my relationship with Dad.

He would head straight down to the hardware store.

On his way, Nigel heard footsteps behind him.

Jeremy Fry.

This was the last thing Nigel needed. Someone seeing him with Jeremy. It would look like he was deliberately hanging out with Jeremy Fry on a weekend, which would be certain social suicide.

Nigel tensed.

'Why are you always just behind me?' demanded Nigel.

'Oh I am quite ubiquitous,' said Jeremy. 'That means –'

'I know what it means,' interrupted Nigel. Quite obviously it meant something like *stalker* or *pathologically annoying human being*.

'Would you like to come over and practise football?' Jeremy asked.

'No,' said Nigel. 'Now could you please go away? I am very busy.'

'Could I have two packets of very hardy balloons?' Nigel asked Mr Paxton at the hardware. 'And one roll of extremely strong masking tape?'

Mr Paxton nodded.

'And do you have rubber tubing about this thick?' Nigel asked, circling his forefinger around his thumb to show how large he wanted the diameter.

'What's it for?' asked Mr Paxton gruffly.

'It's an invention. I need to siphon liquid,' Nigel said, going a deep shade of purple. Surely other great inventors did not have to put up with this? Being quizzed by someone of far less intelligence about things which they could not possibly understand?

Mr Paxton raised his eyebrows and showed Nigel the various diameters.

'That one should do,' said Nigel.

'How long?' asked Mr Paxton.

'About two metres precisely,' said Nigel, imagining the length he'd need to go all the way from the top of his bed to underneath.

Back at home, Nigel found an empty bottle of orange juice in the rubbish. He filled it with water, and then attached the piping onto the neck and carefully taped it on with masking tape.

He pulled the lip of the balloon around the other end and taped it firmly round the edge of the piping.

He closed his eyes and counted to twenty. Then he stood over the sink and studied the balloon.

The balloon had most definitely filled with water.

'Not a drip!' whispered Nigel with enormous satisfaction.

He kissed the contraption. This would most definitely work and possibly secure him a place in the history books.

Then, with extreme care, he placed his conduit to a relationship with his father into his bag.

After lunch on Sunday, Nigel practised the piano. And then the trumpet.

Dad had played both these instruments as a boy, and Nigel was hoping when Dad saw how good he had become that Dad might even want to do a duet.

Then, one hour before he was to leave for his dad's, Nigel did some drawings, dressed as a knight, and entered his brother's bedroom.

Ivan deserved one more chance.

Besides, at the moment Ivan was Nigel's last hope. How could Nigel ruin Mum and Gordon's relationship if he wasn't going to be there in person?

He woke the slumbering Ivan from his afternoon nap.

Ivan's sleepy gaze slid up the plastic sword Nigel had thrust in the direction of his nose and he went cross-eyed as he tried to focus. His head made jerky movements as he dribbled.

'I oo,' he said, attempting to say *Nigel*.

'I am giving you one more chance,' Nigel whispered sternly. 'Do you understand?'

But Ivan was doing a very good imitation of someone who didn't. So good, in fact, that Nigel suddenly felt foolish.

But he did not let this stop him. He went on regardless.

'I understand that you can probably do nothing,' he said. 'And that you probably don't even care. And probably you wouldn't even notice. But just in case there is any part of you that understands, I am telling you that if Gordon marries our mother, our father will never be able to come back. Ever. Do you understand how important this is?'

Nigel waited.

'My point being, if you continue to act all nice to Gordon, Mum will think she is doing the right thing marrying him and she most definitely is not. So if you care about Dad at all, which from the way you have been acting it would be easy to suspect that you do not, will you stop smiling at Gordon? And please stop saying his name too. If you continue, and if I ever find you are intelligent, then I will formally consider you my enemy. Understood?'

Nigel scanned Ivan's eyes for any understanding. Any remorse. Anything.

He waited. And waited.

'And let me remind you,' he explained eventually, 'that when I grow up, I am planning on putting my brain to good use by studying stem-cell technology so I can cure you. This may not mean you could actually feed yourself, or go to the toilet on your own, however one day you might be able to live in assisted accommodation. Wouldn't you like that? And we could play Warhammer, and you could come on beetle-catching excursions with me. I have counted thirty-one subspecies so far. And that is just in this vicinity. You could have proper swordfights with me. But most of all, you could have a relationship with Dad one day.'

Nigel felt a bit choked up. He waited for his voice to sound smooth again.

'And I'll just remind you of all the things I have done for you. I stick up for you all the time at school when kids say you're spastic. And what about when you slipped in the bath and I saved you? And all the times I take such care to make sure you don't hurt yourself during a fit? And when that praying mantis went for your jugular?'

Nigel waited another small interval.

Then Nigel showed Ivan the drawings he had done. The one of a boy in a wheelchair having a fit.

'If you care about Dad, throw lots of these while you're in town with Mum and Gordon,' said Nigel. 'Okay? Every time it comes near you. Then Mum will know you don't like Gordon. And she might call the wedding off.'

Next he showed Ivan the drawing of a face with a smile, and a big cross over the face. Next to it was a face grimacing with a big tick next to it.

'Look miserable,' Nigel insisted. 'Don't smile at Gordon.'

Next he showed Ivan a mouth with vomit coming out of it.

'Throw up lots. Preferably on Gordon.'

And then he showed Ivan a boy in a wheelchair biting the hand of a man with red hair.

'These are all things you can do to help,' said Nigel, scanning his brother's face for any sign of recognition. 'Do you understand? If you can be sick as anything on this trip and totally ruin it for them, that would help a lot. Because I can't tell you what a diabolical imposter Gordon really is.'

Ivan blew a spit bubble.

'Good,' said Nigel, feeling for the first time in the discussion that Ivan was with him. 'That is exactly what I think of Gordon too.'

Then Ivan farted.

'Brilliant,' said Nigel, overjoyed. 'I couldn't have put it better myself.'

This is what he had hoped for from a brother. Intelligent comment. Though of course it was probably just a coincidence.

I, Nigel Dorking, Shall Always Count My Blessings and Be Eternally Grateful.

On Nigel's firm instructions, Gordon drove Mum, Ivan, Nigel and Gilgamesh incredibly slowly to Dad's, so the goldfish water wouldn't slosh.

It wasn't easy for Nigel sitting in the back holding a goldfish bowl with Ivan thrashing about next to him because of the sunlight, and also he, Nigel, was preoccupied, getting ready for the moment when fairly soon Mum and Gordon and Ivan would drive off without him.

Nigel silently thanked Gilgamesh. Even at such a time, he counted his blessings in gratitude for the friendship. Besides Ray, Gilgamesh was his best friend.

Even though Nigel was excited to be going to Dad's, he had never actually stayed the night away from Mum before.

He had some pretty powerful feelings building up inside about that. And some surprisingly powerful ones about Ivan too. Ones like, *Everyone feels sorry for you, but I don't. After all, you're the one who doesn't have to go to school, or play sport. You don't even have to wipe your own bottom, or chew your own food. You get yours mashed, and you get Mum all to yourself all day, every day and you get to go on their holiday. I wasn't even invited.*

Nigel knew this was unfair. For he was going to Dad's. And Ivan wasn't invited to Dad's. But right then he didn't feel like being fair.

Their car stopped.

Ivan was unsuccessfully attempting to bang his head on the car window.

Right then, Nigel couldn't stand Ivan. You've got to be smarter than you let on, thought Nigel. Much.

It was the moment Nigel had been dreading. It was time to get out of the car. All Nigel wanted to do was stay with his mother.

'Kiss your brother,' said Mum.

Nigel dutifully did as he was told, though as he did he took the opportunity to let Ivan know the score.

'You win Mum for now, Ivan,' he whispered, 'but I'll win Dad. And I won't share him.'

As he slid carefully out the car door, holding Gilgamesh, Nigel was aware of another weird sensation.

He hadn't actually ever been away from Ivan before either. Well, only when Ivan was in hospital but that was Ivan being away from him, which was different. Nigel was surprised by the painful ache he felt. And it wasn't made any better with Ivan frantically yelling, 'I oo, I oo!'

Nigel was hoping his mother would not want to see him to Dad's front door. He was hoping that she'd drive off quickly so Babette, the girls and Dad wouldn't have to see Ivan.

But Nigel's hopes were destroyed when he saw Gordon getting out of the car. He stood and gave Nigel a farewell bear hug, putting his huge arms around Nigel and the Gilgamesh bowl.

'Careful,' cautioned Nigel.

Gordon stared into Nigel's eyes, and said in his Orcish whiskery way, 'I'll miss you, laddie. I hope when you get back we can spend more time together.' This was of course all for Mum's benefit.

Naturally Nigel said nothing.

'Nige,' whispered Mum, beckoning him to the front gate away from Gordon for privacy, 'I love you. And I want you to relax. I know your problem has recurred, but I promise Dad won't mind. Get to know your dad, that's an order!'

This was an outrage! How did his mother know? He had been so careful and discreet, washing and drying his bedclothes.

'Mums know,' said Mum, apparently reading his mind. Then she gave Nigel a hint, 'They can tell when they see sheets and pyjamas flapping on the line and they didn't put them there.'

Nigel wanted to deny that his problem had recurred

and to suggest that instead he had developed a cleanliness obsession, but there wasn't time. And quite clearly Mum doesn't know Dad, thought Nigel, if she thinks he wouldn't mind. He made up his mind not to follow any advice of hers in future concerning his father.

Mum opened her arms wide. Nigel decided it would be best to put the bowl down. Mum then gave him an extra-hard squeeze, and lifted him right off the ground.

Nigel said nothing. But after checking that his head was still attached to his body, he allowed himself to feel glad about putting down Gilgamesh's bowl.

Mum had just pressed the gate bell.

That's when they heard the dog. 'Arf Arf.'

Now Nigel was hoping Babette wouldn't answer the door. He really didn't want her to see Mum like this. For sure, Babette would look down on mothers who had tattoos and sons like Ivan.

Mum picked up Gilgamesh.

Nigel hoped in a most unknightly way that perhaps Babette was doing her weightlifting and that the weights machine might have fallen on top of her.

Sadly however, just Nigel's luck, a totally uncrushed Babette answered the door. There were not even any bruises. And next to her was the yapping, snarling sausage dog, baring its teeth.

Did his twin stepsisters have no manners at all?

They had raced and stood next to their mother, gawking up at Nigel's mother with open mouths. Nigel was stunned – they didn't even have the manners to say hello.

Stop it. That's impolite, Nigel wanted to tell them. But he didn't. Nonetheless, he was shocked that Babette had brought up her children to stare at the fashion disadvantaged like that. Particularly when the fashion disadvantaged was also age disadvantaged.

But then the girls saw Ivan in the car. And their eyes goggled and their mouths fell open.

Nigel felt incensed.

'Is he insane?' asked the taller of the girls.

'No,' said Mum in a very friendly way, 'just intellectually disabled.' Then she handed Babette Gilgamesh's bowl.

Babette looked at it icily.

'Reckon you could rest that on your tummy? Having another one or just too many choccy biscuits?' said Mum.

Suddenly Nigel's guts ran cold. He had just seen Babette turn side on and the terrible truth struck him. Either Babette had just swallowed Lotsa, their family dog whole (which wouldn't have surprised him at all), or she was pregnant.

Nigel felt the blood draining out of him. He knew exactly what Babette was up to. Replacing him, Nigel.

Obviously she wanted a boy. This clearly meant war.

Though Nigel reminded himself to remain respectful of his host even though she was his enemy.

'I don't allow junk food in this house,' said Babette, icily referring to the choccy biscuits. 'But yes, I'm pregnant if that's what you mean.'

'Ah. So what are you hoping for?' asked Mum, trying to be chatty.

A human, Nigel wanted to say. *But it's most unlikely given half its parentage.* But he didn't, due to the Code of Chivalry.

'I don't mind,' lied Babette with her fake, cold smile, 'as long as it's healthy.'

Prevaricator, Nigel wanted to accuse her, *You want a boy, and I know you do.* But he didn't, because he knew this was too important. He must be on his best behaviour on his first ever overnight stay at his father's.

Nigel was determined to be impeccable.

That way she, the interloper, could never fault him. Nigel knew that she'd try and turn his father against him at the drop of a fork at the dinner table.

'Put it in the laundry, Nigel,' she ordered him as she held the Gilgamesh bowl back out to him with great distaste. 'I wasn't aware you'd be bringing your animals.'

Nigel knew he shouldn't, but he couldn't help himself. 'Actually a fish isn't technically an animal,' he erroneously corrected her. 'But that is . . . I think.' He looked down at the dog that had plunged its pointy teeth into his trouser leg.

'Lotsa,' said Babette, 'heel.'

The look that Babette shot him was one he was certain she would never allow his father to see. It was one that said, *I want you out of my life, kid.*

And Nigel smiled back at her with precisely the same look. But the word *serpent* substituted for the word *kid.* (If that were possible to do in a look.)

The girls followed Nigel to the laundry.

'Is he dumb?' asked the taller one, still gawking over Ivan.

'For your information,' said Nigel, 'no, he most certainly is not dumb. He is actually very smart indeed. More cunninger than a fox actually.'

Nigel and his stepsisters, Gabby and Janelle, were finally introduced. They were obviously poorly brought up. When Nigel put his hand out to shake they giggled. At least, though, Nigel had to admit, the girls had been excited to meet him. Actually they'd almost bounced off the walls, and he'd sort of enjoyed it too. Even though they were selfish, ill-mannered brats and born from spawn of the Evil One, Nigel couldn't help thinking that they probably were alright, as they seemed very excited he was staying with them. He was even a bit disappointed when Babette insisted they have a bath. What would he do until his father came out of his office?

Babette led him into the sewing room.

'This is where you'll sleep, Nigel,' she said coolly.

Nigel stood and carefully inspected his room.

A camp bed was set up by the window and there was a spinning wheel in the corner. The spinning wheel didn't bother him now, but he knew once it was dark it might, probably about 13 per cent, he decided.

Not that spinning wheels were scary in themselves either, but it reminded him of *Sleeping Beauty*. And that reminded him of *Hansel and Gretel*, which reminded him of *Snow White*, which reminded him of *Cinderella*. And all these fairytales had one thing in common. Wicked stepmothers.

I, Nigel Dorking, Do Hereby Swear to Exhibit Patience and Forbearance at All Times.

Nigel had been sitting on his own for ages now in his stepmother's sewing room, which was to be his bedroom for the next three nights. Even though it was against Babette's rules, he decided to smuggle Gilgamesh into his room. Just for a while.

On his way back from the laundry, while carrying Gilgamesh, he saw, fast disappearing around the hallway corner, one yellow balloon attached to a tube and he almost dropped the fishbowl.

After putting Gilgamesh down, Nigel followed the clip clop of claws on wooden floorboards, and raced after his invention.

'Gotcha,' he whispered as he grabbed the tube from the jaws of his arch enemy's minion, the growling sausage dog. His enemy, her spy.

'Try anything else,' threatened Nigel, 'and all you will be good for is a sausage sizzle.'

'Grr,' it snarled.

He made an oath from that moment on to keep his

bedroom door shut at all times.

Back in his room, after having thoroughly washed his invention, he carefully placed the plastic mattress-saving sheet he'd packed, and re-made his bed.

As he was tucking the sides in, he glanced up and noticed the picture above his bed. The portrait of the little Dutch boy with his finger in the wall of the dam. The boy who was stopping all of Holland from being flooded. It had always been his favourite picture. Father had taken it from home when he'd left.

Nigel knew exactly how that boy felt.

As he put his contraption under his bed he whispered to the Dutch boy, 'There must be no flooding.'

When Nigel was little he always thought that boy was him, except that boy was blond, and Dutch, and older.

Father hadn't come in to say hello yet, even though Nigel had been in his house a whole hour. Would Dad say anything about the mallet? Did he suspect Nigel? Could Dad be staying away to punish him?

But then, Nigel reminded himself, Dad does have an extremely important job to do.

And a knight must have patience at all times.

So Nigel sat, sending his penis and bladder the most important message of his lifetime. *Please behave tonight. This is the most momentous moment of my life.*

'Dinner,' Babette called.

Nigel's stomach started whirring like the hand-mixer Babette was using to whip the mashed potatoes. He was about to set eyes on his most beloved father.

He walked towards the dining room.

He walked towards the table and sat.

That's when he heard Dad's footsteps, right behind him. He would know that footfall anywhere. And that strange little cough Dad always did before he spoke.

Nigel jumped to his feet, spun around and held out his hand.

'How do you do, Dad,' he said as he shook his father's hand.

'Nigel,' Dad said, not meeting Nigel's eye.

Nigel's stepsisters stared at Nigel strangely as he sat back down.

Didn't they know it was polite for a young person to stand when an older person entered the room?

Babette plonked everyone's meal in front of them.

'Oh look,' said Nigel, pointing out the window. The girls looked and Nigel switched his plate with Babette's. Just in case.

'At what?' said Gabby.

'That cumulus nimbus cloud,' said Nigel.

Dad sat down.

'Welcome, Nigel,' he said, inclining his head in his very formal, almost knightly way. The way a noble person might to an esteemed guest. He didn't smile. He wasn't the smiling sort. That kind of behaviour was for grinning idiots like the Orc.

Instead, he tried sending his Dad a mental telepathy message to let him know he wasn't upset by the way Dad'd stayed in his office when Nigel had first arrived.

It worked.

'Sorry I didn't get to see you earlier than this,' apologised Dad. 'I had some urgent accounting to attend to. Bloody tax returns.'

Nigel felt a rush of pure love. Hoping to hide how flushed his cheeks had become he leant forward with his head down to pick up his knife and fork, only to become aware that the girls had gasped in horror.

In Nigel's peripheral vision, he also noted with some alarm that Gabby was mouthing a warning to him while Janelle looked anxiously up at her mother.

'Prayers, Nigel,' reprimanded Babette. 'Don't you say grace at home?'

How come, Nigel wondered, it's always the people who ruin other people's lives and steal their fathers who are the ones to act the most religious?

After saying grace they all ate their food in silence, apart from Babette complaining about her lack of sleep because of how the baby kicked inside her at night.

Nigel silently congratulated the baby on its good taste in hating Babette.

He wasn't used to having someone glare at him every time he accidentally made a noise.

He tried to concentrate on chewing his food thirty times a mouthful.

'Mum, what are we going to call the baby?' asked Janelle.

Horrorhead, Nigel refrained from suggesting.

Instead, he tried sending Dad another mental telepathy message. Just to let him know he, Nigel, wasn't upset by the way Dad was ignoring him right now.

To let him know that he, Nigel, understood perfectly well that his father was not in a position to be demonstrative in front of Babette.

Nigel's insides grinned like the Cheshire Cat. Dad hiding their closeness was only proof to him that he and Dad had a strong bond forming, even without eye contact.

This must be infuriating to her, he thought joyfully.

'In fact,' said Dad after dinner, 'why don't we play the game I invented?'

The girls groaned. Nigel's heart soared. This was obviously what Dad had planned all along to welcome Nigel.

'Do we have to, Mummy?' whined Janelle.

'It's a board game about water facts,' lisped Gabby unenthusiastically.

'It's called Dripial Pursuit,' stated Dad proudly, looking directly at Nigel. 'The idea is to put out a quiz game for kids to raise awareness about saving water. It has questions like . . .'

Dad cleared his throat as if to speak. 'Did you know . . .' he started to say.

Nigel's heart leapt like Mum's favourite ballet dancer, Nijinsky. This was exactly what he'd been hoping for. That Dad might tell them some interesting water facts, just like he used to when he lived with him and Mum.

The girls didn't seem interested – Nigel could tell by the way Gabby rolled her eyes like Mum used to, and Janelle kicked the table repeatedly with her foot.

'Did you know,' his father repeated, 'that 99.5 per cent of all the fresh water on earth is in icecaps and glaciers?'

Nigel shook his head, even though he did already know.

'And,' said Dad, 'that one small drop from a leaky faucet can waste over 200 litres of water a day?'

'Wow,' said Nigel, just like he used to.

'And that we've been using the same water since the dinosaurs were here on earth?' said Dad.

'That's amazing when you think about it,' Nigel

said, trying to make the girls enthusiastic. He hated seeing them hurting Dad's feelings like this.

Nigel really hoped his eyes were shining, just in case his father was noticing him in his peripheral vision. Nigel wanted to let him know that he thought his father was doing a really important job, and that one day he hoped to be a water saver just like him.

Babette yawned rudely, saying, 'Not everyone finds water as fascinating as you do, Len.'

'I find it extremely fascinating,' said Nigel.

Babette glared at Nigel.

Probably, decided Nigel, because things with me and Dad are going so well.

He couldn't wait to seal their bond with the conversation he was certain they would have in a minute when the girls and Babette were busy.

Dad, he'd say, *remember the Knights' Code of Chivalry you taught me? I can still recite it all* . . . And then once they'd really got talking, perhaps then would be the moment to dash to his room and pull out all his certificates from school that year.

And once Dad was suitably impressed, Nigel hoped that the conversation would somehow lead to someone saying something about fatherly and sonly love. And who knew what might happen from there?

Nigel steeled himself and decided he had to go all out with this bonding. It needed to be super-strength.

Nigel sat down on the couch near his father.

'Perhaps, Dad,' he suggested, 'you might like a game of chess?'

That way they could talk about knights and queens and kings. This would serve a double purpose, as not only would they have a chance of bonding but also Nigel knew Babette would not like it at all. He was certain that she did not know how to play chess, as she simply wasn't bright enough.

However Babette surprised Nigel with her counter-attack. 'Nigel, I think it's your bedtime.'

Nigel reminded himself to remain polite, attentive and to exhibit manners at all times.

'Actually,' smiled Nigel, 'my bedtime is nine o'clock and it's only eight thirty.'

'My house, my rules,' countered Babette with her trump card, as she smiled her assassin's smile.

Nigel would gladly have driven a stake through her heart. But instead, he was careful to smile back. He would give her no cause for complaint. He would remain the perfect guest. Though he raised his eyebrows, hoping his father might weigh up the evidence himself, or even weigh in on his behalf.

But Dad cleared his throat and studied his water flowcharts.

Surely though, Nigel hoped, Dad noted that narky tone in her voice? He reassured himself that Dad was doubtlessly thinking, *Is that a nice way for someone to talk to a visitor? Is that a decent way to behave?*

Nigel could see the back of Babette's smirking head as she started to walk triumphantly down her hallway.

'Fine. Oh, by the way, Dad,' Nigel said, in a deliberately pleasant voice to contrast with hers.

He pulled the carefully folded decorated invitation to the trivia quiz from his pocket and handed it to his father.

'It's an invitation to the school trivia quiz fundraiser. I am hoping you will oblige me by attending and of course sit on my table as the guest of honour. Nigel partially bowed. 'It's called the Knight of Knights,' he explained. ''Twas actually my idea. You will have to dress up in your armour, however, which I remind you is at home, awaiting you. Who knows, you could be Len the Lionheart, and I, Nigel the Notorious.'

Nigel could feel Babette freeze. He sensed he had just outmanoeuvred her. Perhaps she was beginning to understand he was not just a pawn she could move about at her will after all.

Dad looked at the piece of paper, mumbled something about looking in his diary, and shoved it quickly into his pocket.

One to me, thought Nigel, wondering how the serpent would strike next.

I, Nigel Dorking, Do Hereby Swear Always to Exhibit Self-Control.

As Nigel dawdled towards his room, he wondered how long a child would get for killing a stepmother. Probably not long, given his stepmother. He might even be awarded a medal of bravery for ridding society of a public menace.

Though, he cautioned himself, I must exhibit self-control.

Even so, he did try to send the baby inside his evil stepmother a message. *Kick her in the duodenum.*

He hoped his father couldn't read his mind, as this anger was a side of himself he preferred not to show. But equally, he would defend himself (in case Dad could mind-read) that he was certain Babette was doubtlessly plotting Nigel's demise.

When he reached his bedroom, Nigel realised this was the final reckoning. Would his relationship with his father make it through the night?

He had a terrible feeling there hadn't been enough bonding yet. Not to survive this – if his invention didn't work and he wet, and Dad found out, that is.

'Grr,' growled Lotsa as Nigel closed his bedroom door in her face.

'Good night, sausage mince for brains,' he whispered.

As Nigel sat on his bed, he couldn't help wishing he had tested his apparatus the night before. But he hadn't thought of it. He had been too preoccupied.

Nervously he held the tube from his apparatus in his left hand, and very gently with his right hand he tried to stuff his penis into it.

'Just go in, penis,' he instructed as he tried to manoeuvre it in again. And again. And again.

He tried twisting it in, squishing it in, and finally decided to make a nick with the scissors in the tube, just to make it big enough for his penis to enter.

It was taking longer than expected, but finally he managed to get the tube around the tip.

'Excellent,' he whispered.

Then six times, he wound the masking tape around, just to be absolutely positive.

If this worked, he could go on camp. Which would mean another three whole days with Dad. This would surely upset Babette! And was probably why she had sent her evil sausage dog to try and steal his contraption!

Then Nigel lay down in his bed and pulled up the sheets and duvet wondering if he'd ever fall asleep. Was he too anxious about his invention? Would he have to think about some of his large words again to help him get to sleep? Words like *copyright*, *multibillionaire* and *genius*?

If he were to make heaps of money then he could dedicate his whole life to curing Ivan.

That's when he got that feeling. The one he imagined Steve Irwin the crocodile hunter would have felt when he realised he had been stung in the heart by a stingray. By a creature he had loved.

Me wanting to help Ivan, Nigel amended his earlier thought, is only if Ivan stops taking my mother away from me.

Just in case Dad was coming in to kiss him goodnight, he switched on the light and placed the balloon under his bed, being careful to hide the plastic tubing under his duvet.

He glanced up and thought he saw the Dutch boy looking a bit stunned.

'It's an invention,' Nigel explained, feeling quite silly talking to a print of a painting. 'It's, well, what you're doing for Holland, I want to do for my bed. After all, all knights must strive to save their King and Country. And their beds if necessary.

'Yes,' he added. 'I wet my bed. Which is most unusual for someone as intelligent as I am, being in the ninety-eighth percentile for my age group.'

Nigel most definitely did not like sleeping in this unfamiliar place. And also, he was used to having an adult tuck him in, or at least bid him goodnight. But it was getting a little late.

It was after midnight now.

Would Dad tuck the new baby in? Would the new baby, the replacement baby, come out already toilet-trained and with a very high WISK score? What if this baby were a prodigy? A genius born with unusual skills that would impress Dad, ones like knowing the rainfall in any country, the level of their dams, the consumption of water in all major towns, alphabetically named, and ancient medieval facts?

Though he reminded himself it would be a slightly evil baby, probably with a large wart that sprouted hairs on the end of its chin, due to her genes. And was more likely to be deeply stupid. Though the twins weren't as bad as he had expected.

It was twenty minutes past midnight now. He did not think Dad would be in to say goodnight.

Nigel found this silence unsettling. He was used to the night-time noises Ivan made. And Mum singing to Ivan. Even if he disapproved of her choice of song, and even though she got most of the lyrics wrong, and hit many bung notes, her voice was comforting.

It was when he was thinking about Ivan's night

noises and Mum's bad singing voice that he found himself being swamped by those same unfamiliar feelings like the ones he'd had in the car, ones that made him feel woozy with an electric-like nausea.

Nigel couldn't help thinking of Mum, Gordon and Ivan all away without him. A tightly knit family group.

He felt intensely alone. And like throwing something.

In front of him stretched a long and lonely night, in the pitch dark, not in his own bed. And thinking about Mum being so far away made Nigel feel like he was infinitesimally small, so unimportant in the scheme of things that he was being flung into the far reaches of the universe, and that he was free-falling.

That's when he knew he had to ring Mum.

Carrying the balloon and tube concealed under his dressing-gown, Nigel crept over towards Dad's office.

On Dad's very tidy desk, he spied Dad's work things, which sent his heart into a flutter. He'd missed seeing Dad's ledger book and Dad's computer. And on the walls, he noted, were some framed paintings the girls had done.

But nothing I have done, thought Nigel with a pang. Or my brother.

In Dad's in-tray he spied a letter addressed to his father 'and family'. So Nigel read it.

This is to confirm that you and your family should be at studio 227 in Bay Street by 7 a.m. on Saturday 5 May for the making of the 'Ablutions Solutions' advertisement. Below are the lyrics for the rap you have okayed.

What could this mean? wondered Nigel.

And then on an impulse, he put it through Dad's photocopier, folded his copy and put it in his dressing-gown pocket. The fourth of May was Ivan's birthday. The fifth was the one-year anniversary of the terrible day Dad left.

Nigel sat at Dad's black-leather swivel work-chair, and dialled Mum's mobile.

'Hello, Nige, it's a bit late isn't it?' said Mum's far-away voice.

Nigel couldn't speak.

'How are you going, lovely?' she asked, sounding a bit concerned.

Nigel still couldn't speak.

'Oh, love, are you feeling a bit homesick?' asked Mum. 'It'll pass, I promise. I'd have called you earlier, but Ivan hasn't been well. In fact, he's been calling out your name all night.'

There were so many things he wanted to say to Mum. But instead, he said in a very whispery voice, 'Mother, did you know that scientists now believe in a theory called the superstrings theory? It's an alternative explanation to the origins of the universe.'

'I oo,' he heard Ivan call out followed by a bout of chesty coughing.

Mum sighed.

'Nigel love, we can talk about that some other time, but can I get you to say hello to Ivan, love? He's been a bit frantic.'

Nigel heard Ivan's whimpering in the background. He was obviously working himself up into a tantrum which would end in an uncontrollable coughing fit. Nigel's heart hardened. Even though he had told Ivan to misbehave, he hadn't meant now. Not when Nigel needed to hear Mum's voice due to being so far away. Even knights of old would have felt this way.

Couldn't selfish Ivan let him have Mum for one phone call? For ten measly seconds? He'd rung Mum, and now Mum was putting him onto Ivan. Ivan, who was with her. Ivan, who would never understand the superstrings theory.

Why did stupid, pathetic Ivan who didn't even know the difference between an igneous and a metamorphic rock always have to come first?

Nigel wanted to scream, *I hate him. Don't you get it, Mum? He's a faker.* And he wanted to scream it so loudly he would split atoms apart. Preferably Ivan's. And Nigel didn't care if he completely annihilated Ivan. Forever.

But instead, he whispered, 'Actually, Mum, I'd better go,' and he hung up quickly.

Now, the feeling he got when he thought of Ivan was surprisingly violent.

'Yap yap,' he heard at his father's office door. And then footsteps.

'What on earth are you doing up at this hour?' asked the ice queen who stood before him in her flowing black nightie, her hench dog at her side. 'And what are you doing in your father's office?'

Nigel could not speak.

'We'll deal with this in the morning,' she said ominously. 'Now to bed.'

Sleep was not happening for Nigel.

Fury and anxiety were getting the better of him.

'I swear I will cut off the head of anybody who gets in the way of my relationship with my father,' he whispered.

I, Nigel Dorking, Do Hereby Swear Always to Persevere, Even in the Greatest Adversity.

Aren't I at Dad's? a still-slumbering Nigel semi-remembered.

He opened one eye to check and felt instantly extremely ill. It was quite clear he was most definitely at Dad's and he had without question done the most terrible deed. He was unquestionably urinating and he was not on the toilet, and he *was* in his father's house.

The nightmare of his life had just come true.

Nigel stared with horror, totally stricken, at his penis, whose very life was poised on the edge of a precipice. It was 5.07 a.m. And his penis was in the actual process of peeing still. And he had so recently sworn to behead anyone who got in the way of his relationship with his father! Could a knight take back a promise?

Then he remembered something really important. 'My invention!' he whispered.

Nigel rolled over. His right arm felt around beneath where he lay to check the sheets, while his left arm snaked down to the floor beside his bed, where he knew a yellow balloon lay. A yellow balloon with a tube attached to it, that was in turn attached to his penis. Then he performed his scientific tests.

His sense of touch told him the sheets were dry.

Relief.

Then, Nigel tested the balloon. He gently squeezed it to make sure the yellow balloon was full of urine. The warm balloon squelched between his fingers.

Nigel felt like doing a Highland fling, though he thought it'd be wise to wait until he didn't have a contraption attached to his penis, and until someone taught him how to do a Highland fling, as he did not like doing things imperfectly.

Instead, he said, 'Excellent.'

Then, taking every precaution not to bump into anyone, Nigel looked either way down the hallway and tiptoed to the loo, holding the sloshing balloon in his hands. There was not one squeak from the floorboards. But there were plenty from Lotsa.

'Arf, Arf, Arf, Arf,' came the piercing yap.

Nigel heard her hurtling around the corner towards him, her toenails clip clopping on the stained-wood hallway. He slammed the toilet door shut just as she started scratching frantically at the door.

'Beat you, you evil tapping fool,' whispered Nigel.

Nigel locked the door with the latch, and switched on the light.

With his left hand, he held the balloon with the urine in it, and pinched it at the top. Then with his right hand he ripped the masking tape from the balloon end of the tube. Then he painstakingly freed the balloon from the end of the tubing.

He worked cautiously, as if he were performing a heart transplant, except of course he would never do that in a loo.

'But so far so good,' he congratulated himself as he emptied the pee from the balloon into the loo.

Now for stage two.

Nigel sat down on the toilet seat. He gave the tube attached to his penis a small tug. And then another one. But it didn't come away. He felt a stab of anxiety.

'Yap Yap,' cried his long-eared adversary at the door. Obviously sending her owner a message in dog code.

Nigel calmed himself and tugged again. Still no good, so he tugged a bit harder. 'Ow!' he cried.

Harder still. No good.

'No,' he whimpered, staring helplessly at his penis.

'Yap yap,' Lotsa continued her onslaught.

'Will you shut up, you stomach-dragging moron?' cried Nigel, exasperated.

'I beg your pardon?' came a voice that sounded just like Babette's from directly outside the toilet door. Nigel yanked up his pyjama bottoms, right over the tube, and vacated the loo as quickly as he could.

'Sorry,' he apologised as he sped past her, head down. And so as not to be untrue to himself, because he wasn't sorry, he said softly '. . . that you're in my life.'

Once safely back in his room, Nigel deliberately plonked himself down on the floor directly in front of the door, acting as a doorstop so no one could get in, not even someone Lotsa's size. Right now, that would be a disaster. Particularly if she grabbed the end of the tube.

Nigel felt ill thinking about it, as he pulled down his pyjama bottoms, and tried to loosen the masking tape that attached the plastic tube to his penis.

'Ow,' he winced. He tugged gently. And then less gently. And then really hard till it hurt like mad.

'It's stuck,' he whispered.

He wasn't sure, but he even thought he saw the Dutch boy flinch.

Then he made a snap decision.

Nigel made a mad dash still in his pyjamas out the back door, through to his father's toolshed.

'I'll have to take more drastic measures,' he whispered, clenching his teeth.

I, Nigel Dorking, Do Hereby Swear to Remain Steadfast.

Nigel scanned the vast array of his father's tools so admirably and neatly hung on his father's workshop wall.

Finally he selected a shiny red pair of wire-cutters. They'd have to cut plastic, he felt certain.

'Calm down,' he instructed himself as he stood on some bricks to get a bit of height. 'Remember you are in expert hands.' The Ear, Nose and Throat specialist had said precisely this to Nigel when Nigel had had his tonsils out.

Then, standing on tiptoe, he carefully placed his penis with the tube on it onto his father's workbench.

It was cold.

Nigel grabbed an old newspaper that was close and slid it under his penis.

'Now, you'll need a steady hand for this,' Nigel spoke as if to an esteemed colleague.

He then placed the wire-cutters in position. Around the tube, ready to snip.

'Please don't let any skin get caught,' he begged no one in particular. It was bad enough when it got caught in his zipper.

After a few false starts, and not being able to look, Nigel plucked up his courage. Even though he felt weak at the knees, he reminded himself of being a knight and how they couldn't afford to be squeamish. Even though his whole body had gone to mush, he braced himself. *Snap* went the wire-cutters.

With enormous relief, Nigel quickly studied his handiwork and realised the wire-cutters had done the job nearly perfectly. The plastic had definitely been severed. True, it was a bit jagged, and the actual cut on the actual tubing was a lot further from the actual penis than he'd planned. There were about five centimetres of jagged tubing on the end of his penis now. But, he congratulated himself, this is quite exemplary for someone with his eyes closed.

Nigel raced to his room to get dressed into his school uniform, only to find his bedroom door open and one fat sausage dog skittling out so fast it skidded on all fours right into the hallway wall.

His heart skipped a beat, for there on his unmade bed, lolling on its side, was Gilgamesh's bowl, water everywhere. Gilgamesh, lying gasping in the shallows still left in the bowl.

Nigel crept with Gilgamesh back towards the laundry.

'Yap yap,' he heard Lotsa deliberately alert the whole household as she snapped viciously at his heels.

'Quiet,' warned Nigel. 'Or you won't be a sausage dog for much longer. You'll be one of those cold-air door stoppers.'

'I beg your pardon?' said Babette. 'What is that fish doing out of the laundry?'

Nigel did not know what to say. So he said nothing.

'Have you nothing to say?' she said.

'No,' he said. 'Obviously.'

Having re-made his bed with the spare set of sheets he brought from home, and having wrapped all his wet sheets in plastic and put them in his school bag to take to Mum's before school, Nigel sat down to breakfast.

He tried to ignore Babette banging on about people who disobeyed rules and who were insolent. She was obviously waiting for Dad to come down to breakfast. And before he'd even sat down she beckoned Dad to follow her.

And then Nigel was summoned.

Nigel saw them both standing at his bedroom door, Babette with her hands on hips, her hair pulled back in a particularly angry style.

Nigel's insides were swooning. What could this be about? Gilgamesh? He'd cleaned up the water.

'Nigel,' said Babette, raising one overly plucked eyebrow. 'Those sheets on your bed. They are not ours.'

Nigel could feel his face flushing vermillion.

'Correct,' said Nigel. 'They are not. They are Mum's. I do not like the feel of other people's sheets.'

'Oh, don't you,' she said.

Now both her overly plucked eyebrows were raised. She had a small smile on her mouth as she gave Nigel's father an *I told you he is odd* look.

Dad was staring at his big toe which was wriggling nervously inside his shoe.

'Well ah, leave our sheets on in future and ah, don't bring that fish into this room again,' said Dad, not very convincingly, as he glanced at Babette to make sure he had said the right thing.

'And don't go to your father's office at night,' she added.

She then looked at Nigel's dad for affirmation.

'Well?' she said, frowning.

How outrageous! Nigel waited for Dad to back him, which he most certainly would. This was an unfair attack.

'Er . . . yes,' Dad said.

I hate her, thought Nigel. I hate her so much.

It must be pretty powerful black magic indeed for

Dad not to see how horrible she is. And for a lowly sausage dog to go over to the dark side.

It was a quarter to nine a.m. when he arrived at Mum's house to get the money to pay the doctor and to wash Dad's sheets. He'd get them from Mum's line after school.

He made his way to his mother's room. She had a few hundred dollars stashed in her top drawer in her bedside table for emergencies.

Nigel opened his mother's drawer and there under her bras he spotted what he was looking for.

He put one fifty-dollar note into his pocket.

'Hey!' cried a muffled male voice.

Nigel spun around. The bedclothes leapt up, and then from under them a tousled man with red dreadlocks.

'Ah,' cried Nigel.

'Hey, dude,' said Ray. 'I was hopin' to catch you. I went to confront my old man last night and couldn't find him nowhere.'

'They've gone away,' explained Nigel.

'Real sorry for scarin' you, man,' said Ray. 'So when are the dudes due back?'

'The day after tomorrow,' said Nigel.

Ray was now sitting on the bed, which he patted, so Nigel sat next to him.

Then Ray pulled out some tobacco and started to roll a cigarette in Mum's bedroom. Mum was the biggest anti-smoker that ever lived. Nigel was about to warn him that smoking was unintelligent and that smoking in Mum's room was especially unintelligent, but decided not to. He wasn't quite sure why. Ray didn't look like the sort of person who would care. Instead, Nigel cleared his throat.

'It must have been pretty bad growing up with him as your da . . . your old man?' Nigel asked.

'Oh no,' said Ray. 'I love the old man. Na, Dad was a cool dude. He rocks.'

Nigel was stunned. So stunned he almost didn't hear the next bit. This would ruin his plan of turning Mum off Gordon, if Ray claimed he was a good dad.

'I'm the problem, man,' whispered Ray. 'I done a real bad thing. Yeah, it was real uncool. Then I ran away. Haven't seen my old man since. See, my mum she was real sick, for ages, man, and he just stayed out. At the pub. Ten in the morning till midnight.'

Aha, an alcoholic bigamist. Nigel could tell Mum this! This was all good ammunition.

'Then she died. I was real mad at him. Didn't understand he was paying for all the medical bills. Like, I thought he just didn't have enough time for her, or me. Too busy at his pub, you know?'

Ray had a far-off look in his eyes.

'That's unforgivable,' said Nigel.

'Yeah well, I bet he'll never forgive me either, man,' he whispered.

What could a son possibly do that a father couldn't forgive? A decent father, that is, frowned Nigel.

'When Mum died, I paid his pub a visit with a few mates,' Ray whispered. He looked white as he spoke. 'Emptied every bloody thing in the place. Over the floor. Crème de Menthe, Advocat, gin, vodka, you name it. If someone had've lit a match that place would have gone up. Even smashed open a keg of beer. You should have seen that amber liquid flying all over the room. Whoosh! Ruined the place.'

'Wow,' said Nigel. 'That would have upset the people who owned the pub too.'

'That was Dad,' said Ray.

'Oh,' said Nigel, very disappointed as this meant Gordon was not an alcoholic. The severity of the act Ray had done to his father hit him with some force. 'Wow,' said Nigel.

'Yeah, wow,' agreed Ray looking dismayed.

Once again they were nodding.

'He knew who'd done it. But he never called the cops. Which means he couldn't have got the insurance, which means it must have sent him broke.'

Nigel didn't know what to say. Even a decent dad might not forgive a son under those circumstances. He didn't like to say it, but he didn't like Ray's chances. Particularly given Gordon was such an indecent dad.

'What did he say when he saw what you'd done?' asked Nigel instead.

'Dunno,' shrugged Ray, 'I shot through. Haven't spoken to him since. Wasn't gunna contact him again. But he traced me and just kept writin'.'

Ray suddenly looked grim. Even sad.

Nigel left him some thinking space.

'What will we do,' Nigel asked eventually, 'if the wedding does go ahead?'

Ray shrugged and scratched his head.

'Dunno. It'd take a bit of getting used to,' frowned Ray. 'I keep thinking it's wrong, man. Real wrong. He's married to my mum, you know? But then I s'pose that was a few years back all that. Maybe he deserves it. A bit of happiness. I dunno.'

Nigel didn't agree, but decided to say nothing.

'So, I dunno.'

Once again they sat there nodding.

'Would you go to the wedding?' asked Nigel.

Ray shrugged.

'Don't even know if I can even face the old man yet.'

'If you want, I'll come with you when you confront him,' Nigel offered.

Ray didn't answer for a while. 'Thanks,' he said eventually. 'But I gotta take a leaf out of your book, dude. There are some things we have to do alone.'

They both thought about this.

Reluctantly, finally Nigel explained to Ray that he had to go, because he'd be really late for school, and that he was staying at his dad's at the moment, so this house would be empty if Ray wanted to stay there.

'Na,' said Ray. 'I'm happy hidin' at me old man's.'

'So,' asked Nigel, 'how did you get in?'

'Oh,' explained Ray, 'your bedroom window was open, man, there was a mattress sticking out.'

'Ah yes,' explained Nigel. 'It is important to air mattresses on a regular basis. It says so on the label. And also, due to getting asthma sometimes, I like to scorch those pesky dustmites in the sun.'

'Hey man,' said Ray. 'Got any deodoriser?'

'Sure,' said Nigel, racing towards the bathroom.

Nigel handed the Orc's deodorant to the Orc's son.

'Good call, exotic garden freshness,' said Ray, who then, to Nigel's surprise, sprayed Mum's room.

Chapter XXVI

I, Nigel Dorking, Do Hereby Swear Never to Betray a Confidence or Comrade.

Nigel waved Ray off at the front door, and both of them headed in their separate directions.

'Take it easy,' called Ray. 'Glad you're in my life, man.'

As Nigel walked down the porch steps, he was surprised to feel a spring in his step. He waved back.

'Hey, I really like your deadlocks,' returned Nigel.

It wasn't until he was at the gate that he actually checked his watch and realised that he wouldn't make it to the medical centre and then back to school possibly until after recess. Nigel turned around.

'Actually, Ray,' he called, 'I need a note to explain that I'll be late for school. And you're eighteen, and a nearly responsible adult who is almost a family member. Would you mind? I've got to go to the doctor.'

Ray looked mildly stunned. Possibly because he'd never seen himself as a nearly responsible family member before.

Ray scratched his head. 'You didn't want to ask your old man?'

'Ah no, actually,' said Nigel.

'Hey, I'm not prying, man. None of my business. I'll write you a note no hassle, just grab me some paper. I know there are things you don't want the olds to know. Not in any trouble, are you? Anything I can help with?'

Nigel didn't like being dishonest to Ray. 'It's something I can't tell my old man,' explained Nigel as they walked back inside and sat down at the kitchen table.

Ray gazed at Nigel with his honest round eyes, and Nigel almost divulged his problem. Something in him wanted to. But luckily at the last second he refrained.

On the way to the doctor's, Nigel sped along with Ray on his charger, protected by his motorbike armour.

He couldn't help grinning at Ray's back as he clung on, his arms around Ray's middle as astride the bike they moved as one against the wind. It's like a ray of sunshine has come into my life, thought Nigel.

The wind rushed at them and right then Nigel felt he could handle anything.

'Well,' Nigel explained to the doctor proudly, 'my possible older-brother-to-be is in the waiting room.'

'Oh if you want he can come in, if you are comfortable with that,' suggested the doctor.

'Ah no,' said Nigel quickly. 'This is a private matter. But may I grab some leaflets on smoking and how it harms you?'

'Certainly,' said the doctor.

'I was simply inventing a party game,' explained Nigel in almost a whisper, just in case people in the waiting room could hear, 'when I slipped and the plastic tubing accidentally fell around my penis.'

Even though he knew it was true that Rule XXXVIII of the Knights' Code explicitly stated that the truth must always be told, he could not risk Dr Maloney telling his daughter Hope.

When Dr Maloney said he definitely wouldn't have to amputate, Nigel was enormously relieved.

And even though it took ages getting the plastic off, it wasn't that painful. He applied some special lubricating ointment that helped make the masking tape less sticky. And then after gently pulling it off he made Nigel promise never to do it again.

Nigel was pretty sure Dr Maloney had believed him about the party invention. The only slightly dodgy bit had been when he'd asked Nigel if he had a bedwetting problem. And if he did, whether he wanted to talk about it.

But Nigel hoped he'd got away with it when he'd answered, 'As if. I am in the ninety-eighth percentile on the WISK test, you know.' He also hoped Ray would find the anti-smoking leaflets he'd tucked into Ray's backpack.

Nigel dismounted the bike, waved goodbye to Ray and walked though the school gates with only a few scavenging pigeons in the playgrounds as his witness. If only all the kids from his class could have seen his very cool and most awesome arrival.

After putting his bag into his locker, he walked only marginally late into his classroom, and was very disturbed to find that instead of Miss Murray, Mrs Pemberton, the Vice Principal, was taking this class.

'Yes?' said Mrs Pemberton in her ugly, brusque, business-like way as she held out her hand for the note Nigel was clutching.

He handed it to her.

The teacher frowned.

'And who is Ray?' Mrs Pemberton quizzed him.

'My brother,' announced Nigel proudly.

A hoot of disbelief made its way around the classroom.

'He is,' retorted Nigel emphatically. Then he added *almost*, to himself.

'Your brother's a spaz,' whispered Bruno. 'He can't write.'

'Bruno,' chastised Mrs Pemberton, who often had

Bruno sitting directly outside her office, which was just opposite the Principal's. 'I will have none of that sort of talk in this classroom, do you hear?'

Bruno nodded reluctantly, but when she wasn't looking he did impressions of Ivan.

'Actually,' said Nigel quite clearly, 'my brother is far more intelligent than you.'

'I beg your pardon?' said Mrs Pemberton looking up from the letter, affronted.

'Oh, not you,' explained Nigel, pointing to Bruno, 'I meant him.'

'I cannot decipher this scrawl,' said Mrs Pemberton. 'In fact, I would go so far as to venture that this was not written by an adult.'

She then handed it to Nigel with such a look of skepticism on her face that Nigel realised she was accusing him of having written his own excuse note.

Nigel felt indignant. He would never do such a thing. That was why he said what he said next.

'It is perfectly legible to me,' and then he started to read it out. He cleared his throat.

It's true, the handwriting was appalling. He had barely begun when the kids started laughing. And continued for the rest of the note.

Dear Dude,

Please excuse my young bro here for being late.

Try not to freak out, cos time is just a human construct. Trust me, he had an appointment he had to attend. Hope it's cool.

Stay calm,

Ray.

PS Trust me, he's a cool dude. He wouldn't bullshit you.

Now the kids were hooting and rocking with laughter. Nigel could feel Mrs Pemberton glaring at him.

'If I was going to write my own note,' said Nigel defensively, 'I would do a far more maturer and more plausibler job than this. And I would most definitely not swear.'

Nigel looked around the class at twenty-three pairs of disbelieving eyes – twenty-four, including Mrs Pemberton's.

'And I do have a brother called Ray. Well he is technically nearly a stepbrother.'

Mrs Pemberton seemed to weigh things up and then she gave a resigned sigh.

'Sit down, Nigel. Given that your behaviour is normally impeccable, I will grant you the benefit of the doubt. But perhaps you could bring your brother to the school?'

'You are in for it,' sneered Hope delightedly.

'Yeah, you'll be expelled,' taunted Bruno.

'Chill out,' whispered Nigel.

Hope and Bruno looked mildly surprised.

Just before dinner at Dad's, Nigel spoke to his mother on the phone, and even though he was normally very careful about what he said, he nearly accidentally blew Ray's whole secret. Mum had put him onto Gordon, and when Gordon asked how he was Nigel found himself saying, 'Cool.'

'What didja say?' asked Gordon.

'Cool, I was just wondering whether the weather is cool over there?' Nigel improvised.

'Oh,' said Gordon, 'you just sounded like someone else for a wee minute.'

At dinner when Janelle handed Nigel the butter, Nigel said 'Cool, dude.'

Babette was over at the sink.

'What's a dude?' demanded Janelle in her piping high voice.

'Actually it's a camel's penis,' whispered Nigel.

'I won't have slang in this house,' said Babette.

'It was Nigel,' lisped Gabby. 'He said it's a camel's penis.'

'Far out,' whispered Nigel, sighing.

'Nigel!' seethed Babette. 'Do not use gutter language in this house.'

That's when Dad sat down.

But he said nothing about Nigel's business card. The one he'd left for him next to his dinner plate. He had meant to show it to Dad ages ago. Instead, Dad carefully slid it into his pocket.

After Gabby's attempt to play *The Pink Panther* theme on the piano that evening, Nigel decided that he'd show them how the piano should be played. This was the perfect opportunity to impress Dad. Particularly seeing his stepsister played so atrociously. So Nigel waited politely until both girls had massacred their piano pieces and then he started playing.

As his fingers travelled down the keyboard unimaginably fast, like the wind, like a concert pianist, he imagined Babette's eyes, absolute slits, while she wished her children had half his talent. He tried to think of modest things to say for when Dad was complimenting him afterwards.

'Nigel,' interrupted Dad.

'Yes, Dad?' he answered, trying hard to suppress a grin whilst awaiting the compliment.

'You are playing *Für Elise* at approximately ten times the speed it is supposed to be performed. Beethoven wouldn't just turn in his grave, he'd rotate.'

Not quite the response Nigel was hoping for. However, he decided, he would surprise his father with his musical dexterity instead.

Nigel snuck off to his room, and back. And while Dad added his goods and services tax Nigel placed himself directly behind Dad, and started to play *The Baby Elephant Walk* on his trumpet.

He had only ever heard Dad yell out loud once before. But this time he also clutched his heart.

Perhaps, Nigel decided afterwards, he should have warned Dad. But it was actually Babette who made the ridiculous fuss. She swished into the living room hissing, 'Will you shut that thing up? We thought it was a truck coming through our window! It's the girls' bedtime for heaven's sake.'

Some people obviously don't understand the finer points of the trumpet, thought Nigel. But without any argument, he put it down and said to his father, 'Perhaps jazz is an acquired taste?'

But Dad didn't answer. Or look up.

Later that night, Nigel lay in bed thrashing around like a trout who'd just swallowed the bait on the end of a fishing line.

How could he avoid wetting his bed tonight?

I, Nigel Dorking, Do Hereby Swear Always to Fight for All Damsels in Distress.

Nigel awoke at 5 a.m. at his dad's house.

The toilet was an unusual place to sleep. And he most definitely did not like the sensation of having a cold, damp backside. Probably, he decided, due to the condensation of the water. And then of course there was the crick in his neck from using the cistern as a pillow. But anything was better than risking wetting the bed.

Nigel sat there, his posterior getting moister and colder and more goosepimply.

Well, that's what happens to disobedient penises and bladders, he thought bitterly. They have to sit up all night on the hard, cold toilet. And it serves them right. Though it's not fair on their owners! Or their posteriors.

He must have finally drifted off to sleep again, because he was startled awake by a loud rapping on the toilet door.

'Who's in there?' demanded Babette.

'Me,' stammered Nigel, still semi-asleep.

Nigel flushed the toilet, ducked out and past her without looking up.

'I cannot use our ensuite or I will wake your father. And next time, show some consideration and do not flush, as that also wakes your father.'

Nigel waited sleepily in his bedroom for her to finish, refusing to nod off. Then he snuck back in.

He hated feeling the warmth of the toilet seat from her bottom on his.

Once again he was awoken by a loud knocking.

'Who's in there?' complained Babette again.

'It is I, Nigel,' he said, vacating once again.

Nigel left his father's house very early that morning. He could not stay at Dad's another night. He was being tortured by sleep deprivation. He would have to find Ray and ask him to stay at Mum's with him.

'Ray,' called Nigel urgently.

He knocked on his mother's bedroom door.

But no answer.

He also needed to ask Ray if he'd come down to the school to see his class teacher. And if he could stay with him tonight.

Nigel searched everywhere, but sadly Ray was nowhere to be found.

So he raced over to Gordon's shed and scribbled a quick note. He didn't knock in case Ray was sleeping.

Dear Ray,
I am having a few problems at school. My teacher needs proof that you exist. Could you come down to school please? I did say you were my brother. I hope you don't mind. Also it's not just the Vice Principal, the kids don't believe you are my brother either. (Well nearly.)

Thanks, dude.

By the way, you are cordially invited to stay with me at my mother's joint tonight.

Nigel

(Please.)

He would ring Ray when he got back to Dad's, and leave a message on his mobile phone.

Nigel sat sleepily in class. At least Miss Murray was back today. Of that Nigel was extremely glad.

By afternoon Nigel's yawns were getting bigger and more frequent. Night-time was looming. Where could he stay?

Just in case he didn't manage to get onto Ray, he decided as a last resort he would have to find a friend. One whose toilet he could sleep on, seeing that was so impossible at Dad's.

Until this moment he had never been at all keen on the idea of friends. In fact, he had carefully avoided cultivating friends for good reasons:

A) They would not understand about Ivan and would stare at him.

B) They often made strange sucking noises which made Nigel's skin crawl.

C) They did not share his interests, e.g. in water facts and medieval knights.

D) They were usually not very intelligent and had smelly lunch.

E) They wanted to play games their way.

F) Most of their games were very boring and childish.

G) They often picked scabs which was absolutely disgusting. And scratched their dandruff onto their desk lids, and then counted the bits.

H) They also teased other people for no discernable reason.

I) They might want to come over on weekends and take up valuable time.

J) They might ask him to their parties, which Nigel did not like. The last one he had attended was in grade one, Bruno's in fact, where they played particularly stupid games like pin the tail on the donkey, and pass the parcel, and musical chairs, where there was no prize for intelligence.

However, now he had to risk it. He had to acknowledge that his situation was desperate.

Nigel looked around as he sat in class for any possible friends. Is it just me, thought Nigel, or are most of these kids totally repulsive and without any redeeming qualities whatsoever? There was not anyone who came even close to being a candidate in his whole class. Possibly his whole school, and his town.

People like Newton and Pythagoras and Achilles probably didn't have a lot of friends either. They probably wouldn't have had time, as doubtlessly they were far too busy being geniuses with all that entails.

However they probably had never been in such desperate straits. As they probably were not the unhappy owners of recalcitrant bladders and penises.

Nigel scanned the room, looking for the kid most likely to have parents with good bladders, so he could sleep on their toilet uninterrupted. A kid who never had to go to the toilet during class.

Perhaps he would be safer also with an unpopular person. One with an annoying personality, as they would be desperate.

But he couldn't spot a likely candidate.

And then he realised. Of course. It would have to be Jeremy. That was his only option. Though a most distasteful one.

This was only a back-up. He crossed his fingers that Ray would get his note.

He knew the other option was to make up some lie and stay at Mum's alone, but he also knew that most people his age and even much older ones, and probably knights of old did not like staying alone in the dark. So he wasn't in bad company.

Just then Jeremy came racing into the classroom.

'Miss Murray,' he said. 'Mrs Bent would like to see Ni– '

'I know,' Nigel interrupted, hoping to cut him off mid-sentence so Jeremy would not utter the rest.

'Mrs Bent,' continued Jeremy Fry doggedly, 'would like to see Nigel Dorking, right away.'

I am not a violent boy, thought Nigel, in fact, I am a pacifist, and he remembered the Knights' Code Rules XXII and XXIII, about exhibiting patience, forbearance and self-control, but surely he could make an exception in Jeremy Fry's case? I would happily put him out of all our misery in a way that involved a lot of pain. Jeremy Fry was the most annoying person alive on this earth today, and possibly for all time.

Nigel glared at Jeremy. What an outrage, what an

assault on his dignity. How would he handle this – Miss Murray and the whole class knowing he, Nigel Dorking, was seeing the school psychologist?

'Only total mentals have to see the psychologist,' whispered Bruno as Nigel stood up.

No, I cannot have Jeremy Fry as a friend, decided Nigel. Under any circumstances.

Chapter XXVIII

I, Nigel Dorking, Do Hereby Swear Always to Listen to Others, Even to the Dull and Ignorant; for They Too Are Important.

'Excuse me, Miss Murray,' said Nigel on re-entering the classroom. 'But Mrs Bent, the school psychologist, would like to see Bruno McGann.'

Bruno's face twisted. Nigel moved towards his seat, head down.

Miss Murray then continued. 'We need to work out who is sharing tents with who on this camp. Now most of you already have chosen partners. Perhaps you, Nigel Dorking, could share a tent with Jeremy?'

Jeremy was beaming. Nigel was not. Respect for all living things, Nigel reminded himself. Even Jeremy.

For the last hour, they were given their assignments for English and told to work in groups.

'Nigel,' called out Miss Murray, 'if you have no one to work with, join Jeremy and Stella.'

'Not fair!' cried Stella. 'Why do I have to be with the losers? Why can't I be with Hope?'

'You'll do as you're told,' said Miss Murray. 'Hope is a bad influence on you.'

They did not get much done in class as all Stella did was complain about being in a group with the dorks.

'Stella,' said Miss Murray. 'You are on notice. You had better pull your finger out or I will have to talk with your parents at parent–teacher night.'

It was just before the bell.

This was a gamble but Nigel decided to give it a try.

'Perhaps we should work on this after school?' he suggested. 'As we did not get a lot done in class.'

'Certainly,' said Jeremy enthusiastically.

'Oh great,' said Stella, rolling her eyes and banging her head on the desk in despair.

'Stella?' chided Miss Murray.

'In fact,' Nigel made a further suggestion. 'You could both come over to my place so we can put in extra time?'

'What an excellent idea,' Miss Murray said, overhearing. 'And you will of course join them, Stella. As you have been the one holding them back.'

And then Nigel frowned.

'Oh no,' he said as if suddenly remembering

something, 'Dad has an emergency on tonight. What about either of your two places?'

'I'll ask Dad,' said Jeremy.

'No way,' glared Stella.

'Dad doesn't mind,' called Jeremy after school as he skipped over, giving them both slips of paper with his phone number and address printed neatly. 'Come at five p.m. After my French horn lesson.'

Nigel checked at Mum's for Ray but Ray wasn't there. He then left a message on Ray's answer phone. But the automated voice said, 'This mobile phone is out of radio range.'

While Nigel was at home, he slipped the Orc's spare deodorant into his bag, then he went to Gordon's. But still no luck.

Back at Dad's, he dialled Jeremy. Better to wet the bed at Jeremy's than Dad's.

'Hello. It is me, Nigel. Perhaps it would be easier if I stayed the night?' he suggested. 'I like to put quite a bit of work into projects and work late into the night.'

'Yes, I do not like to hand in shoddy work,' agreed Jeremy.

After Jeremy confirmed it was fine with his dad, Nigel went to his room to pack his plastic sheet.

Nigel asked Babette to explain to Dad where he was going, and then set off.

Stella was irate when Nigel met her at Jeremy's front door.

'Thanks for nothing,' she scowled. 'Staying the night? Was that your dumb loser suggestion?'

'Well,' explained Nigel, 'there is a lot of work to be done.'

This, Nigel had not counted on. Obviously Jeremy had called her and Stella was now staying the night too.

Jeremy answered the door.

'Next time, and there will never be one,' said Stella, 'do not ask my mother if I can stay the night. Ask me.'

To Nigel's astonishment, at dinner, there, seated at Jeremy's very kitchen table, was Miss Murray.

What was Miss Murray doing at Jeremy's house? Probably, decided Nigel, either giving tips to Jeremy's poor father about how to train his son to be less of a nuisance in class or to check up on Stella to make sure she didn't hold Nigel and Jeremy back with their project.

Yes, this made perfect sense.

Stella baulked when she saw Miss Murray, but then she turned her focus on Nigel.

'Ooh! Nigel's blushing,' she teased.

'It is just quite hot in here,' explained Nigel sternly.

For the rest of dinner he did not look at Stella.

Jeremy was doing all the talking. 'Did you know that fish don't have eyebrows?'

'Yes, actually I did. And did you know,' said Nigel, 'that on average Americans eat over 18 acres of pizza a day?'

'Yes, I did,' said Jeremy. 'And did you know that if you yelled for eight and a half years, you would have created enough sound energy to heat one cup of coffee?'

'Yes, I did actually,' said Nigel. 'And did you know that Ancient Egyptian priests used to pluck out every hair on their body? Even including their eyebrows and eyelashes?'

Stella was rolling her eyes. 'What about their rude bits?' she asked.

'That, I do not know,' said Nigel. But at least Jeremy did not know that either, which left Nigel not in the inferior position.

'How very interesting,' Miss Murray had said.

And when she dropped her serviette, Nigel managed to quickly retrieve it for her, before Jeremy had a chance. He also took the opportunity to glare at Jeremy.

Even if he was going to camp, no way would he share a tent with Jeremy Fry. Not after this appalling display. This is exactly what Jeremy would do, probably try and impress Nigel's very own father. Such people had no moral fibre. And did not understand friendship.

Stella, Nigel and Jeremy sat at Jeremy's desk in his bedroom.

'Luckily, because of my father,' Nigel explained, 'I already know a lot of water facts for our project.'

'I know a lot of water facts too,' said Jeremy.

'I would say I would probably know more,' said Nigel, 'as my father is a plumber and has actually invented a game of trivia all about water.'

'Help me,' cried Stella as she dramatically banged her head on a nearby wall.

'Did you know, for instance, that you can refill a normal size glass of water approximately 15,000 times for the same cost as a six-pack of Coke?'

'Yes, I did,' said Nigel.

'I can't believe you two,' exploded Stella.

'And I can't believe Jeremy knew that,' said Nigel in a low voice.

'Caught in the middle of the battle of the nerds,' sighed Stella.

'I did know,' said Jeremy. And then, 'I have a suggestion. Why don't we both write down our own water facts, and Stella, you can research what happens to water once it goes down the drain, okay?'

'Oh gross,' she grimaced.

But a true knight puts his compatriot's welfare before his own.

'Stella,' Nigel suggested nobly, 'would you like it if we did your work for you, and you could watch *The Biggest Loser* on television?'

'Yes!' she said glaring at him as if to say, *what took you so long?* She flounced over to the television in Jeremy's room, switched it on, and sat cross-legged about ten millimetres away from the screen. And then her parting shot, 'I could have done this at home, you know.'

Nigel had hoped this gallant gesture might result in her being kinder to him at school. Particularly if there were to be an unforeseen accident tonight. But now he wasn't so sure.

I, Nigel Dorking, Do Hereby Swear Always to Act Honourably.

While Jeremy brushed his teeth and Stella watched television, Nigel quickly grabbed the plastic mattress-protector from his bag and put it on his allotted mattress and re-made the bed. He fully intended to spend the night on their toilet anyway. But just in case.

'Did you know,' Jeremy confided in Nigel once they were in their pyjamas, and Stella had taken her turn in the bathroom, 'that Miss Murray is having a baby?'

'I beg your pardon?' gasped Nigel, the breath knocked out of him.

'Yes, in fact, she is leaving the school in six weeks for maternity leave, because she is feeling very sick.'

'I do not think so,' frowned Nigel.

'Oh yes,' said Jeremy, 'it is official. They have been interviewing new teachers to replace her.'

Not his Miss Murray? Leaving? Pregnant?

'To whom?' asked Nigel.

'Dad,' said Jeremy, 'of course.'

Nigel lay in his bed, his insides spiralling.

Was it possible? Could Miss Murray be having a baby out of wedlock? This was appalling. Not only did it mean Miss Murray was imperfect, but if she had done it, got pregnant and so had Babette, could this mean Mum might do the same? Why had this not occurred to him before?

At least now he had something that would keep him awake long enough for the other two to fall asleep, so he could sneak off and sleep on Jeremy's toilet.

Mum getting pregnant would wreck everything. And how could Miss Murray go off with someone so lowly, so unworthy? And with such a ridiculous moustache? And how could she just leave her class like that? This was shocking, diabolical. It was the equivalent of a queen deserting her loyal subjects. A mother deserting her own children.

Poor Nigel, how much more was he expected to bear?

No, he decided, he would not believe it. Not of his Miss Murray.

Nigel woke with a bleak feeling in his abdomen.

For a while he could not work out where he was. It was not his bed at Mum's or Dad's.

Finally he remembered that he was at Jeremy's. And Stella had stayed the night.

But he wasn't on Jeremy's toilet as planned.

And he was definitely mid-stream.

He tried to stop but it was too late.

Nigel held the bundle of wet sheets close to him. He was very relieved that he had managed to sneak his plastic mattress-protector onto the bed. Now, it was neatly in his bag, wrapped around his wet pyjamas, in the plastic bag, with a knot in the top so the ammonia fumes would not escape.

He was very glad he had thought to bring clean clothes, and the Orc's deodorant.

'It was the glass of water beside my bed,' explained Nigel in the hallway to Mr Fry. Though Nigel had to admit Jeremy's dad's face looked just like it looked when he was listening to Nigel's often elaborate stories about why he had forgotten his sports uniform, and the tragedies that had beset him on his way to school.

Nigel's face felt hot, which alerted him to the fact that it might be pink, or red, or even purple. So during breakfast he ate in silence, with his head down, as if staring intently into his cereal.

He was surprised at the extent of his longing for Mum's return, which luckily was to happen that very evening.

Nigel's heart beat like bongo drums as he entered the classroom. Miss Murray bestowed a smile upon him, a smile he once might have cherished, but not now. For he had just glanced at her side on, and there in front of him was the terrible proof. One bulging stomach. Worse than Lotsa's.

How could he not have seen this?

Quite clearly she was with child. Or she was a stomach-dragging sausage woman. And the latter he did not think likely.

And even though Mr Fry had shown him hospitality, Nigel felt vehement contempt for him. How dare he steal her?

Nigel, who had always disliked sport, now despised it, passionately.

He stared out the classroom window. He felt wounded, as if he had been traitored. She, a small light of his life, had just been extinguished. She was leaving. And he, Nigel Dorking, could do nothing to stop it.

By lunchtime Nigel had not looked directly at Miss Murray once. Or at Jeremy. Nigel studiously avoided his gaze.

Just because he had stayed the night at Jeremy's didn't make them friends.

Instead, he sat at his desk, feeling lousy.

He could barely think of Mum without tears springing unbidden to his eyes. How could he have compared Mum to Miss Murray unfavourably? Mum might yell, and she might swear, and she might even have tattoos, particularly short legs, purple hair and drink beer, but Mum would not ever leave.

Never.

She had promised.

Mum was the one person he could count on. Wasn't she?

What if she had a baby? Would the Orc tempt her away with her new family, leaving Nigel and Ivan orphans?

And as he sat in class Nigel's heart started to ache. It felt like a torturous infinity until he'd see Mum. Even though it was only six hours and eight minutes.

Tonight he would be in his own bed. And she would kiss him goodnight. And he would beg her not to get pregnant.

Nigel's part of the talk was going well. Though it was very annoying having to share his facts with Jeremy.

'Water is a precious resource,' he said, his voice trembling only a bit with nerves. 'Like all the important things in life, it is limited. There is only so much to go around. Do not let it go right down the plughole. It would be like thinking that love is limitless for instance.' And as he said this he shot a hurt look at Miss Murray. 'Or time,' he went on. 'My father, for example, can't be in two places at once, as he is very busy saving people from plumbing disasters, and saving the other most precious resource we have in our lives. Water. So if he doesn't come on camp that will be why. And did you know,' Nigel moved on quickly, 'that 20 per cent of people do not know where tap water goes when it disappears down the drain?'

Then Stella explained, stumbling over a few words she had never come across before, 'It goes down the drain for treatment at sewerage plants, and then out into the sea.'

Nigel then explained that there were various methods of saving water, including using the economy cycle on dishwashers, not putting dishwashers or washing machines on until the load was full, and getting dripping taps fixed.

And before Nigel had even finished, Jeremy interrupted with other methods of saving water including installing rain-water tanks, low-flow showerheads and mulching gardens.

'Petser your parents,' said Stella with no conviction as she had not understood why she was saying this.

'It's *pester,*' said Nigel.

She shrugged as if to say 'whatever'.

'And make sure they do these things, because it is our future at stake,' said Nigel. 'The future of our planet.'

Jeremy then stepped forward again.

'More water facts. Fact two, people need about 2.8 litres of water a day (from drinking or eating) to maintain good health.'

Nigel stepped forward, 'Fact three, a person can live without water for approximately one week, depending upon the conditions.'

Stated Jeremy, 'Fact four, the average family turns on the tap between 70 and 100 times daily.'

Nigel, 'Fact five, water makes up almost 66 per cent of the human body, and 70 per cent of the brain.'

Jeremy, 'Fact six, water is unusual in that the solid form, ice, is less dense than the liquid form, which is why ice floats.'

Nigel, 'Fact seven, water covers nearly three-fourths of the Earth's surface.'

Jeremy, 'Fact eight, most of the Earth's surface water is permanently frozen or salty.'

Nigel, 'Fact nine, over 90 per cent of the world's supply of fresh water is located in Antarctica.'

Jeremy, 'And fact ten, salty water can be desalinated for use as drinking water by going through a process to remove the salt from the water.'

All in all, the group presentation had gone very well indeed.

'Excellent,' smiled Miss Murray as she clapped.

But then Hope piped up, 'Youse forgot water fact eleven. If you stay at someone's house and you wet the bed they don't ask you back.'

'Hope,' reprimanded Miss Murray. 'Out. To the Principal's office, straight away.'

'Not that anyone has wet the bed at someone else's house,' said Jeremy, glaring at Hope.

Stella was smirking.

'Can I be excused?' asked Bruno.

After the bell, Nigel emerged from his classroom blinking beneath a brooding, cloudy sky and to his horror saw Bruno writing in big bold letters in yellow paint across the inside of the red brick school fence, *Nigel Dorking w–* , and Nigel knew exactly what was coming next.

I, Nigel Dorking, Do Hereby Swear to Lay Down My Life for a True Brother.

The kids all seemed to be staring way up at a point over the brick wall right above Bruno.

It was quite an incredible sight. The moody sky above the brick school fence was all lit up.

Then Nigel heard a group gasp go up.

Sticks of fire were moving along the top of the school fence towards the gate. Everyone ran towards the spectacle. Including Nigel. There, right in the centre, on top of the school gate, was Ray!

Ray grinning, juggling firesticks.

'Wow,' cried Hope as Ray suddenly added a fourth firestick to his juggling.

'Hey, can you show me how to do that?' cried Bruno.

'Sorry,' cried Ray. 'Trade secrets, man. Can only tell family. Nigel, where are you, bro?'

'Here,' called Nigel from the back.

The mesmerised and stunned crowd parted to let Nigel through.

'Far out, man,' grinned Ray when he saw Nigel. 'I've come down to the school, like you asked. Where's the teach, man?'

The whole time Ray glared at Bruno. Bruno, who did not dare continue to paint his horrible graffiti.

'Excuse me,' boomed the voice of Mr Bower, the Principal, from behind Nigel. The crowd of kids parted and turned to face him. And Bruno's face drained of blood.

'Hey cool,' said Ray. 'Good to see you again, dude. Sorry I can't shake yer hand . . .'

Some kids laughed. But Mr Bower did not smile.

'I'm just a bit of a do-anything guy these days,' Ray continued unfazed. 'Want any light bulbs changed? Fences painted? Want a go of these?'

But the Principal did not look as if being called *dude* was his favourite thing. Or as if he wanted to offer Ray a job or to juggle firesticks.

'Busking outside this school is illegal,' he said sternly, 'and firesticks are doubly illegal.'

'Cool,' said Ray, stopping. 'What about people spray-painting your walls?'

Now Ray was pointing at Bruno. Caught yellow-handed.

The kids watched as Mr Bower escorted Bruno to his office.

'Wait for me, will you?' Nigel asked Ray.

There seemed to be a lot of yelling going on. And finally Bruno emerged red eyed.

Mr Bower now beckoned them in.

He looked pretty serious. Then he looked up.

Mr Bower was beaming. 'Ray, my boy!'

'Did you go to this school?' asked Nigel after a while.

'Sure did,' grinned Ray.

'Now show me,' said Mr Bower, 'how to use the firesticks. Without lighting them up, of course.'

So Ray did. Then Mr Bower had a go.

'Cool,' said Mr Bower as he tried and they all fell to the ground.

Ray has that effect on people, thought Nigel proudly as he waved Ray and Mr Bower goodbye.

Nigel was enormously relieved to see Mum again, and had forgotten what a strong hug she had. And what a wonderfully flat stomach. One that appeared to have no baby inside it.

What also really surprised him was how delighted he was to see Ivan.

'I oo,' Ivan seemed to cry out, as if to say, *Nigel, I missed you so much!*

But he was far less pleased when he saw Gordon, especially with his arm around Mum. And especially when he spied that ring on Mum's finger.

Even though he wanted Ray as his brother, he did not want Gordon as his stepfather. End of story.

They'd only been home twenty minutes and he had already kissed her six times. 'That is disgusting,' said Nigel. 'And quite germy.'

Nigel had a quiet, stern word with his brother while Mum and Gordon unpacked.

'Ivan,' he explained. 'You were under strict instructions to make sure they didn't get any closer. It doesn't look to me like you threw enough fits. Except for while I was on the phone to Mum. And now they are closer than ever!'

But Ivan just drooled.

I, Nigel Dorking, Do Hereby Swear Never to Accept Defeat.

Nigel closed the closet door behind him and walked smack into Mum in the hallway.

'Nige,' said Mum. 'What's the matter, love? You have been acting a little oddly, even for you.'

'I am not the one addicted to kissing strange men,' he said. 'And don't expect me to come to your stupid wedding. I hate him. He has sucked you right in. Just like *she* sucked Dad in. Well, I am not sucked in. And by the way, if you have another baby I am leaving. Oh, and also, I'm not going on camp with Dad either.'

Nigel strode as calmly as he could to his bedroom and then flung himself face down on his bed as doubtlessly many a knight had done in moments of defeat.

Life is cruel, thought Nigel bitterly as he buried his face in his pillow.

Nigel heard Mum creeping towards his room. He then heard the door open. And felt her weight as she sat on the bed next to him.

She didn't say anything at first. She put her hand

on Nigel's head. Nigel wanted to roll over and face her but he couldn't.

'Nige,' said Mum, 'I'm not planning on having any more children. I'm delighted with the ones I've got. But, love, did you get to spend any actual time with Dad over those three days?'

Nigel breathed deeply, as if a lot of air might compress his feelings and stop them all spewing forth.

'Mum,' he said, 'Dad is extremely busy.'

'Yes, love,' said Mum as she stroked his hair. Nigel wanted her to go away now. He did not want to discuss this. Mum would not understand.

She sighed deeply, as if to repress her feelings too.

'Nigel,' she said. 'Part of the reason Dad and I couldn't be together was because . . . how can I put this? Dad doesn't really understand people. Or feelings.'

This, Nigel did not want to hear.

'Look, different people are for different things. Some explore. Some invent, some save others, some have a lot of love to give, and some are for plumbing.'

'And Dad is all of those things,' said Nigel, 'which is why he is so busy.'

'No, love,' said Mum. 'Dad is mainly for plumbing. It's all he thinks about, love. It's his life. It doesn't mean he doesn't care. He does, in his own way. But he's different to other people. Dad's . . . well, he's just not a people person.'

To Nigel this was treachery being spoken. Unforgivable and wrong.

'Listen, my little knight in shining armour,' she continued. 'I know it's hard, but it's best if you get to know him yourself. Then you might understand and not take it personally. Go on camp with him, love. You've been desperate to spend time with him.'

Nigel said nothing.

'Make it happen, love. It'd be the greatest test of a true knight I reckon. To find the courage. See your dad for who he really is.'

And then she reminded him about knights and hope and other virtues.

'And, love,' she added, 'don't be offended by this, because I am certain Dad wouldn't reject you if he knew about you-know-what. But there are ways of dealing with bedwetting.'

'Enuresis,' Nigel corrected her. 'I am already seeing the psychologist at school. But I need to be cured sooner than that. Camp is the day after tomorrow.'

That was when Mum handed it to him. The packet of nappies. Ivan's nappies.

'They work for Ivan,' said Mum coaxingly. 'When he can bear to have them on. They'd work for you. You'd just need to be discreet. But then, knights are.'

Nigel stared, appalled.

'Many people wear them. Even adults. Probably

mayors, doubtlessly the odd president, poet, and prime minister,' coaxed Mum.

'Had they actually been invented in olden days,' she said quite reasonably, 'I am certain knights in battle would have worn them, as it would have been difficult to always get their armour off in time.'

That night, in the privacy of his own room, Nigel put the nappy around his private parts. He tore away the sticky strips and taped the adhesive to the absorbent underpants, otherwise known as a nappy.

It fitted.

He then pulled on his pyjamas, and checked in the mirror. It was impossible to tell. Mum was right. No one would know.

Worry one had been dealt with.

Now for worry number two. Would it actually hold the litres of urine someone his size made?

The very next morning, with a capsizing heart, Nigel checked his sheets.

Nothing! The urine had definitely not leaked out!

'Yes!' he whispered, punching the air triumphantly. 'Camp, here I come.'

I, Nigel Dorking, Do Hereby Swear to Trust in Knightly Valour, and Banish All Doubt.

It was the night before camp when Nigel spotted them. They were on the living-room table, ivory-coloured invitations with gold wavy edges, and gold embossed formal writing that said, *Kelly and Gordon request the pleasure of your company to celebrate the occasion of their wedding on 4th June.*

Horrified, Nigel raced to the phone.

'Ray, it's me, Nigel,' he said to the message bank. 'This is urgent. I have just seen the wedding invitations. June the fourth. This is really happening. What can we do? See you, bro.'

Nigel then raced to the kitchen to talk sense to his mother.

'Mum,' Nigel challenged her. 'Why do you have to get married so early? I just saw the invitations.'

'Oh, Nige,' laughed Mum. 'It's not early. And that's just a sample. We have to decide on what sort of invitations we want.'

'But why June?'

'Not this June, Nige,' said Mum. 'June next year.'

Well at least that gave him more time to split them up.

'I oo,' called Ivan.

'Alright,' said Nigel. 'I will play with you. But on one condition. That while I am on camp, you give them hell. Once they are married, Mum will have no time for you. If we don't split them up, they'll probably replace us both with more kids. So, if you can act at all, act your guts out. This wedding must be stopped.'

Ivan seemed to agree.

Nigel lay in his sleeping bag in his tent in his back yard trying to blot out possible images of Mum with a new baby, and instead imagining the deep talks he and Dad might have. The bonding things they might do in their tent at night.

That's if I can shut Jeremy up, thought Nigel.

He imagined Dad being impressed when he, Nigel, said *No, no, Dad, allow me to put up the tent.* And *Care for a brew in the billy can?*

Nigel switched on his torch and into his diary wrote all the things he and his father could do together on camp. Including an act together for the talent show. A water facts act. Yes! Nigel smiled into the darkness as he imagined Dad being impressed by his own vast and extensive knowledge.

Now he felt so excited, he feared he would never get to sleep.

So to calm himself down, he recited from memory, out loud, every single rule from the Code of Chivalry for Modern Knights. All forty-one of them.

Nigel woke. It was barely light. Birds were tweeting.

It's camp day, he remembered with a jolt. Today's the day! Today I will see my beloved father once again. Face to face, without Babette or the girls. Just me.

Nigel felt a lump in his throat at the very thought.

Would Dad get there?

Yes, Dad had given his word. A true knight, Nigel told himself, does not go back on his word.

Dad had taught him that. The night before Dad left Mum and him and Ivan.

Trust is very important. After all, if the knights of the round table had let doubt plague them they would have lost all their battles.

As he soaped under his arms in the shower, Nigel imagined Dad being back and felt the missing jigsaw piece from his heart fall into place. Life would suddenly be wonderful, complete and safe again. Like in the olden days.

'You are my holy grail, Dad,' he whispered under his breath as he turned off the tap.

The milk gushed onto his cereal as Nigel calculated that in less than twenty-three minutes he would be re-starting his relationship with his knight in shining armour.

'Nigel,' said Mum, 'your bowl is overflowing. And I think you're dribbling.'

'Oh,' said Nigel, wiping his mouth.

After mopping up the mess, Nigel could not suppress the smile that kept leaping onto his lips. For once, Nigel was looking forward to the day.

'Remember, Ivan,' whispered Nigel, across the table while Mum was busy showering, 'I just want to remind you that the next few days are crucial. Those fits I heard you do on the phone when I was at Dad's were good, but not good enough. Give them hell. All the time. Okay? We shall prevail.'

And Nigel kissed his brother.

As Nigel waited out front for Dad to arrive, he felt he knew how knights might feel once the tournament had begun.

It was exactly 7.30 a.m., as Dad had requested.

'Don't worry, love,' said Mum as she waited with him in her dressing-gown. 'That is one thing about Dad, he is always prompt.'

Nigel was glad he'd be travelling in the car with Dad. He didn't like the idea of the bus, with the other kids and their dads. Nigel had heard of kids who got motion sickness and threw up, and Nigel was very sensitive to smells. And particularly to vomit that swished from one end of the bus to the other, getting all over one's feet and personal belongings.

In fact, he gagged just thinking about it.

And there at 7.30 on the dot was Dad.

Nigel climbed up into Dad's white charger.

Mum waved from the curb as they drove off.

'Dad,' said Nigel, 'did you know that the honeybee kills more people worldwide than all the poisonous snakes combined?'

'Ah, no,' said Dad.

After the success of his first fact Nigel wondered whether he should launch into another one immediately or wait a while for maximum effect.

But then he started to worry.

Nigel looked around the vehicle for Dad's rucksack.

'Ah,' said Dad in his matter-of-fact voice, 'you may have noticed that I have not packed anything. I left it at home.'

Nigel was enormously relieved to hear that. He thought that perhaps Dad was going to say he wasn't coming after all. Though Nigel was surprised that his father would forget something. His father rarely forgot anything. Except Nigel's last birthday and Christmas. Dad was normally very meticulous.

'That's fine, Dad,' said Nigel, glancing at his watch. 'We have time to drop by your house.'

Dad cleared his throat again. He didn't look entirely comfortable. His big toe was moving nervously in his shoe.

'Well, actually,' he said, 'Nigel, I can't come. Something urgent has come up.'

I, Nigel Dorking, Do Hereby Swear Always to Accept My Fate with Fortitude.

They were silent all the way to school.

Weird conversations ran though Nigel's mind. Ones where he said things like, *What's wrong with me, Dad? Why don't you love me? Dad, could it be possible that you are afraid of the Evil One? Why do you do everything she says? What about me? Why don't I matter? Surely I have a right to you. After all, I was first!*

Instead, he stared out the window at the patterns the light rain made as it ran up the window.

Dad dropped Nigel outside the school and drove off, leaving Nigel on his own, seemingly unaware that the other parents who weren't attending camp were all waiting to wave their kids off. He didn't even get out of the car to explain to the teachers that he wouldn't be coming.

'Jeremy,' said Nigel, 'can I borrow your mobile phone?'

'I'll get my dad's,' said Jeremy.

'Ray,' whispered Nigel after the signal to leave a message. 'He didn't come. He didn't come on camp.'

'Nigel!' called Mr Fry. 'Your father just rang to say he couldn't make it, but don't worry, you can still come. We'll have a great time. I've called your mum, and both your mum and dad are happy for you to join me. I'm with a few boys whose dads couldn't make it, so you're not alone and I'll be keeping an eye on you. Bruno's doing the same. So, into the bus.'

Nigel found an empty seat. Then Jeremy plonked himself next to him.

'Did you know,' said Jeremy, 'that only female ducks can quack?'

Nigel stared out the window.

'And that no two spiderwebs are the same?'

'And that only inconsiderate rude pests keep talking all the time when other people need quiet?' said Nigel.

Jeremy gave Nigel a hurt look.

Perhaps something very important had come up for Dad, Nigel thought as he sighed deeply. Something unimaginably big. Quite clearly his father would not break his word lightly.

Perhaps Dad was trying to teach me a lesson, thought Nigel. Was it about not allowing oneself to hope too much? Was it about learning to deal with life's disappointments? Was this to develop Nigel's character as a true knight?

But his insides did not believe his brain.

Nigel helped Jeremy and his dad set up their six-man tent.

'Didn't your dad come, Dorko?' sneered Bruno.

Nigel narrowed his eyes but said nothing.

'Get lost, Bruno,' said Jeremy. 'Neither did yours.'

Nigel spent the rest of his day inside the tent. It was too wet for any activities anyway. The others might like huddling together in the main tent. But he did not.

As Nigel lay in his sleeping bag, he wondered what precisely the kookaburra thought it had to cackle about. It wouldn't be laughing, he decided, if it had brains enough to comprehend global warming, and how one day that would mean the death of all living things, including it.

It was pouring outside too. Even if his father had come, Nigel knew there would have been nothing they could have done, except maybe bond.

Nothing could entice Nigel out, not even the campfire that night. Though Jeremy's dad kept checking on him and so did the Principal.

All Nigel wanted to do was lie in his sleeping bag

and stare bleakly around him. What was the point in anything?

His feelings were too big. He tried not to let them happen by refusing to let certain thoughts surface.

Particularly any thoughts about Dad leaving Mum and him and his brother, or about Dad not coming to Father and Son Night. About how when Dad did finally come he hadn't even said hello. How he hadn't given Nigel a lift home. How Dad had missed his birthday. And Christmas. How when he'd stayed at Dad's, Dad hadn't made any time for him. And now this.

And even though he knew a true knight would always accept his fate with fortitude, he did not want to.

It was all unthinkable. But, Nigel forced himself to think, why had Dad never stood up to the Evil One on his behalf?

The words he did not want to think were, *My father does not care. He is not a hero. My father is a coward.*

'There's a great campfire out there,' said Jeremy's dad cheerily as he poked his head in and tried to tempt Nigel out.

'I do not like rowdy company,' Nigel claimed.

Nothing would budge him from his gloom and misery. Particularly when he heard Jeremy Fry saying to his father, 'Did you know that the average Australian will eat 17 beef cattle, 92 sheep, 4,005 loaves of bread,

165,000 eggs, half a tonne of cheese, 8 tonnes of fruit and 9 tonnes of vegetables in their lifetime?'

This should have been Nigel and his dad. And it was *10* tonnes of vegetables.

The unsettling sounds of the boys and dads bonding around the campfire didn't help his mood. Particularly when he heard Jeremy regaling them all with facts about terrible accidents at camps. Ones he, Nigel, had learnt.

Anyway, he decided, camping is a foolish activity. A mistake never to be repeated.

'There's toasted marshmallows,' Jeremy's dad announced, popping his head in again.

But Nigel, who wanted to explain to him that toasted marshmallows were in fact a dentist's nightmare, and would rot your teeth more quickly than Coca-Cola, found he couldn't utter a word.

'Fine,' said Mr Fry. 'But if you want company just let me know.' And then he winked.

It was that wink that did Nigel in. It's what he'd always wanted Dad to do, to wink.

He hoped no one could hear him. But he could keep his despair inside no longer.

It must have been hours later when Nigel heard a familiar voice, one he had not imagined he would hear on camp. His heart raced.

'Hey, bro,' he heard Ray call. 'Where will I find my main man Nigel?'

Nigel flew from his tent.

'Ray!' he called.

Nigel joined them around the campfire. That night, Ray told them all hair-raising tales.

Then later, when they entered the tent in the dark, Jeremy decided to tell them a few facts about the origins of the Universe.

Finally, when it sounded like the others were asleep, Nigel lifted his backside into the air, and tried to position his nappy under him.

But he froze when the plastic crackled really loudly.

He held his breath until he heard Ray lightly snoring again. Then slid the nappy across under him and tried to pull the plastic tags on the nappy open.

Rip, went one.

'Shhh,' whispered Jeremy. 'I have very sensitive hearing.'

Nigel tried to do the other one slowly.

R-R-R-R-R-R-I-P-P. It was worse than trying to eat a packet of crisps in a cinema.

Mr Fry sighed.

Nigel then tried to wiggle his pyjama bottoms off. But the harder he tried not to rustle his sleeping bag the noisier it got.

'What have you got in there, man?' asked Ray sleepily. 'Two wombats mating?'

'Sorry,' Nigel whispered. 'Just trying to get comfortable.'

He gently raised his hips to pull down his pyjama bottoms. But the plastic nappy crackled underneath.

'Will you stop it?' said Jeremy far too loudly. 'I have a sleep disorder. Did you know that quite a large percentage of imaginative people do? It's called insomnia.'

'Put a sock in it, Jeremy,' said his father.

Nigel's body fell back flat onto the ground, his heart beating fast.

Please, penis, Nigel sent a mental telepathy message, *this is now a desperate situation. I promise if you're good I'll take you to some really good toilets. There are some great ones around these days. Motion sensitive and electrical, so they automatically play music when you go in. And the doors open and close when you press a button. I'll do anything.*

He lay unable to sleep, dreading the morning. Then he had an idea.

He sent his penis another message in his politest mental telepathy voice.

Penis, I'm sorry about being a bit bossy lately. I can see you're doing your best. It's not your fault. I know you're really trying. And you're doing a really good job. In fact, if you were a sprinkling system on a timer that was set to water regularly at night, you'd be doing a brilliant job.

All I have to do, he told himself, is not roll over. The nappy is in place.

He fell asleep with his fingers and legs crossed.

Nigel woke, mid-stream.

He quickly put his hand under him to see if the nappy had caught it. But it hadn't. It had just soaked his sleeping bag. And pyjamas.

Nigel crept out of his tent.

He was twenty minutes from camp, hanging his sleeping bag on a tree when he heard crunching behind him.

Nigel turned.

It was Bruno.

Nigel's insides quaked. He could have run. He could have called out for help but he didn't.

'Not so brave without your biker mate,' jeered Bruno.

Then Bruno pushed him.

Nigel heard the crunch underfoot of gravel. Ray appeared.

'Everything alright?'

I, Nigel Dorking, Do Hereby Swear Allegiance to Those Who Put Their Selves in Harm's Way to Help Others.

Back in the tent, when the others had all gone bushwalking, Nigel sat with Ray.

'I wet the bed,' said Nigel, the words tumbling out.

He fully expected Ray to reject him. To walk away. What he didn't expect was for Ray to put his arm round him.

'Hey, I feel real honoured you told me. That can be real awkward,' said Ray, nodding.

Nigel wondered what he meant.

At breakfast Bruno waited until Nigel was serving himself, then he called out, 'Hey, everyone, Nigel wets his bed.'

For the second day Nigel hid in his tent.

'It'll be cool,' said Ray. 'You'll see.'

But Nigel had no intention of coming out of that tent again. Not until home time.

Ray didn't hassle him. He just joined the others at

the campfire that night. Nigel heard him out there on his mouth organ.

'Hey, tell us some more stories,' begged the kids.

'Oh na,' said Ray. 'I'm feelin' real disappointed.'

'Why?' they chorused.

'Go on,' said Reece. 'Those stories were awesome last night.'

'Oh, I don't like it when people bullshit, man.'

Nigel could hear it all.

'You know, the way you're treatin' Nigel is crap. I bet you've all wet the bed.'

Suddenly it was very quiet.

'I have,' said Ray. 'What's the big deal? Most people have at some stage.'

Obviously they must all look stunned, thought Nigel, his heart thudding.

'Oh come on, I'll tell youse mine if youse'll tell me yours. What happened to me was pretty funny. Anyone else ever done it?'

Silence.

Ray laughed. 'You bunch of scaredy-cats. Come on.'

'I have,' piped up Jeremy.

'Typical,' said Bruno.

'Bet *you* have, dude.' Ray winked at Bruno. 'Otherwise you wouldn't carry on so much, man. That's the dead giveaway.'

Strangely Bruno shut up.

'Hey there's no shame in it. It's cool. It's just a bodily function. I'm not havin' a go. I'm not.'

'It's happened to me,' called out Reece.

'I'm not saying anything,' said Mr Bower. 'But did you notice no one wanted to share a tent with me this year on camp?'

This made all the kids laugh.

'It's because the stories around the campfire were so scary last year,' he grinned.

The dads and kids all laughed again. But a bit uncomfortably.

'When did it last happen to you?' asked Jeremy.

''Bout six months ago,' Nigel heard Ray admit.

Nigel found himself getting out of his sleeping bag and walking out of the tent and sitting on the log beside Ray.

Ray's face looked honest and his eyes shone in the flickering light.

'Only happened to me once, at my girlfriend's parents' house. First night I met them.'

The kids all looked appalled. Like they had at the gory bits of Ray's stories last night.

'Oh no,' laughed some of the adults.

'Yeah, can you believe it, man? I know it happens to most people at some stage in their lives but man – that was bad – pretty uncool timing!'

'Go on,' his spellbound audience agitated.

'So I'm out to impress, right? Anyway, they make all this fuss about the guestroom. How it's got a new mattress. They hope it's comfortable and all that. Anyway, eventually I go to bed. I have this dream. You know the one where you dream you're on the loo?'

'Yes,' chorused heaps of voices. 'I've had exactly that one.'

'Me too,' whispered Nigel.

'So I'm letting go big time, right? This isn't just a trickle, man, this is Niagara Falls, full strength. So anyway, I wake up, and I'm still going.'

'Yeah,' called out a few of them. 'I hate that.'

'So the bed is flooded, man. So I get up at five a.m. and drag my mattress outside. My plan is when they all wake I'll just explain that the mattress needed airing, and seein' it was real sunny, it was a good day for it.' Ray winked at Nigel. 'Anyway, what I didn't plan on was fallin' asleep on the couch, and wakin' three hours later with the rain pissin' down.'

The audience was now groaning with apprehension. And Nigel remembered telling Ray about his mattress. He wished he hadn't lied. To Ray of all people.

'So their new mattress is totally sodden. I'm draggin' it back in when they all come down for breakfast . . .'

'Oh no.' Everybody clutched their sides as they imagined their own humiliation under such circumstances.

Ray started to giggle. Now he was rocking as his whole body was racked with silent laughter, and tears rolled down his cheeks.

It was infectious.

'And you'll never believe this – my girlfriend wouldn't speak to me.'

'What?' cried Reece. 'What a loser!'

They were all appalled.

'Shallow,' said Mr Bower.

'I'd reckon,' said Ray. 'No great loss. I told her to chill out. But she was too uptight, man. I reckon if someone can't hack a bit of a bed wet, then they're not worth it, hey?'

Nigel felt like he imagined knights of old felt when they had been saved by another noble knight who had even risked his own life.

'Hey,' said Reece, 'when I did it at Nanna's, I tried to hide the evidence by getting rid of it with her hairdryer, but then she came in and caught me.'

Everyone laughed.

'That's nothing,' said Bruno. 'I did both at my nan's. And blamed it on the dog.'

They all looked a bit astonished at that.

'Well,' said Nigel eventually, 'I was so embarrassed, I invented this wetting machine, but the problem is, the tube got stuck on my penis . . .'

Their faces drained of blood when Nigel described

chopping the plastic off his penis with his eyes closed.

Bruno had to leave the group because he was feeling giddy.

Nigel started telling them about going to school with it on.

The kids were all hooting. Nigel's story was going down well.

Though even Nigel was surprised at the bit where he ended up at the swimming pool about to dive in on sports day and the tube showed beneath his bathers. But campfires were a place for tall stories.

Back in the tent that night, before Jeremy and his dad rejoined them, Ray said, 'Hey, man, I hope when I said people who can't handle a bit of a wet weren't worth it that you didn't think I was sayin' your ol' man ain't worth it. No way. It's just maybe he can hack more than you might think?'

Nigel thought about this, and decided that for once Ray was wrong.

'And by the way,' Ray whispered, 'good on yer, bro. Wow. I'm glad I came.'

'Ray,' whispered Nigel, 'why are you so good to me?'

'After what you've done for me? It's nothin', man.'

'What have I done?' asked Nigel, astonished.

'That kid, the one I told you about ages ago, who

reminded me of you, the one I hadn't seen for ages. He's back.'

Nigel looked at him in the torchlight, not comprehending.

'That kid is me. I'd just forgotten about him, that's all.'

Nigel stared at him.

'I'm going to do it, Nigel. I'm taking a leaf out of your book, man. I'm going early in the morning. I'm going to try and do something about my relationship with my dad.'

Nigel didn't want to dampen his spirits so he didn't say, *Well, sometimes it doesn't work out.*

Nigel woke with Ray tapping him.

'Gotta go,' he whispered. 'It's been awesome.'

'Careful,' Nigel called after him. 'The rain is pretty heavy.'

Ray turned, winked, unzipped the exit to the tent, zipped it back up after him, and set off.

Ray's biker outfit reminded Nigel of his own armour. Of the day he had worn it to Dad's.

Nigel heard the bike revving, and the roar of its engine.

He listened until he could hear it no longer.

He hoped desperately for Ray that everything would work out, wishing only that Gordon had been more worthy. But life, he had learnt at his tender age, was not full of happy endings.

Suddenly without Ray it felt dark, and wet, and Mum was still getting married, and he didn't have a relationship with Dad.

Nigel tore up the water facts script he had written. The one he had intended to do with Dad for the talent show.

Chapter XXXV

I, Nigel Dorking, Do Hereby Swear to Fight with Knightly Valour for the Honour of Those I Love.

'If you want company just let me know,' Mr Fry said again the next night as he'd poked his head in to check on Nigel.

He was really very nice. Even if he was a sports teacher with a handlebar moustache who had stolen Nigel's lady.

'Darn wet patches on pillows,' said Nigel, turning his pillow over.

And when he heard Jeremy and Mr Fry doing their act, with Jeremy pretending to be a ventriloquist puppet sitting on his dad's knee, and all the kids' laughter, poor Nigel's body was silently racked with sobs.

Just when he least wanted to see anyone, and when Ray needed Gordon in town to confront him, Nigel heard the entrance to his tent unzip, and then a familiar loathsome voice.

'Hello, laddie,' it said.

What was *it* doing here? This was an outrage. Gordon was ruining things for everybody.

No way did Nigel want Gordon to see him feeling so low about his dad, because wouldn't that be perfect for Gordon? This'd be Gordon's big chance to ride in on his white charger and prove to Mum how great he was!

Not on Nigel's life.

This is beyond pathetic, scowled Nigel. How obvious. And obnoxious. No way would Nigel let on to the Orc that he hadn't been coping. Or give that knuckle-dragger even a whiff of a chance to save him.

'You shouldn't have come,' said Nigel, glowering at Gordon. 'I don't want you here. I hate you.'

'I canna hear you,' cried Gordon over the sound of the rain that was suddenly pelting down hard on their tent. It was almost deafening.

'Go away,' Nigel yelled.

'No,' yelled back Gordon. 'I know you're not pleased to see me, lad. But I had to come. Don't worry, I'm not here trying to replace your dad, if that's what you're thinking . . .'

Nigel did not want to speak about his father, and he definitely did not want to speak to Gordon about him at all. He despised being forced into a position of having to have a heart to heart with Gordon of all people; because it reminded him even more that Dad wasn't there. And thinking about that made his eyes well up with tears. And no way did he want Gordon to see him cry. But there was something that urgently needed to be said. Something that Nigel suddenly had no power to keep inside him.

'Well, you couldn't replace him if you wanted to, you idiot horrible stinking pig,' screamed Nigel. 'Why don't you just die? He's the only father I'll ever want. You're Ray's dad. And he says . . .'

Nigel realised he'd accidentally almost given Ray away. That is when he felt the desperate sobs making their way up inside him again, so he turned and ran. He didn't know where. He just had to run. Out of the tent, and into the darkness.

'Nigel,' he heard Gordon yell after him. 'Not that way. The river's in full flood.'

But Nigel had run into the deafening rain.

How could he, Nigel, have betrayed Ray?

He'd sat for ages, shivering and clinging onto that branch high up in the tree.

He did not like to look down into blackness where he could hear water, wind, and see only darkness. It made him giddy.

Nigel did not like being wet, sodden or stuck – and he could tell he was stuck by the way his legs could not reach the branches below him.

And even though Nigel was a knight-in-training, he had to admit he was far too scared to climb down the tree in the dark. And in the howling wind.

Not to mention of course the branches being so slippery. It would be very foolhardy. Even daredevils would not be so stupid.

'Good will prevail,' he whispered authoritatively, to still his wildly beating heart.

How had he even managed to get so high, seeing he was afraid of heights? He clung on.

Nigel was not at all embarrassed about being afraid of heights. He was sure genetically it had been to his own ancestors' advantage. For example, most people who did not have these particular life-preserving genes had probably died out, due to being blown off mountain peaks.

He felt sure the survival of his own ancestors was due to intelligence and their ability to cling to solid objects.

It was then he saw what he knew to be the tail end of the Southern Cross constellation twinkling from behind a purple cloud. And this reminded him of the moles on Dad's back.

'It certainly wasn't bravery,' he whispered bitterly.

Nigel did not know how much longer he could cling on. From where he sat, high up in the gum tree, he could now see Gordon, who looked quite small from this perspective.

'Nigel!' Gordon bellowed.

But Nigel did not want Gordon to find him.

For he did not want Gordon to see him like this, up a tree and unable to get down.

No, he would sit up here quietly, and refuse to answer the Orc's cries. That would punish him. Even if he, Nigel, were freezing, and scared witless, still it was worth it.

For it had just occurred to him that this was his big chance. It would be so perfect if, because of Gordon, he, Nigel, disappeared. Died, even. That would serve the Orc right. Mum would be so furious with him.

Perhaps though, he revised his plan, instead of actually dying he would let the Orc know where he was eventually and refuse to come down until he had extracted a promise from him that he would not marry Mum.

'Nigel,' Gordon was yelling after him. 'The river is dangerous. Please let me know where you are!'

Nigel watched his jacket that'd got caught on the branch below. The jacket he'd had to wriggle out of, because he'd been unable to disentangle it.

It blew about in the strong winds. Its arms filled like windsocks. Then suddenly with a crack a large branch from above fell, and broke the branch underneath. The jacket hurtled down, with the branch. Into the dark, swirling waters below.

Nigel had often had this terrifying falling sensation in dreams. He wanted to cry out now but found he couldn't.

As he clung onto his branch, Nigel saw Gordon.

It's true the river was wild, but nowhere near as wild as Gordon. Even though the ground was a long way down, the wind carried Gordon's voice right up.

Nigel was stunned. Gordon was yelling, furious, raising his fists to the sky. He seemed to be staring in the direction of Nigel's jacket, which was being tossed about in the swirling waters.

'Oh no, that's Nigel's jacket,' he cried.

Nigel heard some real Scottish swearwords and Gordon telling God what he'd do to Him if anything happened to Nigel.

Nigel had always thought Gordon was a pacifist. And an atheist.

If God were at all smart, thought Nigel, He should be quaking in His boots. Nigel had never heard a man so angry.

Then Nigel saw Gordon fling off his coat and dash like a maniac into the water.

'No!' Nigel screamed, as he saw the water swallow Gordon whole. Nigel saw Gordon no more.

Nigel's insides felt like they were being liquidised.

They swirled.

Nigel clung on.

Then in the distance, right out in the middle where the fast-moving water ran like rapids, Nigel saw Gordon re-emerge.

'Gordon,' Nigel only just managed, as he was all choked up.

'Nigel?' he heard Gordon call his name as Gordon tried to stay afloat. 'Was that you? Nigel!'

'It is I!' Nigel called. 'Up here.'

Nigel saw Gordon make a grab for his jacket, and swim back to shore.

He's a powerful swimmer, thought Nigel.

Now Gordon had spotted him way up the tree.

'Nigel, you wee wretch,' he heard the Orc cry. 'Why did you not let me know earlier? You can be a right pain in the proverbial backside. Sometimes, lad, I could kill ya. Honestly.'

I, Nigel Dorking, Do Hereby Swear to Honour Friendship above All and to Know a True Friend by His Deeds.

Gordon was on the branch below, looking up. He climbed higher and higher. 'It's alright, lad,' he said when eventually he almost reached Nigel's dizzying height. 'You could have slipped, Nigel. Anything could have happened. You can be a right little so-and-so sometimes. But I'm real glad you're okay.'

Nigel did not correct him and say 'really glad'.

'Let go and I'll catch you.'

Nigel wondered if the Orc might deliberately drop him, after what he'd said earlier. Perhaps this was his way of making sure Nigel plummeted to his death.

Should he trust him?

'Nige, I'm too much of an oaf to climb any further. Reckon the wee branch might break under me. We'll have to be quick.'

Nigel had no choice. He had to trust him. His enemy. He was now officially too tired to hang on.

How could he slide his arms round Gordon's neck and retain dignity?

'You can do it,' said the Orc.

Nigel did.

He let go, and fell. Into Gordon's arms.

'Got ya,' cried Gordon. 'Now hang on.'

Just for a short while he decided to give in, and rest his head on Gordon's chest.

That's when Nigel heard Gordon's heart beat.

He hadn't expected Gordon would have one of those. A heart. Kerthump kerthump. He hadn't heard that sound for ages. Not since he was little, when he used to sit on Dad's knee and watch TV. In a flash he remembered all the noises, the stifled burps, the swallowing, the gastric juices bubbling, the indigestion. All the wonderful chest and stomach noises.

And Nigel felt wetness on his cheeks. Then warmth, as Gordon pulled his big, dry coat round Nigel.

'It's okay, lad,' said Gordon. 'It's okay. You just hang on, and I promise things will all look better by the light of morning.'

Nigel heard a branch breaking. Gordon quickly moved his foot and manoeuvred his body round the other way.

But his weight was too great, and Gordon's foot slipped as he lost his grip.

Nigel tried to grab onto branches as they started to slide. It was such a long way to the swirling black waters below.

Falling. Fast.

'I won't let go,' cried Gordon as his great hulking body fell.

When Nigel came to, he heard the creaking of leather. The squelching of boots.

Nigel didn't speak. Words were too far away. They trudged on in sodden silence, Gordon's arms grasping Nigel all the way.

Nigel started to fall asleep. Falling, falling.

'We're not far from the bus noo,' Nigel heard Gordon explaining to him.

Nigel hadn't intended to speak. His mouth seemed to operate of its own accord.

'Why did you save me?'

Gordon looked at him, astonished. His eyes looked round and honest just like Ray's. 'Why would I not, laddie?'

'Ray said –' Nigel started to whisper as they neared the bus.

'You saw him?' asked Gordon. Kerthump.

Nigel could hear Gordon's heart beating so loudly it was like a big bass drum being beaten double time.

He felt Gordon's chest heaving and his grip tighten.

'Ray wants to see you.'

'I canna tell you how happy I am, laddie.'

Nigel woke, dry and in the van with Gordon.

'I let you sleep, laddie,' said Gordon. 'I explained it all to your principal. We're on our way home. I didna want to worry you, lad, but I need to take you to the hospital. Your wee brother's a bit ill, Nigel. That's why I came on camp.'

'Oh,' said Nigel.

Nigel felt extreme guilt.

'What's wrong with him?' he asked lamely. For he knew exactly what was wrong with his brother.

'It's pneumonia, laddie. That's why I've come to get you. Your mum's at the hospital waiting for us.'

They went straight to the hospital in the city. When Nigel arrived at Ivan's ward in the hospital, Mum threw herself at him and sobbed. And even though he was very happy to see her, he was too desperate to see Ivan. Just in case, he needed to tell him to pull it back a bit. Fast. He had never meant to upset Mum like this.

Nigel had never hoped that Ivan was faking it this much before. For it was unbearable to think about if he were not.

'Mum,' whispered Nigel. 'He'll be alright. I promise. Do you mind if I have a word with Ivan on my own?'

Mum looked surprised, but agreed and did not follow him into intensive care.

Nigel put on the white outer garments, washed his

hands in the supplied disinfectant, and approached his brother's bed.

He was shocked when he saw Ivan attached to a drip. And the respirator. It's impossible, thought Nigel, for someone to have shrunk in such a short space of time. Nigel knew it hadn't been that long since he'd seen Ivan but he looked so fragile. So small.

'Ivan,' whispered Nigel.

Ivan stirred.

'It's me,' whispered Nigel.

Ivan's eyes flickered open.

Then Nigel sought out Ivan's hand and held it.

'Ivan,' said Nigel urgently. 'I'm sorry. I know I told you to act sick but I'm really hoping this is just a bad case of overacting. It is, isn't it? If it is, please, I take back everything I said, okay? This is way too much. The stress will probably give Mum a heart attack. Pull it right back. Right now. It's okay. I've changed my mind about Gordon. Gordon isn't so bad. He is most definitely not an Orc.'

Nigel sat in Gordon's van as they drove home. Mum had not wanted to leave Ivan alone that night, so she had stayed behind.

The strong winds buffeted the van about.

Nigel hated Mum being so distressed. What if Ivan really was sick?

Gordon was concentrating hard just trying to see in front. The rain was bucketing. Gordon slowed right down.

'I just thought you should know. I am hoping the reason my brother is so ill in hospital is because I ordered him to act really sick and wreck any time you spent with Mum so you would realise we didn't want you there.'

Nigel's voice had become a whisper. Even as he heard his own words he knew that Ivan was not faking. He had known all along.

'Can we go back to the hospital?' he whispered.

'Your mum asked me to make sure you got some sleep, laddie. She said she'd call if there was any real worry tonight. Ivan needs to sleep too.'

'Okay,' said Nigel.

Chapter XXXVII

I, Nigel Dorking, Do Hereby Swear I Shall Never Harbour Envy, Fear or Hatred in My Breast, but Instead Shall Live a Pure and Noble Life.

'Gordon,' said Nigel as they neared home. 'You know how I mentioned Ray earlier?'

'Yes, lad,' whispered Gordon, gripping the wheel, his knuckles white.

'You haven't seen him yet?'

'No, laddie,' said Gordon, surprised. 'Why?'

Nigel knew his brother-to-be had every intention of confronting Gordon.

'He's here,' whispered Nigel. 'It's just I am not at liberty to say exactly where.'

'He's here?' cried Gordon, his face lit with joy.

'I'll give you one clue. He has the most brilliant red motorbike.'

It was late to be visiting anyone when Gordon knocked at his own shed door. Nigel stood near him.

A tousled Ray answered the door. Gordon switched on his torch. Ray blinked. At first he didn't seem able to focus. 'Dad?' he whispered, stunned, like a rabbit caught in headlights.

'Laddie,' said Gordon. 'You came! I am so glad. I know you think I'm angry at you. But I'm not. Not one bit. In fact, you did me a huge favour. I packed it all in. All that working hard. Life is about the people you love. And the animals you love. And you taught me that.'

Nigel saw them hug.

'You don't care about the pub?' asked Ray.

'I don't give a rat's,' said Gordon. 'I told you that in the letters.'

'I thought you were just saying that so I'd come and see you.'

'No, laddie.'

Nigel looked away. This was a very private moment between a father and son.

It was 1 a.m. when Nigel finally got to bed again.

His insides were twisted. Surely if a father could still love a son who deliberately wrecks his pub, then did it not follow logically that a father should be able to love a son who undeliberately wets his own bed?

Nigel imagined himself at the hospital, by Ivan's side, announcing that Dad didn't care that they wet their beds after all, and that he wanted them both to come and stay the night.

He imagined Ivan angrily rejecting the idea at first, but then Nigel coaxing him.

He imagined wheeling Ivan into Dad's. Dad running towards Nigel. He imagined the joy in Ivan's heart, and he even entertained the possibility that this would cure Ivan. That Ivan might even get up out of his wheelchair and run!

Though he knew that was sheer fantasy, still, love could work wonders.

There was something he must do. The very next morning.

Over breakfast, when Nigel was eating cereal, he wrestled with himself, but decided to do it anyway. After all, as a knight one must always show loyalty to one's friends. And both Ray and Gordon were not just friends, they were family.

It is the gallant and right thing to do, he told himself. And Gordon had shown himself to be worthy. And it was important for him to know that no son was perfect.

'I have enuresis. In case you don't know, that is a bedwetting problem,' he said.

'Oh,' said Gordon. 'I appreciate you tellin' me about your waterworks, laddie. That's quite a common problem. It goes away with time, so I read.'

Nigel was glad to have Ray with him. He could tell Mum really liked Ray too.

And when the nurse said officiously as she looked Ray up and down, 'Only family may come into the emergency ward,' Nigel said quite sternly, 'He is family.'

'Hey, little dude,' grinned Ray. Nigel could tell Ivan liked him, by the way he dribbled not just from one side of his mouth, but right over his bottom lip.

Nigel told the others he would join them in the canteen and then stole in again to see his brother. He wanted to catch the specialist.

'Can I ask you a few questions?' Nigel interrogated Dr Forsil.

Nigel spoke in his most *I will probably be a doctor one day too, so you can use technical jargon with me* type of voice.

Dr Forsil sighed and looked at his watch.

'Can I ask you,' said Nigel, 'about my brother Ivan? I am suspecting that even though he is like he is, don't you think that if people believed in him and if he tried an awful lot harder, like with maximum hardness, that he might do a little better, educationally speaking?'

'No,' said the specialist. 'I think, sadly, nothing can be done for Ivan in that department. At the moment the most we can do is try and keep him alive.'

'But what if I were to do stem-cell research, and find a cure?' Nigel demanded of the retreating specialist. 'Would that not help?'

'No one will be able to cure your brother,' said the specialist firmly. 'Not even a stem-cell research scientist. I am sorry, but I have rounds to perform.'

'Perhaps I will speak to one of the more senior specialists in the area then,' said Nigel reprovingly.

'I am the senior specialist in the area,' corrected the doctor. 'And I am very sorry to be quite so blunt, but you'll have to accept your brother the way he is.'

'Which is how?'

Well, due to birth trauma he has cerebral palsy with intellectual disability. Now I really must go.'

Nigel stared at the retreating figure in white and then at his brother Ivan. Ivan, who according to this doctor would always be like this. And Nigel kept on staring.

When he was able, Nigel whispered into Ivan's right ear.

'Ivan, I don't know what's wrong with me. I'm sorry. It doesn't actually matter how you score on the WISK test. At all. All that matters is that you get better. Please? I don't care if we can't make you intelligent. Okay? I don't care of you can't ever walk or run and play knights with me, and I definitely don't think you're a traitor, either. And you can be a knight, okay? Just get better . . .'

'Mum,' said Nigel before Gordon drove him home, 'has Dad been in to visit Ivan yet?'

Mum shook her head.

I, Nigel Dorking, Do Hereby Swear to Always Speak the Truth, No Matter How Painful.

When Nigel arrived at his father's that evening he was ready to erupt.

He was met at the front door by Babette, also ready to erupt. And Lotsa, who growled.

'What is the meaning of this unannounced visit?' Babette demanded.

Nigel pushed past her, and headed towards his father's office, Lotsa yapping at his heels.

'How dare you wreck my family,' he accused.

That seemed to shut Babette up. But not Lotsa.

'Grrr.'

'Your father is busy,' called Babette, regaining the power of speech, as she raced in front of him and tried to bar his way. 'He has a very full week coming up.'

But Nigel was too quick.

'Be gone,' he ordered as he pushed past.

He knocked loudly on his father's office door. And when he, unbidden, thrust the door open, he was greeted with a stern cold stare from his father.

'Dad,' he said, 'I need to tell you something. A few things in fact.'

'I am in the middle of something very important, Nigel,' chastised his father.

'So am I,' said Nigel.

He stood there, his father's accuser.

'Your son Ivan is in the hospital. And you haven't even been to visit him yet. And you're his father. You are not Len the Lionheart, you are just a pathetic, selfish sperm-donor. You are no father. I always thought it was our fault, my brother's and mine. But it's not. There is nothing wrong with us. It's you. You don't know how to be a father! You do not deserve us.'

Nigel hadn't intended for his voice to shout. Or for torrents of tears to cascade down his cheeks. They came as hard and fast as the water from that burst fire hydrant all those weeks ago.

But he did not care.

'You can have stupid Babette.'

It was then Nigel remembered she was standing directly behind him. But he did not let this throw him off.

'Oh and just so you know, we both wet the bed, Ivan and me. Oh, and by the way, that water main, I was the one who did that. I busted it with that mallet.'

Dad looked deeply shocked.

'Yes, I am a water criminal. It was the only way of

getting you to Father and Son Night.' Nigel defended himself, and accused his father at the same time. 'You should be ashamed.'

'It doesn't surprise me,' came Babette's voice from behind him.

'No disrespect,' said Nigel, 'but shut up.'

And then to his father, 'And don't bother coming to the fancy dress trivia quiz dressed as a knight,' he stormed, 'because I don't want you to. You left me, now I am leaving you. Goodbye. You have no son. And that includes Ivan.'

Then Nigel turned and slammed his father's office door behind him and walked straight into the thin-lipped Babette again and his two stepsisters.

'Do you wet the bed?' gasped Janelle.

'Yes,' said Nigel. 'What of it?'

Then he ran out towards the front door.

'Yap yap,' barked Lotsa at all the commotion.

'To you,' said Nigel, just managing to keep his voice under control, 'I owe an apology. It is not your fault your stomach drags along the ground. My mother has short legs too, and she finds it hurtful when people make jokes. Now, could you let go of my leg?'

Nigel shook the dog off, and walked out the front door. One he was sure he would never enter again.

He climbed into the special bus with Gordon, ready to go home.

'He is no longer my father,' said Nigel, staring grimly ahead.

That night, Nigel did not cry at all when Gordon sat on the side of Nigel's bed and put his hand on Nigel's back.

'One day, lad,' suggested Gordon after a long while, 'you might find it within your heart to forgive your dad. He's just made differently, I think.'

'I will never forgive him,' whispered Nigel. 'Not ever.'

The gates to his heart had already clanked shut forever and he did not have the keys any more.

Right now, his feelings were too big to talk about.

'Well, take me,' whispered Gordon. 'I stuffed things right up with my family. I was a real lousy dad. But people can learn. Soometimes it's people's own kids who end up teachin' people the most important things.'

Nigel had an impulse to correct Gordon and say, *Actually it's 'really' lousy dad.* But he didn't.

Suddenly, incorrect pronunciation didn't seem to matter. Gordon might make grammatical mistakes but he had been a good dad. And still was. He had never left his son.

Right then, Nigel felt like he would do anything for Gordon. Absolutely anything.

Gordon said goodnight, tousled Nigel's hair and winked.

'Gordon,' said Nigel. 'Do not tousle my hair and wink. You are not my father.'

Gordon switched out the light.

Nigel rolled over to be closer to Gilgamesh. The only bit of Dad he still had left. He pulled his pillow right up to his bedside table. Right beside Gilgamesh's bowl, and he put his arms around it.

That is how he fell asleep.

When he woke, he decided he didn't care that his bed was wet. He lay there not opening his eyes.

At least I have you, Gilgamesh, thought Nigel, as he tentatively opened one eye. Even if I don't have a father any more.

At first he couldn't make sense of what had happened. Gilgamesh's bowl was on its side, and there was water everywhere.

Where was Gilgamesh?

Nigel threw back his covers. No Gilgamesh. Where was he? Where?

That's when Nigel saw him. On the floor. Near Nigel's sodden slippers. Lying there.

Nigel dived on him. Scooped him up tenderly.

'Gilgamesh,' he cried out. 'Gilgamesh.'

Nigel heard footsteps. The door opened. It was him, Gordon. He saw the bowl upended, and Nigel cupping Gilgamesh in both hands.

'He needs water,' cried Nigel.

Gordon came running back with a jug of lukewarm water, and he filled the bowl. Nigel plopped Gilgamesh in, but he didn't move. He floated on the surface.

'No!' cried Nigel.

But Gilgamesh was not breathing. He lay on his side, floating on the top.

Nigel had just lost his best friend in the world. The one he told all his secrets too. The last part of his dad.

'Murderer,' Nigel accused Gordon, regretting it before it had even escaped his lips. 'If you hadn't turned the light off last night this would never have happened.'

Gordon turned and left the room.

Nigel stood staring towards his window, where on the sill a lone ant searched for its trail. Another ant scurried along, possibly looking for ant one, but they seemed to miss each other. It was carrying a particularly heavy load. Possibly a breadcrumb from yesterday's toast, which Nigel had left out for a pigeon.

Nigel glanced up, wondering where the pigeon was.

Now ant one was heading down the wall towards the Orc's deodorant, which lay on the floor.

Nigel picked the deodorant up. He hugged it.

'Gordon,' bellowed Nigel as he flung himself onto his bed.

'What on earth,' cried Gordon. Nigel heard Gordon's giant footsteps, hurtling up the stairs three at a time. His door flung open.

'It's all my fault,' sobbed Nigel.

'No, laddie, it's not your fault. It's never a bad thing to love someone. In fact, it's brave. Always.'

Then Nigel finally sobbed, worse than when he'd first found out Dad had left them. This is far worse, thought Nigel, his body wracked with heaving sobs.

It was a strange feeling. Having someone lie down on the bed next to you. Particularly when you had never even allowed them to hug you before.

Nigel felt his whole body go limp in his stepfather's arms. The sobs kept coming. Big, loud sobs.

Then, to Nigel's astonishment, he heard strange sounds emanating from his stepfather.

I am not the only one, Nigel realised. The pillow seemed awfully wet for just one sobber.

Eventually, when he could trust his voice to speak, Nigel asked, 'Gordon, are you really descended from real knights?'

'Yes, laddie,' he sniffed. 'But they probably weren't blubbergutses like me.'

'I don't think you're a blubberguts,' said Nigel.

Mum wailed behind the procession, just like women did in medieval times when a much loved person had passed away.

Nigel said a few words in Latin at the funeral, and then they lowered the large matchbox lined with cotton wool into the ground directly outside Nigel's bedroom so Gilgamesh would be near where he had once lived.

And even though he missed Gilgamesh, and he had no father, Nigel saw he had Ray and Gordon.

And Nigel smiled at Ray. It was a pretty generous thing to do, to share a dad.

Later that night, as he was going to sleep, Gordon came in to check up on Nigel.

'So, why doesn't my dad know how to be a dad?' Nigel asked. 'How could he leave his own kids?'

Gordon frowned and thought for a while.

'Well, put it this way, laddie. I reckon most things, including being a blacksmith, a baker, or a quantum physicist, have to be learnt. What was his dad like?'

Nigel pictured his grandparents.

'Grumps was niceish,' said Nigel. 'But Mumps always said he'd been mental since he'd served in the war.'

'There's your problem,' said Gordon. 'He wasn't there when your dad was a wee lad . . .'

Nigel shook his head.

'No, he just had Mumps,' said Nigel, 'who was

horrible. A long time ago when Ivan was tiny, Mumps and Grumps were babysitting us. Ivan had had a fit. So Grumps had him on their double bed and Ivan wet.

'Mumps came in and yelled and screamed at Ivan. Even cursed him. And it wasn't his fault. It was Grumps's for putting him there. Ivan always wets after a fit. They should have known better.

'Anyway, I waited for Grumps to step in and own up, and stand up for Ivan, but he didn't. Instead, Grumps cowered, so I said, "Leave my brother alone. He can't help it." And Mumps hit me. Really hard, many times.'

'You poor kid,' said Gordon with sadness. And then as an afterthought, 'And your poor dad.'

'Mum never let Dad's parents babysit us again. Yeah, Dad had the most awful parents in the world,' said Nigel finally.

'Kick it to me!' Nigel heard himself calling.

Ray kicked the ball to Nigel. They were playing keepings off Gordon in the front yard.

And Ray had promised afterwards to give Nigel a few good footy tips, for the match tomorrow week. The day after the Knight of Knights.

Nigel was rather surprised to be enjoying this game.

Chapter XXXIX

I, Nigel Dorking, Do Hereby Swear Never to Look Down on Those Less Fortunate than I.

It had been almost three weeks since Gilgamesh had died. And Nigel missed him more than ever.

It was 7.30 p.m., the night of the big trivia quiz. The Knight of Knights.

Mum and Gordon waited in the kitchen. Nigel, who should have been dressed in his armour, wasn't. Instead, he lay in bed, the armour strewn over the floor.

His mother came in to see him.

'I don't think I'll go tonight,' he explained. 'Sorry you got special babysitting for Ivan.'

'Nigel, what's wrong, love? Why don't you want to go?' asked Mum.

'Knights are irrelevant,' he said. 'I don't want to be one any more.'

Nigel heard Mum leave the room, and then eventually the door opened and the bed sagged as he felt Gordon's weight next to him.

'Don't you want to fight your dragons any more, young Nigel?' asked Gordon.

Nigel shook his head.

'I don't believe in them. It's childish.'

'Maybe,' said Gordon. 'But the way I see it is the world needs knights like you, lad, now more than ever before. With or without your armour.'

Gordon stared into Nigel's eyes.

'How about coming tonight? Just for the fun. Poor old Guinevere is all dressed up and nowhere to go! Will you go, lad? For a damsel in distress? For me?'

Nigel thought for a while. Gordon really seemed to want him to go.

Nigel nodded.

Was this the time to ask, he wondered? He'd had a question forming inside him. A very important question.

'Gordon,' whispered Nigel as he rolled over and faced him. 'Can I call you Dad? I've asked Ray and he doesn't mind.'

'What did he say?' asked Gordon.

'He doesn't mind sharing you, if I don't mind sharing Mum.'

Gordon laughed.

Nigel's heart beat fast.

'Lad,' said Gordon gently. 'I'd be honoured if that's what you want. But I'd like to remind you that you do have a dad.'

'No, I do not,' stated Nigel categorically. 'He is just the sperm-donor.'

'Okay, lad. Whatever you call me, Nigel, I'd be honoured to have you as one of my wee lads, eh, sonny?'

Gordon dropped Nigel and Mum off at the hall, and said he wouldn't be long.

As Nigel entered the hall, which was full of medieval knights and dames and squires and knaves, he still felt like he had a hole in his heart in the shape of Dad.

Mum looked good. Except for the AC/DC inside a heart tattoo on her upper arm, she really did make a great Lady Guinevere.

Nigel sat down next to Mum and she squeezed him supportively on the knee.

'This'll be fun,' she whispered, trying to coax him into a good mood.

Nigel's insides did not collapse like a house of cards when he saw his stepdad's seat still sitting empty.

For he knew Gordon was on his way. Gordon was not the sort to leave him in the lurch. He would most definitely be here. Very soon, in fact. It's just that Gordon was so busy with his work at this time of year.

'Do you mind?' asked Jeremy who was dressed as a knight also. 'May my father and I join your table?'

'Of course,' said Nigel. It was unknightly to be unwelcoming.

Jeremy and his father sat.

Where was Gordon?

Even Mum was looking around anxiously.

Nigel started to wish he had not allowed himself to become so attached to Gordon.

He was foolish to have set himself up like this.

Nigel was just wondering whether he could bear to stay, without his new father, when Mr Bower, the Principal, strode out onto the stage followed by Miss Murray.

That's when Nigel spotted Gordon. All dressed up like a serf.

He strode over to their table, beaming.

Nigel grinned. He had no idea he'd be quite so glad and so enormously relieved. Though he couldn't help feeling a bit disappointed. He had secretly hoped Gordon would wear Dad's armour. That would have been fitting.

That's when Nigel heard the clank clank clanking. Nigel turned around like everybody else in the hall, his heart in his mouth.

And sure enough, there was a knight of sorts walking down the aisle. Pushing Ivan in his wheelchair.

A very tall knight. With an upside-down metal silver bucket on his head with a slit cut out where the eyes were, so he could see. And it looked like sawn-off downpipes on his arms and legs, and part of Mum's old corrugated water tank for a middle.

The knight was tiptoeing so as not to interrupt the Principal any further which made everyone laugh. Typical Ray, laughed Nigel. Well, a tiptoeing knight in armour is a funny thing to see.

And grinning ear to ear, Ray pushed Ivan in his wheelchair.

Nigel's heart soared. And even though lots of people had turned their heads and were staring at Ivan, Nigel didn't care one bit.

'Hey, Sir Ivan,' called Nigel. 'Sir Ray, over here.'

So that's why Gordon was late, realised Nigel. He was helping Ray make his armour.

Even so, this was not good enough. Nigel glanced at his watch, to give Gordon the hint that this was not acceptable behaviour. Even though he was technically only three minutes and four seconds late.

Nigel shot Ivan, Ray and Gordon a welcoming smile. Then Ray sat down with them.

Ray nodded the way a real knight would. He was obviously getting into the part.

'Welcome,' said Mr Bower.

All the tables were set up with microphones for the quiz.

Mr Bower read out the rules of the quiz. Each table tested its buzzer.

Nigel tested theirs.

The gong was sounded, and the Knight of Knights had begun.

Nigel felt the adrenaline kick in.

Mr Bower fired the first question. 'In medieval times, who could train as warriors?'

'In medieval times,' piped up Jeremy Fry, who'd hit the buzzer first, 'any man who trained to fight could become a knight.'

'Correct,' said the Principal. 'Question two, what age would a boy leave his home to go and live with a knight and learn to use hand weapons?'

Jeremy was first on the buzzer again.

'At age seven.'

'Correct. What would happen at age fifteen?'

Jeremy replied, 'At age fifteen, a page became a squire. He served a knight in his home, trained to fight on a horse, and rode to battle with the knight.'

'Correct.'

Ray grinned at Nigel and gave him the thumbs up.

Jeremy must have answered twenty-two questions correctly in a row now. He wasn't letting anyone else have a go.

Someone ought to tell him, thought Nigel.

Twenty-three questions now.

Jeremy gave Nigel the thumbs up. 'We're killing them,' he said boastfully.

Doesn't he know that one should never gloat, even in triumph, thought Nigel.

And Jeremy answered yet another question.

I wonder if he'll ever give anyone else a turn, thought Nigel in utter disbelief. What a know-all. What an outrage, hogging all the questions!

Nigel saw Mum rolling her eyes good-humouredly.

The Principal asked another question.

'Now, tell me, in medieval times what was a caparison?'

'Um,' said Nigel. He knew this one. He reached forward. But that's when Ivan's hand seemed to fling itself towards the buzzer.

'Buzz,' it went.

Nigel saw Gordon laughing and grabbing the microphone and putting it to Ivan's lips.

'I oo,' Ivan grinned right into the microphone.

Mr Bower was uncertain what to do. So he said, 'Ah, incorrect.'

And even though Nigel could have saved the day and got their table a perfect score by saying, *It's actually the decorative covering worn by jousting horses at tournament*, he didn't. He was too busy laughing about Ivan, like the rest of the people in the hall. Well, most of them. Except for Jeremy Fry, who was glaring outraged at Ivan.

He really doesn't get it, thought Nigel.

Chapter XL

I, Nigel Dorking, Do Hereby Swear Always to Show Forgiveness in My Thoughts and Deeds.

So far it was nil, nil.

Jeremy Fry was thrilled – Reece had been kicked in the head in the first quarter of the match, which meant as the reserve Jeremy was getting to play St Ives.

He trotted onto the field grinning, his team scowling.

Nigel did not join in with the scowling. After all, he decided nobly, it wasn't as if Jeremy had asked for that personality. No one would ask to be like that. And to be fair, it was not Jeremy's fault his dad stole Miss Murray. After all, Nigel could never have married her, as she was a bit old. And even though now in retrospect he realised it might have been great if Miss Murray and his ex-dad had got together, at the time, he had been trying to get Mum back together with Dad.

And so except for his obnoxious personality, Jeremy was forgiven.

Nigel smiled at him. After all he knew how it felt not to be wanted.

And at least now he had Mum and Gordon and Ray who were all there barracking for him, Nigel. Nigel could see them cheering, even though he hadn't marked or kicked a ball yet.

And okay, so he didn't have Dad, and Jeremy had his dad, but Jeremy's dad only had eyes for Bruno.

Poor old Jeremy. No wonder he was such a try-hard.

There he was on the field, jogging in fast motion.

Nigel saw the oval football high in the air, twirling against the blue sky. And now the ball was coming down, hurtling towards him.

He jumped up, remembering Ray's advice, *Don't be scared of the ball*, and Nigel marked it. The crowd were cheering.

Nigel saw he was near the goalposts.

He lined the ball up for a goal. But there in his peripheral vision he saw Jeremy, desperately leaping about.

And to this day he has no idea why he did it, but he handpassed it to Jeremy.

Jeremy fumbled the ball, but accidentally re-caught it at the last second.

He can't miss from where he is, hoped Nigel. Though, there was one small part of him that admittedly wished Jeremy would.

But through the goalposts sailed the ball. Jeremy

looked stunned, as did his dad, and, Nigel noted, there on the sidelines was Miss Murray, clapping with glee.

Bruno and Reece and Hope and all of them were now carrying Jeremy around on their shoulders, calling, 'We are the champions.'

Jeremy had been a lot less annoying at school the last few weeks. That is why Nigel had invited him to his brother's birthday party.

Gordon and Ray had just given Ivan his birthday present. A shiny new whizzbang wheelchair. Bright red, to match Ray's motorbike, but with a few adjustments.

That's when Nigel realised. That's why all those wheelchair parts were lying around on Gordon's floor at his place that day. Gordon was making a specially modified wheelchair for Ivan.

What a wonderful job! The way he had inlaid those cushioned tall sides, that slid right in next to Ivan's torso, and the adjustable padded tray, and the neck supporter. It was amazing.

And Mum had given Ivan some new clothes and a DVD. Of his favourite show, the test pattern.

'Yes, I have one quite similar,' said Jeremy.

Nigel frowned.

And then Jeremy gave Ivan his gift.

Nigel helped Ivan unwrap it. It was a small Warhammer figure in armour.

'It's plastic,' explained Jeremy, 'so he won't hurt himself.'

'Actually,' said Nigel, 'he might put it in his mouth so it is best if I look after it. And it will work well with my army as I actually collect that army, the Empire.'

'Oh,' said Jeremy. 'Well I collect the Khemri. Would you care for a battle?'

'Yes, certainly,' said Nigel. 'Though I should warn you, I do have a fairly impressive army.'

'Actually, so do I,' said Jeremy.

'And I am a very skilled player,' warned Nigel.

'So am I,' said Jeremy.

Poor Jeremy, thought Nigel. He is very competitive. And it is not his fault he has such an unlikeable personality. Given I am so lucky, in that I have a much better personality, I should try to be a good role model for him.

Yes, Nigel decided, he would show Jeremy the way. He would be magnanimous. Not that Jeremy would understand that word. He would pretend he did, but of course he would be faking.

'That would have been a very good choice of present,' said Nigel kindly, 'particularly if Ivan had been smarter, and able to control his movements. Under those circumstances it wouldn't have been a dangerous gift that he might possibly kill himself with at all.'

'Thank you,' said Jeremy, beaming.

It is a good feeling to show friendship towards someone who is quite undeserving. But appreciative.

On the dot of 2 p.m. the doorbell rang.

Nigel had not wanted to do this. He had not wanted to invite his ex-father. But it was clearly so very important to Gordon and Mum that Nigel had grudgingly allowed them to send his ex-father an invitation. For Ivan's sake. And Nigel insisted they invite his stepsisters too.

And then Mum had done a foolish thing. She claimed you could not invite the whole family, and not include Babette.

So she, the viper, had been invited as well.

Gordon went to answer the door and when he did, Nigel saw his ex-father, standing there in full view, his stepchildren standing behind him, but no Babette.

And even though he, Nigel, had not wanted her to come, he felt furious.

How dare she! After his family had been so forgiving and so magnanimous. She would not get away with this!

Dad waited there expectantly as if he were hoping to be invited in.

Then, for the first time since the blue bear episode, Nigel saw his ex-father walk over the threshold. Right through the front door at Mum's.

For so long, Nigel had longed for this moment. And now he didn't feel a thing.

'*C'est la vie,*' said Nigel grimly. Then he explained to Jeremy who was standing next to him 'that means *That is life*, in French.'

'I know,' said Jeremy.

But Nigel was certain that was untrue.

Nigel noted that his father had turned up exactly on time. At 2.00 p.m., as suggested on the birthday party invitation Gordon had sent Dad. Not 2.03 p.m. or 1.58 p.m.

'You've got a cactus in your front yard, same as us,' said a delighted Gabby.

A prickly look crossed Mum's face.

'I must say, Kelly,' said Dad to Mum, 'it was a good idea taking that squeaky old side gate off.'

Mum didn't know what he was talking about.

Nigel's ex-father then handed Ivan a present (also suggested on the invitation, in quite big writing actually. And underlined.).

Gordon was grinning like a maniac. Even Mum managed a smile for Dad. But Nigel remained stern.

No way was his ex-father going to be forgiven just because he happened to turn up to one birthday and bring one lousy present.

'Well, what are you waiting for, lad?' cried Gordon. 'I canna bear the suspense.'

Nigel helped Ivan unwrap the birthday paper from the present, so the paper could be used again. And there inside was a real knight's chain-mail top. One in Ivan's size.

'Thanks,' said Mum on his behalf. 'Isn't that fantastic, Nigel?'

But Nigel said nothing. He even felt annoyed at Ivan for grinning at their ex-dad.

While the candles of Ivan's birthday cake were being lit, Nigel still said nothing. He didn't need to impress his father.

Even though he knew heaps of cake facts – for instance, the reason we light candles on birthday cakes is because the ancient Greeks used to take cakes, which were round to represent the full moon, to the temple of their goddess of the moon, Artemis, and they are said to have placed candles on the cake to make it look as if it was glowing like the moon – Nigel kept his mouth closed.

Instead of speaking, he tried to work out what he'd wish for. On Ivan's behalf, of course.

'Did you know,' said his ex-dad, much to Nigel's annoyance, 'that the biggest actual cake ever was in fact an oatmeal cake, built in Bertram, Texas during the Labor Day weekend in 1991? And it was a 43-layer cake that was more than 5 feet tall, and weighed 533 pounds, and served 6,123 people?'

'No,' said Ray, looking stunned.

'And did you know,' said the ex-dad, 'that in America, 20 acres of cake are consumed every day?'

'Len,' said Mum.

The candles were all lit now and they'd started to sing 'Happy Birthday'.

'Did you know,' said Jeremy, 'that "Happy Birthday" is still in copyright?'

'I did,' said Nigel crossly.

'Wow,' said Ray.

Nigel helped blow out the candles for his brother and as he did he also helped him make a wish.

My wish for Ivan, thought Nigel, is that one day, when he is a man, and so am I, say when we're about forty-three or so, that we might start to forgive our ex-father.

On second thoughts, he decided, make that forty-seven and a half. He's got to put in a lot more effort before we'll even consider it.

'And did you know,' his ex-dad continued, 'that on Christmas Eve in Japan they like to eat fried chicken and strawberry shortcake?'

'Yuk,' said Mum, pretending to dry retch.

'And did you know,' said his ex-dad after Nigel had cut the cake for Ivan, 'that the Germans invented birthday cakes, and celebrated birthdays with a cake called *Geburtstagtorte*?'

'No,' said Jeremy, obviously mightily impressed.

Nigel repressed a sudden urge to say to his ex-father, and Jeremy, if you tell other people facts all the time, it might make you look smart but it is incredibly boring for everybody else, well to 97 per cent of people anyway. And telling them statistics is worse. Apparently 99.9 per cent of the population hate that.

Chapter XLI

I, Nigel Dorking, Do Hereby Swear Always to Remain Faithful to My Pledged Word.

Later that night, when it was still Ivan's birthday, Nigel woke at the allotted hour. He woke Jeremy, the first friend he'd ever had to stay the night.

It was time for their secret ceremony.

Dressed in his knight's armour, Nigel grabbed the chain-mail top Dad had given Ivan, and headed towards Ivan's bedroom.

Ivan didn't appear to be at all surprised to be woken, and dressed, and then sat in his wheelchair.

Nor did he appear surprised to be wheeled out into the night air.

He looked mildly pleased when he saw the full moon, and grinned at it like it was an old friend.

He did not even mind putting on the chain-mail top.

Jeremy watched as Nigel stood opposite Ivan. Ivan, with the moonlight in his hair.

Then, just as it approached the bewitching hour, Nigel took his own plastic helmet and leggings Mum had made and his plastic sword and gave them to Ivan. They couldn't get the leggings all the way up but they were over Ivan's feet. Ivan did chuck a wobbly about having a helmet on his head, so Nigel hung it off his new shining wheelchair. He bound the sword to Ivan's arm.

They waited for midnight.

All they could hear were the bats in the distance, Mum snoring, and the occasional possum fight.

They rehearsed the dubbing of the new knight.

Then the time had really come.

Midnight.

'Ivan the Terrific,' said Nigel, solemnly holding Dad's old sword, which glinted in the moonlight. Then he gently touched Ivan's left shoulder and then his right and then his left again. And so doing, Nigel uttered these words, 'I give you my armour. For I do not need it any more. Ivan Dorking, because this I have promised you, and I do stand by my word, by the powers vested in me, I hereby dub thee knight.'

'I oo,' grinned Ivan, brandishing his plastic sword and nearly putting out Nigel's eye.

Nigel lay in bed, almost too excited to sleep.

Perhaps his plan was foolish.

Perhaps his judgment was in grave error, but he decided that would be too unusual. This would be an act of bravery. Of standing up for his brother's rightful place. Something he should have done long ago.

This was his quest.

The next morning, Nigel Dorking got up early and started this, the last chapter in his story so far.

It was the first Saturday of the month, and he was about to head off to catch the bus with his brother. But before he left there was one final task to perform.

Nigel found his voice recorder.

Dear reader, this is me talking into my voice recorder. No longer will I write in the third person. From now on, I shall refer to myself as I. After all, 'tis I, Nigel Dorking.

This is who I am. I shall not pretend. I feel now as if I have matured so much, and am well on my way towards becoming a man. (Perhaps this has happened already!!!!!! Though that would be unusually young!!!)

But it could explain what I plan to do next.

But before I set forth upon my adult journey, there are a few things you might want to know.

In the early hours of the morning I woke Ivan. 'You have an appointment with destiny,' I explained, 'and I think you should keep it.'

I quickly dressed Ivan into his armour, and gave him his breakfast, and his medications. Then, I explained to Ivan, 'This trip is partly because I may have rejected Dad, but I cannot speak for you, Ivan. And also to make up for that first time I went to Dad's without you. That was unbrotherly. Today I make amends.'

Just before opening our front door and stealing out into the year's first mist, on this crisp blue May morning I wrote my mother this letter.

Dearest Mother (and Stepfather! And not you, Ray! But thanks for keeping this a secret. And sorry for waking you so early. I just needed someone else's opinion.),

I should have explained my plans to you, but today is May 6th.

And in case you don't know what that means it is one year exactly since Dad left.

So today, I am taking Ivan to studio number 227. You may not know this, but today is the day Ablutions Solutions is making their advertisement. Dad is making it with his family. And Ivan is in his family. Do not come and get us! Ivan will be fine. I promise.

I have even written them a new rap song if they will let Ivan join in. With a little help from Ray.

Got a leak,
What a bummer
Hey man let's call a plumber.
Need to go?
But got no loo?
Len Dorking is the dude for you.
Keeps prices down
And water bills too
Ablutions Solutions
Is the Solution for you!

I am now dictating this on the bus. It helps me not to worry when I concentrate on my autobiography.

Today my brother and I are in public alone for the first time ever, and I am happy for the world to know, this is my brother.

I must say, I could not believe how courteous the bus driver was. He got right out of the bus and helped me on with Ivan and his wheelchair.

I have deliberately not worn my armour today, because I think there are situations where it is inappropriate, and braver not to. Though it is different for Ivan. He is younger and his is just new and also knights wear armour to protect themselves. And today Ivan might need all the protection he can get.

I am amazed by how well his new medication is protecting him. He has not had one fit so far. And as

I pointed out to him even knights of old would have had epileptic fits. So he is not to worry, as if one occurs I can look after him.

One lucky thing for Ivan having his particular disabilities is that if Dad does reject him, which is quite probable, given Dad's love disability, I bet Ivan won't even care. Actually, he probably won't even know. I am more realistic about Ivan these days. But if Dad does reject him, he will have to face me. And I am not afraid any more.

Well, not very.

Here we are. Waiting out the front of the studio, me and Ivan.

It is now 6.58 a.m.

My heart is pounding like a galloping steed's hooves as I await their arrival.

There in the distance. I am certain it is Dad's vehicle. Sorry, correction, my ex-dad's.

Oh be still, my beating heart. Why do I feel so ill?

Remember, Nigel, even though you are here as a warrior you must remain courteous at all times, even to the Wicked Witch of the West, and to say exactly what you have rehearsed. Which is?

I believe you are filming the ad for Ablutions Solutions here today with your family? Well, my brother is here to be in that advertisement, as he is part of your family.

He does not mind being seen with you publicly even though you have a love disability. Hopefully you will not mind being seen with him. In fact, you might have something to learn from him.

Oh, by the way, here is the rap I have written. Just in case you are interested. Ivan can jig along to it quite well. We were practising on the bus.

I can now see it is most definitely my ex-dad's car from the numberplate. And my ex-dad's face from his features.

He is looking a bit stunned.

Babette wears an expression that would make a glacier look warm and inviting. She is glaring at Dad. The girls' mouths have fallen open and Lotsa is going nuts.

Any second now.

I must do this. We must.

Ready, Ivan.

That man is your father.

That baby inside Babette is your half-brother or sister.

You must take your rightful place.

Will I, Nigel Dorking, have the courage?

What is that? That familiar noise. That streak of brilliant ruby red? Just across the road? Behind Dad's vehicle.

I can do this.

Here we go, Ivan . . .

For you.

I am now pushing Ivan's wheelchair towards them . . .

Dear Voice Recorder,

This is the end. Not of my life of course but just the story so far.

And that, dear Miss Murray, is my autobiography, which I commend into your hands with the red nail polish. As you will have noted I have striven always to tell the truth in an uncompromising way, in the hope that others who might share my problems might know of my courage and hence take heart!

If you enter this book for any literary awards, I do not mind. In fact, I would only be flattered. (The Nobel would be a good one, and perhaps the Pulitzer?)

By the way, I am not hurt at your choice of

name for your baby as I think 'Nigel' would have been a bad name for a girl. Raphaella is much nicer. Perhaps the next baby.

Oh, and perchance do you have a godfather in mind?

Oh, and many thanks to my friend Jeremy Fry not just for typing up this manuscript (though 'tis much appreciated) but also for being part of my journey to self-knowledge.

Jeremy is not just typing this up because he is my friend, but also because I explained to him that I am myself such a quick typer and that I could probably type up all my voice notes in probably just over two days. And that would not even be me typing my fastest.

And Jeremy said he could probably do it in one day and twenty-three hours and probably less. And he is trying to prove it.

Jeremy is quite lucky to have me as a friend. Other people who brag quite that much do not have friends at all. Take Bruno and Reece. They are now the least popular people in the whole school. At least Jeremy and I, Nigel, have one friend – each other.

As his friend and mentor, I hope through typing up this manuscript that Jeremy learns invaluable lessons about sentence structure, grammar and bragging, as this would help him enormously. After all, knights are always virtuous, and modesty is a virtue! And also friends help each other out. I wonder if Jeremy will ever know the acts of friendship I have shown him. Probably only when he types this bit. It might start him thinking!

But even so, despite his many faults, many many thanks for his dedicated one-finger typing, which I suspect will have taken him possibly weeks longer than it would have taken me, but thankfully it has freed me up and allowed me to get on with my self-portrait which I hope to enter into the Archibald Painting Prize.

By the time you get up to this bit, Jeremy, sadly the closing date for entries will have passed for the Archibald's so don't even try, but good work! Also, to enter, your portrait needs to be of someone famous, which I will be when my autobiography comes out!

By the way, I have decided to do my self-portrait by the beach and to call it *Boy in Front of Expanse of Ocean Lit by the Golden Sunlight Glittering Like Diamonds on a Bejewelled Sea as the Foam on the Azure Waves Comes Riding in Like White Horses.*

Adieu.

Nigel

Glossary

Some multi-syllabic words I, Nigel Dorking, use frequently (and don't even need to look up in a dictionary as they are second nature to me).

Note from Publisher
The following glossary has not been proofread (and reflects the standard of the rest of the manuscript before proofreading). Mary-Anne Fahey claimed she was 'over it', and after paying her rates we didn't have the budget for anyone else.

Valient	Fearless. Or a yob's car.
Portentioius	With tragic foreshadowing (Not to be confused with someone who is up them self like Jeremy Fry. That is pretensious)
Prevale	A more majestic version of 'Win'.
Indignatories	Very Important People
Embecilic	Stupid (Like most of the kids in my class)
Infantessimal	A very tiny infant.
Interpretating	Translating for people who aren't very good with language.
inheritate	People you get your jeans from. (Not Just Gene's)
Spewrious.	Questionable and slightly sick (hence the spew)
Unirrational	How adults behave quite a lot.
Unsensible	Also how adults behave quite a lot.
Repitative	A common bad trate of adults.
Unrevelent	Not anything to do with what is being disgust. Also, *unirrelevent.*
Cunninger	Like cunning but even more so.
Impressioned	How you feel when someone uses language exceptationally well.
Sincearely	What you write at the end of letters – when you really don't mean it.

Aluminate	To highlight in a rust proof way.
Maturer	Like mature but more so.
Plausibler	Even more beleavable
Prosteriors	Bottoms
Exceptational	How I am referred to quite a lot. (Quite exceptational)
Suspicioning	When you suspicion somebody of something.
Intelligenter	How I am compared to the other kids in my class.
Literarsy	What they do not teach in schools.
Antidisestablishmeantarianism	A word I use a lot.
Uninnapropriate	When something is not appropriate
Eminent	(See page 74) Very soon

Author's postscript

Ah Dear Reader,

'Tis true that being a nearly published author of an autobiography has its perks, e.g. enormous respect from strangers in the street (once you tell them), and stepmothers who suddenly for the first time ever give you a Christmas present, but there are also hardships. For instance, dealing with the publishing company.

It was quite obvious to me that I, Nigel Dorking *was the perfect title, and I strongly suggested this to them in my very first draft. Below however are the other titles they made me come up with, before they finally settled on the very first one I had suggested. It is enough to make a boy reconsider being a famous author one day, and to choose being a famous scientist instead. Luckily forbearance is something knights are quite good at. And not saying, 'I told you so, idiots.' (Which of course I never would.) (Though if I were Jeremy, I might.)*

A Knight's Tail
A Portrait of a Boy as a Young Man
A Story of Valour and Triumph: An Autobiography, by Me, Nigel Dorking, Grade Six
Ah! *Mon Ami* (*My Friend* in French)
Alas and Alack

Bad in Bed
Being Me
Beyond His Years
Brain
Busting

Chivalry Now, By A Modern Day Knight

Dorking, My Childhood
Drip

Excalibur, My Pen

Farewell Childhood
Frequently upon a Mattress . . .

Gallantry, Chivalry, and Modern

How Novel
Humbly Yours (Note a Very Fat Book for Someone My Age to Even Read Let Alone Write!!!!)

I
I Can Make Puddles
Incomple
Incomplete – a Partial Autobiography of My Life Till Now
Indefatigable (to Save You Looking This Up in the Dictionary It Means Tireless, Persistent, or Steadfast)

Insufferable (A Story About A Boy, His Indominable Spirit, And His Valiant Refusal To Give In To Suffering, Written By That Very Boy Nigel Dorking Grade Six)

Kith and Tell

Modestly Yours: A Story Of Chivalry, Courage Hope and

My Autobiography by Me, Nigel Dorking (Obviously, Else It Would Be a Biography)
My Manifesto (A History Of My Universe Up Till Now)
My Metamorphosis (as Opposed to Kafka's)
My Tragic Life So Far in Words.
Mything Dad

Nigel D
Nigel Dorking at Your Service
Nigel Dorking – Drought Buster
Nigel Dorking Holds His Own
Nigel Dorking Is (Not) Up Himself (Actually)
Nigel Dorking Legend
Nigel Dorking Unplugged
Nigel Dorking, Drought Buster, Doer of Knightly Deeds, and Library Monitor (On Tuesdays)
Nigel Dorking, Scared Dadless
Nigel Dorking, Self Diagnosed Possible Virtual Child Prodigy
Nigel Dorking's Holy Grail
Nigel Dorking's Inferno (One Boy's Journey to Hell and Back)
Nigel Dorking's Knightly Deeds
Nigel Dorking's Night-Time Crusade
Nigel Dorking and the Dark Knights . . .
Nigel Dorking's Most Terrible Recurring Knightmare
Nigel Dorking's Number One Problem
Nigel Dorking's Quintessential Guide to Redemption
Nigel Dorking's Remembrance of Things Present
Nigel Dorking's Unfinished Business
Nigel Dorking's Worst Knight Ever

Obviously
One Boy Caught Between Heaven And Hell, Childhood And Manhood, Mum And Dad, Medieval Times And Google . . .
One Boy's Incredible Story of Redemption, as Told by Himself
One Little Australian

Such Is Life

The Extraordinary Canvas of My Life So Far
The Fickle Finger of Fortune and Fate
The Good, the Bad and the Particularly Ugly Stepmother
The Life and Times of Nigel Dorking
The Nigel Dorking Chronicles
The Not Quite Complete Works of Nigel Dorking (As He Intends to Write Many More Bestsellers)
The Orc, the Witch and the Empty Suit of Armour
The Pen Is Mightier than the Sword (NOTE TO PUBLISHER – PLEASE MAKE SURE THE WORDS *PEN* AND *IS* HAVE A BIG SPACE BETWEEN THEM!!!!!!!!!!!!!!)
The Rich and Colourful Tapestry of My Life So Far
The Thrust and Parry of My Life
The Universe and My Part in It
The Unseen Bits of Nigel Dorking
The Wee Knight
Through this Visor
Touchée! A Modern Day Story of Gallantry, Chivalry and Plumbing
Twinkle Twinkle
'Twas
'Twixt

Unauthorised: My Autobiography
Unputdownable . . . What You Won't Be Able to Do to This Book When You Read about the Story of This Boy with the Indomitable Spirit
Unspeakable (A Story of a Boy Mature Beyond His Years, and the Hand Cruel Destiny Dealt Him)
Untold

Wee of the Never Never

Author acknowledgements

I, NIGEL DORKING, WOULD LIKE TO ACKNOWLEDGE THOSE WHO HELPED ME IN THE TELLING OF MY STORY, BUT ACTUALLY WHEN I THINK ABOUT IT NO ONE DID.

LUCKILY I HAD THE FORCE OF CHARACTER TO STICK STEADFASTLY TO MY DREAM ALL ON MY OWN.

IT IS TRUE JEREMY DID THE TYPING BUT THAT IS MERELY MENIAL.

THERE WAS OF COURSE MISS MURRAY, BUT SHE DIDN'T ACTUALLY DO ANYTHING EITHER. (MUSES GENERALLY ARE NOT EXPECTED TO.)

THE ONLY PEOPLE I SHOULD COMMEND ARE PENGUIN BOOKS FOR HAVING THE FORESIGHT TO SEE BEFOREHAND MY GREAT POTENTIAL (WHICH WAS PROBABLY QUITE OBVIOUS SO IT WAS PROBABLY NOT THAT FORESIGHTFUL NOW I THINK ABOUT IT.)

AND ALSO FOR BEING SO SMART AS TO SEE ITS FULL POTENTIAL AS A FAT INTELLIGENT BOOK FOR ADULTS THAT IS CONSIDERED HIGH LITERATURE, AND THAT SHOULD SIT PROUDLY ON THE SHELVES (AND ON HIGHSCHOOL AND EVEN UNIVERSITY SILLYBUSES) WITH PATRICK WHITE, SHAKESPEARE, AND KOFKA. (BUT PROBABLY NEXT TO DOSTOYEVSKI AND DICKENS AS MY NAME STARTS WITH *DO*. . .)

THIS I LOOK FORWARD TO SEEING IN ALL GOOD BOOKSHOPS.

A word from the proofreader

I, Mary-Anne Fahey, would like to thank so many people for their continuing emotional support over these difficult months of proofreading *I, Nigel Dorking*.

I thank my children, Tom Fahey and James McFadyen, for understanding when Nigel insisted that me and them going away on family holidays might compromise his book. And their friends Lisa and Kate, who as a result had to stay home for their holidays too.

I thank my partner, Morris Gleitzman, for his tolerance and good humour when night after night I was on the phone to Nigel.

I also thank my late mother Stephanie Podger (whose funeral I was unable to attend due to urgent dictation updates from Nigel).

My heartfelt thanks also to Julie Watts for spotting my proofreading potential, and to Lisa Riley and Laura Harris for helping me to realise it. (I am hoping I will make a lot of money as Nigel assures me that proofreaders are generally quite rich.)

And a special thanks to the delightful Catherine McCredie (very rich as she is a senior editor!!!), whose support, inspiration, and unerring expertise as a skilled mediator, steered me and Nigel away from many an imminent irretrievable breakdown in communication, and of course to the ever-lovely Jane Godwin (extremely rich as she is a head publisher) for her counselling and belief in me during those dark moments when I doubted my abilities, and for taking us on extremely interesting outings (particularly to Dorking Road).

Many thanks also to Debra Van Tol, Hamish McCredie, Penny Matthews, Kate Chisholm, Katrina Webb, Sharon Neville, Janet Raunjak and Peter O'Connor for psychological services. And of course Wolf Blass for their extremely fine product.

And to Debra Bilson and David Altheim for their artful contributions, and for making my name as big on the cover of *I, Nigel Dorking* as Nigel's own, even though he was dead against it.

And of course many thanks to Julia Ferracane, Kristin Gill, Sally Bateman and Louise Ryan for all their hard work in trying to boost my very sagging public profile.

Many thanks also to Peg McColl from Penguin Australia.

I would also like to thank: Ted and Rhoda Waterman; Alf and Elva Waterman; Moina and Valentine Podger, John and Bronwyn Podger, Mark Podger, Peter and Carol Waterman; Iris Evans; Jean, Hector, and Bob McFadyen; Jane, Laurie, Harry, Ellen and Isobel Angus; Georgie, Don and Eddie Saunders; Bobbie, George, Phillipa, Prudence, Georgie and Cookie Stent; Nick, Mary, Bridget, Joe and Lotsa Waterman; Kathy, Jack and Beth Nielsen; Kim Waterman; Tony and Charley Chicken Brewster; Francie, Rusty, Harriet, Billy and Kittykottie Walker; Jutta Goetze; Sue, Bill, Jasper and Max Garner-Gore; Prue and Baddie Cameron; Bernie Wynack; Lynton Daehli; Bob Swinburn; Frances Monaghan; Patrick and Jean Kittson-Cook: Ted and Anne Robinson; Andrew and Dianna Cameron; Ruth Shoenheimer; Linda Hall; Ramona Koval; Veronica Elkins; Mrs Murray; Cathy and Terry Grearly; Ruth and Mark Higgs; Cath Pirrie and Lou; Wendy Lawson and Beatrice; Vicki Warren and Michael Yenko; Ian, Jessica, Claire and Jo McFadyen; Keith, Harriarti, Raphael and Bella Fahey; Les, Des and Sarah Fahey; Michael Fahey; Sophie, Ben, Pam and Phil Gleitzman; Cas, Friday and Lauchlin McFadyen; Arie Snabel; Claire Jennings; Paul Jennings; Mr and Mrs Yamada and their judo academy; Bill Livingston; Mark and Di Mitchell; Dr Mel and Bronwen; Nick Gleitzman; David, Michael, Kate, David and Jessica Watt; Lisa, Dennis, Andrew, Luke and Nathan Harnetty; Michael, Elaine, Sean, Caillan, Finn and Aidan Watt; Sandi, Wayne, Louise and Charlie Tuddenham; Badcat; Squeaker; Kitmus Podger and Cockie. And the goldfish. (Of course.)

I would also like to thank Sarah Hughes and Penguin UK for taking Nigel into their hearts.

About the author

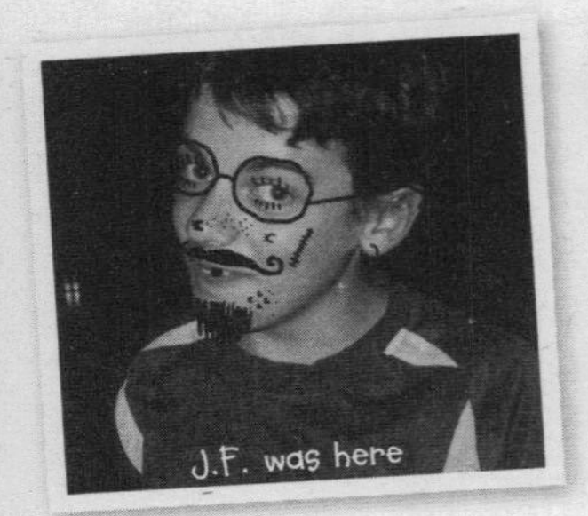

Nigel Dorking lives in Camelot Heights with his mother, brother, stepfather, stepbrother and his new goldfish. He is currently tossing up whether to call it *Gnothe seauton* which is Greek for *Know thyself*, or *Moby Dick* after the famous great white humpbacked whale. However he is a little concerned that those less literary and more ignorant might laugh immoderately at the word 'Dick'. So for now he is calling it *I, fish*.

About the proofreader

Mary-Anne Fahey has robbed banks, murdered people, jaywalked and had a bum lift. And that was just in her television career.

Her other talents include bad ventriloquism, even worse Irish dancing, and terrible tongue tricks, all of which she can be coaxed to perform at the drop of a banknote.

Even though she has danced and sung with Kylie Minogue, and snogged Sylvester Stallone, still there was something missing from her life. Then she found proofreading.

She has two children, two cats and eight very demanding goldfish and is incredibly young, rich and beautiful.